TO

Anna Rashbrook

THANK YOU

Margaret Connor for all her typing and helping me with Tom.

At the end of the book are tasters for my other books. All set in countryside with romance, drama and a strong Christian message.

Do come and join me on:

https://booksbyanna619772285.wordpress.com/

Author page on Facebook@horsesandogs

Twitter: Anna Rashbrook@AnnaRashbrook

And my book group on Facebook: Horse Books For Grown Ups

CLARE
1993

Clare pushed her toes firmly into the shoes and sighed with relief as her heel followed in. She tried to wiggle her feet but the patent black leather gave no ground. Unsteadily, she stood up and placed the cover on the typewriter.

'Flipping thing!' she glared at it and the pile of unfinished letters. Everything wait until Monday. She was really past caring, so what if it meant another lecture from Eric, she could take it...or maybe she just wouldn't come back! As she began to close the door on the silent office, her reflection scowled back at her from the glass. Clare jumped because for a moment because she didn't recognise herself. The permed yellow waves were the worst part. The flattery of the Hairdresser still hadn't convinced her that she didn't look like anything but a clown. The make-up didn't help either, she saw the smears caused by a day of frustration behind the wilful typewriter. That was enough, she stuck her tongue out at the reflection, slammed the glass door within an inch of smashing and marched to the stairs.

On the top step, the fickle shoes betrayed her, and a heel turned, sending Clare sliding down the steps until her grip on the bannister halted her flight. She sat on the stairs, rubbing her bruised calves, muttering every curse she knew. She pulled off the hated shoes and slung them down the steps. They bumped and leapt, and she wished them in pieces, but as they reached the bottom Clare remembered the long walk home. Anxious for their safety, she followed them down, and with a sigh of relief, entombed her feet again.

The cold, dirty winter wind swarmed down the road, hurling litter like darts around Clare's sore calves. She winced as a piece of newspaper grabbed them then flew manically on. Evening was coming. The lights of the shops and cars became beacons of colour in a dull grey scene. Shivering, Clare pulled up the thin collar of her jacket and began her walk.

There was nothing in the cheap streets to cheer her up. Dull shabby shops policed by secretive turbanned assistants talking in their own dialects, take-aways surrounded by their own litter and discount shops daring to be the cheapest around. The air was full of car noises and music competing from each shop; the smell of cooking onions, car fumes and filth was everywhere.

The sheer monotone of each day suddenly struck Clare; the fixed routines, the inane chatter of her workmates, their lives centred about boys, music and sex. Didn't they ever read a book? A speeding car flashed past, soaking her wounded legs. With each punching step, the angry, fed up and bitter thoughts she'd kept in check for so long, boiled over and engulfed her. What was she doing here far away from home in this ugly polluted city?

Phil, oh Phil, why can't we leave this dump? Thinking of him stemmed the trickle of tears, and things perhaps weren't quite so bad. It was still difficult to take in the fact that they were together. It had taken months of trying every trick she could imagine to catch his attention. In the end, she had, he'd liked her, taken her out, even suggested he move in. Clare thought of all the new clothes he'd lavished on her transforming what Phil had suggested was a bit of a dowdy old frump into a stunner. Clare became aware that the rain was spoiling her precious curls, turning them lank and lifeless. Belatedly, she pulled a plastic hat from her pocket. Finding it was a surprise, usually, she was so disorganised. Clare glanced at her watch, if she walked on quickly, she'd have a good half an hour to get herself sorted before he returned. Perhaps they'd go out for a meal, but no, she acknowledged it would probably be the Pub, and that infernal fruit machine. At least they'd be together. What would he do if she took a book?

Test of endurance over, she stood at the door of No. 32, searching for the elusive door key. She saw Mrs B's television, its colours dancing through the net curtains. Dancing? Top of the Pops! It was Thursday, not Friday. Keep Fit night. All her plans flew out into the night air as now she'd have to ring the office and warn Phil not to pick her up before he left. At last, she found the key and fitted it in the lock.

As usual, the door stayed stuck until she put her shoulder to it and heaved, and as usual, she nearly fell into the long dark corridor. The ever-present smell of cabbages and babies was overwhelming, so she ran, breath held to their door, key at the ready. Shutting the door behind her, she sighed out in relief, and smelt the aroma of fresh roses from the pot-pourri. The shoes went flying to hide under the cabinet, her coat closely following. Guiltily Clare remembered Phil's tidiness, picked it up and hung it on the correct hook. The neon light in the kitchen was savage to her street worn eyes. The heap of unwashed dishes made her want to run. Clare dithered. Hair, phone or washing-up? Hurriedly she dialled the office only to get the engaged tone. She waited a while in case she got through, glancing at her reflection in the mirror, seeing with relief that the curls were quietly returning to their correct positions. Clare slammed the phone down, and quickly washed the smeared makeup off her face. If he came back now, she'd at least be presentable. Drying her face on a tea towel, she again tried the office. It rang and rang. Dismayed, she prayed he wouldn't be too cross at his wasted journey.

The washing-up became a priority, she wanted no fuel for arguments. She piled it all in the sink, as the geyser began to hiss and bubble. Plunging her hands into the soapy water, Clare reflected on how nice it must be, to be at home, to keep everything in pristine order, preparing meals with time and care. No belting around with a hoover, five minutes before work. To be a wife.

Through the hissing water, another sound began to attract her attention. A persistent clicking seemed to come from the sitting room. Hands dripping, Clare peered into the darkness. The red and green flashes of light gave the answer. A long finished record turned silently on. Puzzled she put the machine to rights, she was sure it was turned off last night. Something rustled against the wall adjoining the sitting room. Phil must already be home! The sore throat of which he'd complained must have grown worse. Relief rushed through Clare. Poor man, sore throats were so miserable. She rushed back to the kitchen to check her hair and make two mugs of coffee. Carefully balancing them against spills, she made her way to the bedroom.

'Hi love - that sore throat got worse?' She stood in the doorway testing his reaction. The bedside light clicked on, and two mugs of coffee hit the white carpet, spreading pools of glistening brown. Clare sank to her knees in disbelief and shock.

Two faces stared guiltily over the edge of the quilt, Phil's dark hair and the blonde tresses of a complete stranger.

'What the blazes are you doing here?' roared Phil before Clare said a word. There was dead silence seemed an eternity.

'What do you mean me? This is our flat. How could you Phil? Why?' Clare wailed. He had at least the grace to go crimson, while his friend pulled free of the covers and began to search for her clothes. They watched her in silence. When she rose to leave, Phil reached out, kissed her roughly and murmured something in her ear, to which she smiled and nodded, yet she didn't have the courage to look at Clare as she fled the bedroom and the flat.

Clare was surprised at the dead calm she felt. The shock was all her worst nightmares enacted, but somehow it felt a relief. She didn't know what to say, do or demand, she was witless.

'Look, it had to come,' Phil avoided looking at her. 'I mean, I have never been tied to anyone. You should have seen that it was nice to be here while it lasted, but I've met someone new. All good things come to an end. I'm sure we can work things out like adults.' The placations tripped convincingly from his tongue.

'Anyway, look how you've changed. You've got all those lovely clothes and a hairdo. Some bloke will be after you in no time.' He even managed to smile.

'I was going to tell you this weekend anyway, things have just - well come forward a bit.' He burbled on, convincing himself of the rightness of his actions.

Clare was in a stupor of disbelief. How could someone, who'd seemed so caring and loving turn overnight into a louse? All the endearments and the promises had been lies. Mum was right, no man, least of all someone from a town, was to be trusted. She almost laughed at the homily from childhood. Clare was tired, bone-achingly tired, with her knees soaked in the puddle of cold coffee. She wished for the energy to tell him exactly what she thought of him, but his placations were like a battering ram to her emotions; her willpower vanished. She was sick of being here, the town, her job, him. She was going to move away, move on, leave it all behind, seal it up in a box and bury it.

Finally, Clare summoned up the energy for words. 'Phil, get out of my sight,' she interrupted in a calm drained voice. 'You can get your stuff in the morning, but for now, just get out of here, before I find the energy to tell you exactly what I think of you.'

He had sense enough to shut up and obeyed with the alacrity of a schoolboy being let home early. Clare hauled herself out of the coffee, onto the bed and watched him dress. Her cold, unwavering glare finally unnerved him. He began to tumble and drop his clothes in haste, colliding with the mystery blonde For the first time, Clare saw the thinness of his arms, the over-manicured fingernails, the receding, weak chin, what on earth had she ever found attractive in him? The relief was overwhelming as they left, Phil still fumbling with his jacket.

Yes, it was time for Clare to go too. But where? Away from this mess into clean air where there was room to breathe and rest. Sylvie's.

She was finally going to take up the invitation that had so often been extended. Decision made, Clare concentrated on not thinking too much and just getting on with packing.

The first thing to do was to sling all the stupid clothes. Yes, she admitted that now, they were cheap tat. Rapidly, she stripped to underwear, then rummaged for the cardboard box shoved to the back of the wardrobe, to where her 'Oik' clothes were buried. The jeans and jumpers were dusty and a little damp, but so, so, comfortable. Clare felt every muscle in her body slump as if back into an old mould when she put them on. The tatty trainers were a joy to her tortured feet. The suitcase rapidly filled with all her old clothes, anything new, bought by Phil was slung in a heap on the bed.

In the bathroom, she had to wade through Phil's collection of aftershaves and deodorants to find her shampoo and soap. A little, malicious thought crept into her head, she would never be able to say to Phil all the things she wanted to, and anyway, it would probably go in one ear and straight out the other. Actions speak louder than words. She was embarrassed by the childish giggle that slipped out, but it didn't stop her. Bottle after bottle, pound after pound poured down the sink, and by the end, the stink was making her cough, but every last drop was down the drain.

Clare began to collect her possessions from around the flat. It came as a surprise to realise, just how few they were, and they had mostly been pushed in a corner or shoved in a drawer by Phil. How could she have been so blind? The sitting room was dominated by the stereo, squeaky clean, every dial precisely set after hours of juggling. The malicious spirit within her set the knobs twirling, and it was simple to push the stylus askew with a stabbing finger. Clare found her books, shoved behind the LPs and for a second was filled with pure hatred for Phil as she saw the twisted spines. She breathed in deeply to try to regain control, this wouldn't do. Just then the radiator gurgled in the corner and another scheme for revenge sprang to mind. Reverently, she took the records from the shelf and stacked them against the heater.

The electricity meter in the kitchen was nearly empty, so Clare shoved the waiting pile of 50p coins into her jeans pocket, along with the rent money from the jar. Enough. All her actions were as petty and as small- minded as Phil, but to her stunned mind they felt infinitely sweet. Clare now wanted to run from the scene of her crimes. It was enough to imagine his reactions. The scent of roses now seemed cloying and suffocating.

She dumped her suitcase and bags of oddments and reached under the smart damp jacket on the coat rack for the last piece of her old self, the dull, black duffle coat. Putting it on felt like a mother embracing a child. Clare relaxed into its musty warmth. One last hurdle. Clare tapped cautiously on Mrs B's door. As if she'd been stood waiting, Mrs B's familiar, trusting, bleary-eyed face looked askance at Clare.

'You're off then?' Clare nodded, thankful that there was no demand for an explanation. 'Well, shame you're going. Got the rent?'

'Phil will pay tomorrow - it's his turn anyway,' Clare avoided her gaze.

'Well, if you're sure. Want any stuff forwarded on?'

Clare shook her head and handed over the key.

'Bye then, Good luck love,' Mrs B shut the door. She was used to the comings and goings in the flats and had learnt not to ask questions, but this girl had seemed different. Never mind. Now she'd have to make sure she caught that shifty looking Phil in the morning for the rent.

The world was dark outside the flats, full of rain and mist. Clare began the trudge to the bus stop, thankful that this time her steps weren't in pain. The rain soon began to soak the old coat, sending a trickle of cold down her back. It was a fight to concentrate on the task in hand, deliberately blanking her mind because she kept on thinking of other things she should have said, and that was futile. There would be time to adjust to the pain when she was safe, but now she didn't want the sardonic city to see her distress. Pity from passers-by would somehow bind her to the city because they'd remember her and wonder why. She wanted to be free of its clutches.

All the buses went to the station, so the agony of waiting was short. Clare looked at hoardings, bags, newspapers, anything to distract herself. Now she really did want a good cry, to sob and scream. The bus ride was steamy and cramped, and her bags seemed to have doubled in weight as she trudged up the mountain of steps to the station foyer. Busy, wet people rushing home to creature comforts, pushed past her, knocking her off balance, leaving her trailing behind. They got to the ticket office first, so she had to follow their slow shuffle to the desk. Finally, she was eye to eye with the glass plate.

'One way to Bathurst,' she demanded and thrust the 50p meter coins through with cold clumsy fingers. The next quest was to find the train which she achieved by leaping in front of a porter so that he had to stop. Twenty minutes lay in front of her escape. Hunger suddenly grabbed her attention. Clare realised she hadn't eaten since the meagre slimmers' lunch at midday and wanted to cry when she saw the Buffet doors shut. Then she felt stupid and went to find a kiosk.

Like a child with a watering mouth, she scanned the trays of long-forbidden delights, they were all so appealing, she didn't know where to start. In the end, she picked two off each shelf and further demanded crisps and a can. Clare ignored the censorious glare of the plump woman inside. She would enjoy every mouthful.

The allotted platform was empty, a diesel-filled wind blowing in from a tunnel. Seeking occupation, Clare rearranged her bags keeping the battle for concentration going. Straightening up, she caught her reflection on the shiny side of a cigarette machine. This time it wasn't a stranger, because she didn't have to hide from it. That hair! Ponytails and clips would fix it.

A blast of air heralded the train; doors banged, people rushed. Clare savoured the moment because it was goodbye, she'd only ever come back here if it were on her own terms. She slammed the carriage door with a sense of triumph, and grabbed a corner seat, thrusting the curtain across the window, she didn't want to see her face that much. In her rummaging, she'd found an old favourite book. Contentedly she settled to its familiar tale, absorption in its words blanking and nullifying all the terrors of the present. The book and the chocolates soothed the journey's course, so it was with a jolt that she realised the train was pulling into Bathurst.

The duffle coat chilled her as she stood on the platform, but now the night was cold and starlit. What was she doing here, Oh Phil, why did it have to happen like this? Taxis were non-existent, and the buses had long ago returned to the depot. Yet Clare relaxed a little, it was only a short walk, then she'd be able to let go, shoulder her misfortune onto Sylvie, get it out of her system.

The air was as clear as the sky. Clare breathed in deep lungs full, to find it tainted only with mud and cow. She began the struggle down the road, her aim was from lamppost to lamppost, their beacons warning her of potholes and puddles. When they were passed, Clare began to lurch about, feet and legs getting soaked, the starlight wasn't enough to guide her way. Shivers began from deep inside, it seemed as if she were heading for an abyss.

She narrowly missed bumping into a large truck, parked in the lane, so she kicked it in frustration. How much further? Then she saw a white painted handrail and sighed in relief. The bridge ran over the ditch to the cottage. Not much more girl. She lurched across and up the uneven path. Clare couldn't find the bell so she hammered instead.

'Sylvie, for heaven's sake,' she wailed. 'Wake up!'
A light came on inside. In the hall, catches clicked, and the door opened, blinding her in the radiance. Clare prepared to hurl herself at Sylvie, and release that bottled cry. To tell all to the only friend she had ever made.

'Sylvie - you just won't believe it!' She took a step forward, still dazzled.

'Oh, crumbs. Isn't this No.3? Clare was faced with the bulk of a man, no diminutive Sylvie.

'Yes it is, but she's in Australia,' he stated.

'I'm sorry,' Clare muttered in utter confusion. Picking up her bags she turned back down the path. Where on earth could she go now? Did the pub have rooms? The abyss really was engulfing her now. The long-held tears were escaping, she tried not to sob out loud. She faltered at the gate. Which way?

'Now stop!' A heavy hand was laid upon her shoulder, and she spun round to face the man.

'Don't go tearing off like that. If you're one of Sylvie's many friends, I'm under strict instructions to let them all in!'

Clare found her bags taken away, and herself propelled back up the path. In the warm glow of the hall, he dumped her bags and courteously helped her with the sodden coat. He gestured to the living room door. Clare, peering through the glaze of tears, saw the room lit by the blazing burner. The familiar settee was in the corner covered in a faded quilt, the mountains of books, piled behind it. Its familiar welcome finished Clare, she ran to the settee, hurled herself into its warmth and howled. Great, stomach wrenching gulps, engulfed Clare, her nose blocking and eyes aching. The storm quickly blew over, leaving her hollow and shaken. She began unsuccessfully to search for tissues. Just then the kitchen door banged open, and the man walked in with a laden tray. He handed her a kitchen roll, and she mopped up.

'I'm sorry. I don't know what you must think. I've never done anything like that before. I've just left my boyfriend, and I needed somewhere to go. I didn't know about Sylvie. I suppose I should have phoned. I'll find somewhere else in the morning.' The words tumbled out.

'Look, don't worry. Sylvie's away for several months and I'm just the cat minder. She briefed me to expect people dropping in. It's no problem. Stay as long as you need.' He handed Clare a steaming mug. She took a swig and nearly choked on the whiskey in it, but the warmth created was too pleasant, so she supped on and inspected her host.

He had the tanned look of an outdoor man, with ragged curly black hair. His eyes were deep set and hooded, behind a classical roman nose. It was strange, she reflected, his voice was nicer than he looked. He was plump too, his blue jumper was stretched tight over a rounded tummy. Draining his mug he stood, and she realised he was very tall, almost reaching the beams.

'Stay as long as you need,' he again stated. 'Help yourself to coffee and things in the morning. I'll be out until quite late.' He was gone, thundering up the stairs.

Clare sighed drowsily. What was she going to do? Somehow she didn't feel too worried. Funny bloke that. Wonder why he'd said stay as long as you need -not want? Perhaps he was shy. Clare realised the whiskey was colouring her thoughts. It took a herculean effort to leave the settee, especially when she felt the cardboard dampness of her jeans. She closed the Wood burner then tottered upstairs.

The spare room was also comfortingly familiar, equipped with more quilting and stripped pine. To her surprise, like in a Hotel, her bags were there. Clare rapidly stripped to T-shirt, shedding soggy clothes all over the floor. Quickly, she dived under the quilt, sleep coming instantly to her anaesthetised mind.

Tom
1983

Tom stood in the aftershock of the slammed
door. Echoes of curses and the sweet smell of
casserole wafted around him and from inside he
heard Douggie answering back to his mother's
shrill voice.

Shimmering dayglo stripes on his new
shoes caught Tom's attention, and he waved
them around making patterns in the dimming
evening. He glanced at his watch, it was too late
now, he'd never get back in time to be safe.
Listlessly, he turned out his pockets and the
small change in his plump hands added up to yet
another portion of chips. Slowly he walked along
the empty streets, not daring to look through the
windows at the domesticity within. Most people
were home now and the blare of the news,
cooking smells, occasional shouts of laughter
engulfed him in a fog of pain. Why not me? Why
me?

The moon shone wearily in the pale
October sky, half-clad trees catching its reflection
on sagging leaves. Tom shivered, feeling the
thinness of his pullover. The blare of light from
the Chip Shop was a familiar comfort, Gladys
winked and shoved some extra chips on his
portion. Two leather clad youths walked in, loudly
demanding their orders and Tom found himself
back on the street.

Munching at the bland, limp chips, he
ambled to the park. It was sombre and cheerless
in the dim light, his footsteps echoing sadly down
the path to the swings. Here lay memories of
baby chuckles, giddy swings and gentle hands
that comforted after a tumble. Light days before

this dark. His hurt became taunted with anger and he swung around to face the terraced streets.

An hour to go at least before the coast was clear. The street was still as people fell into the lethargy of midweek. A weariness, not of his years or comprehension sapped him and he sank onto his doorstep. He didn't mind the cold hardness against his bruised back, it was some sort of shelter. He huddled against the warmer wood, watching with envy the warm lights within the houses. Unwillingly, he dozed. A shriek of feminine laughter and his support fell away from behind him, With wildcat reflexes, he shot away from the door and hid behind a parked van.

The man who came out of the door was burly and dark, a bull of a man who knew he had nothing to fear. Yet he spoke a farewell in a hushed tone to the woman now framed in the hall light. She wore a pale green bathrobe, her rich red hair cascading around her face. To Tom, she looked like a photo from a glossy magazine. The man's car revved up then sped away as she began to close the door.

Slowly, testing the quietness, Tom left the protection of the van and sped to the rapidly closing door.

'Where were you then?' the vision demanded.

'I told you. I had tea with Douggie,' he said in mock exasperation.

'I don't remember. Next time, be in before he gets here. I can't relax when you're not in.'

Tom bit back an angry remark and tried to duck past in case of another blow. At a glimpse, the woman still looked young but to Tom, the faint flecks of grey in her hair were streaks and the faint creases around her eyes, caverns. Trapped in the corridor he shrieked,

'Why, why can't it be like before?' he demanded.

'None of your business, you're looked after, so shut up!' Her hand half raised to strike him but then she struggled past him into the kitchen and reached for cigarettes.

'He won't be back this week - shall we go to the flix tomorrow?' she offered in a whining tone. Tom was still young enough to clasp straws, however meagrely offered, so he nodded. Then he saw the wad of notes on the table. For a second he caught his mother's eye, she reached for the wad, peeled off a couple and handed them over.

'Buy yourself something nice after school,' she murmured. He raced away, thundered up the stairs, and in the bathroom turned the taps on full blast. He felt so cold, so dirty, he wanted to scrub himself clean, but before he stripped, he shoved the money firmly into his jeans' pocket. It set the rules for the next few years.

CLARE
1993

There's a chicken in the flat! Clare sprang up
thumping her head on the sloping roof then sank
down again nursing her head as she realised it
was outside. Opening her eyes sent a cold black
dread sweeping through her, making the hair on
the back of her neck stand up. Her heart raced to
match the sensation until she took deep breaths
and willed herself calm. This was ridiculous. It
was all over, finished with, yet still, the memories
of the previous day flooded her, two startled
faces, melting records and clear bright stars in
the night sky. No!

She leapt up again, this time avoiding
the roof and pulled the curtains apart to inspect
the day. From her bedroom eyrie she saw the
front garden filled with bronze, glowing
chrysanthemums, and at their feet were dying
summer flowers, their colours muted and drab.
An oak tree stood in the garden with a few brown
tinged leaves still hanging on, pointing to the
cloud laden sky. Outside the gate stood the
maligned truck, and beyond that, miles of hedges
and fields, all clothed with the drab brownness of
early winter.

A white cockerel sprang into view,
coming to rest on the handrail by the gate. He
began to brace himself for another yell. At that
moment, the front door banged shut sending
judders throughout the house. Clare's host
strode down the path and lunged at the cockerel
as he went past it. The bird flew off with a hen
like cackle into the garden and away through the
hedge. Clare laughed out loud at seeing him

echo her sentiments. He heard her peal of laughter and turned to give a flick of a wave and was gone; the truck leaving a thin cloud of smoke floating in the air. Clare leapt back from the window, remembering her lack of clothing. Had she embarrassed him? Shivering, she sank back under the covers. For want of better company, Clare addressed the room.

'Well, my girl. This won't do. You're in the middle of nowhere, in a friend's house except the friend isn't here, with a man you've already embarrassed. No job, no transport and not a lot of money. It's all your own fault, perhaps you should go home.'

Once again she saw with crystal clarity, the scruffy farm hidden in a gap between two large Midland towns. Piles of corrugated iron, bricks and wood all waiting for never started projects. Rickety buildings so deep in trampled straw that the animals had to duck to enter them, an endless succession of mud smeared pigs scampering about. Thin black and white cows, stealing food from each other, always gathered around the feed shed, trying to break in. Dad, waistcoat flapping in the breeze, chugging about on the tractor, trying to look busy. Mum, struggling through the mud to find the few eggs. The practical image she could take but it was the mental torture of her childhood years that made her shudder. Silent hours spent in the cold chapel, not daring to fidget. The monotony of learning verses, the horror when she forgot. Dull black Sundays when nothing was allowed to be done. There would be no light or hot food even in the depths of Winter. Endless Bible readings. The pony. Her pony, which had died, because it dared to get into trouble foaling on a Sunday.

She hadn't been really aware of her difference until adolescence hit. Most of her friends at school were of farming families, and so all were familiar with the grind of harvest and the squeal of the dying pig. The difference was that they were freely allowed to go to Youth Club, and on jaunts to the city cinema. Come with us they said, and a couple of times she had, but the beating that followed hadn't been worth the pleasure. In the end, they stopped asking, left her alone, kept her out of their conversations about boys, make-up and pop. Clare had planned her flight in the years of loneliness and had struck during harvest just when they were least able to chase after her to bring her back. She'd stolen all the money hoarded in the china jug above the aga. She felt only a tinge of regret, it seemed a just payment for the years of misery.

In the city, hundreds of miles from the farm, it had been easy to find a flat with her bounty, and with an address, the jobs, night school, friends. That was history. She brought herself back to the present with a start. There was no going back, there would never be any forgiveness for the lamb returning to the flock, a just punishment for running astray.

The city was just as bad, Clare reflected. There she was bound by the attitudes of the crowd she ran with. They'd taught her a lot, about drinking, clothes and morality. She had willingly followed them and it had been great fun at first. Many times she had thought smugly of what her parents would do if they saw her now.

Phil was one of the crowd, her only boyfriend and lover. Had he ever loved her? It seemed impossible now; in spite of all the things he had once avowed. Had he seen her desperation and used it, had he been aware all along of her clumsy chasing? Had she ever loved him, or was it the desperate devotion of a spaniel for its master? Clare shivered under the blankets.

In this cold light of day, Clare realised that her capitulation to all his ideas and demands was grounded in naivety and fear. Fear that if she didn't do as he wanted she would lose him. That wasn't love, how had she managed to kid herself for so long?

Her own self-deception had caused all this. Now, from this minute on she was going to listen to that nagging inner voice, she'd ignored for so long. Trust in her instincts. Put herself first, just as she'd set out to do when she left the farm. Certainly now she had been given another chance to get it right; only this time with no blunders. Her quest for love was done with, she hadn't found any of the emotions she'd read in the novels, so it must all be lies, fiction. Nothing to do with real life.

'Am I hardening up?' she demanded of the room. Shouldn't she be weeping and crying because of the blows she'd been dealt? No, suddenly she felt sorry for Phil and his narrow-minded cronies. They'd spend the rest of their lives treading the same small circle. She even wished the new girl joy in him, she couldn't hate him now. Had he found the little things she'd done around the flat? Guilt overwhelmed her, she didn't want to imagine his rage, but she'd have to live with the guilt because she wasn't about to go back to apologise.

At last, Clare began to warm up, and calm down, even feel a bit smug at the ease with which she'd dismissed all the pain, betrayal and grief she'd been dealt. Away from the physical grime and squalor of the city, she dismissed her inner feelings. As long as there was nothing to remind her, she could push it to the back of her mind and forget. The lack of replies to her questions was a comfort, from now on all the answers would be her own.

Then she remembered all the minor complications and leapt out of bed in eagerness to tackle them head-on. Clad once more in jeans and jumper, she tackled the array of curls. She found pins and elastic in the drawer beneath the mirror and brushed and pinned and tied them all into submission. She smiled at the friend in the mirror and made her way downstairs.

The kitchen was cosily warm, every surface was cluttered with the masculine mess, beer cans, tools, unwashed plates. Someone else who was habitually untidy. Why put something in a drawer when you'd need it tonight? In spite of her feast of the previous night, Clare was ravenous, so she plundered the kitchen, and made toast and coffee. She ate with bovine contentment, feet resting on the aga rail. Having sorted her emotions out so easily all the other problems must surely follow suit, it just showed how unhappy she must have been and just not realised it. The phone rang...

Clare jumped, she'd forgotten its presence and its links to Phil. Had he found Sylvie's number on something she'd left behind? No, it was unlikely; Sylvie had fled to the country long before Clare had joined 'the gang'.

'About time too, Alex. Some cat minder you are, you're never in!'

'Sylvie!' Clare squealed.

'What the blazes are you doing there - not ditched yet another job?'

'Well sort of, I left Phil last night.' Clare said with pride.

'Good! He always sounded a jerk. I can't be too long. Is Alex about?'

'No, he left not long ago.'

'Darn. You'll have to pass this on then. I'm staying out here for another six months. I've got a really lucrative assignment on a big paper. Get Alex to write and say if he'll stay until then. There's no point phoning, I'm all over the place.'

'Okay. I will. Is he one of your crowd from the college?'

'No, he's a mate of Ted's. He'd been living in an old shack in the marshes - you know what it's like to rent around here, so we've done each other a favour. He's quiet but allright. Stay as long as you wish. If Alex can't stay on as cat minder you can. I've got to go, I'm out of coins. Write soon, Alex has the address.' The line went dead.

Yellow sunlight trickled through the glass pane of the front door, inviting Clare out. Pausing only to find a pair of wellies from the pile under the table, Clare lifted the catch and burst out onto the empty garden. The air was mild and soft, scented with natural, earthy smells, no reek of the decay in the city. She strode along the track, now openly courting the puddles, enjoying their novelty after so long away from the country. Never again would she wear skirts, never again would she work in an office Clare vowed with conviction.

The mud dance halted as she saw once again the loathed typewriter and the bland faces of her workmates. No regrets at the loss of their companionship. She would keep her own company now. Mrs Jones, the Boss would be waiting, right now, to tick her off for unpunctuality, ready to sneer at any excuse. She would be defeated at the end of the day and have to find a new victim. Practicalities swamped Clare. She would have to at least ring the office and explain, give her new address. No! Phil would be able to track her down that way. They would send her P45 along with the last wage slip to the bank, then she'd transfer the account. That would neatly cover her tracks. Gleeful again, she took off down the lane. In the distance, a train hooted and began its clattering approach to the station.

The village was small, its original need for a station dating back to the days of private railways. The cluster of cottages, uniform in their local stone, had been discovered soon after the Agricultural population had moved out by the fore-runners of the 'Yuppies', and they'd kept the station and village alive to the extent that the village was growing and people were screaming at the planners to keep its rustic integrity. The shops were based around a small supermarket, the rest being traps for the unsuspecting tourists and the weekend gardeners.

Clare was surprised to find a wide range of goods in the supermarket. No village grocer here. There would be no need to range far afield to stock her larder, so she picked out basics enough so that she wouldn't infringe on any of Alex's supplies. How would he take her decision she wondered? With a start, Clare realised she'd made up her mind subconsciously because so many things were falling into place that everything pointed to her staying. All that needing sorting now was work, so at the checkout, she grabbed a local paper. The trek back up the lane was at a more decorous pace now she was laden with goods.

On her second entry to the kitchen, she felt like giving it a good clear out, but caution held her back. She still had to face telling the news to Alex. Last night seemed an aeon ago, the whiskey had blurred the edges of her memories. Despite her resolve, it was with trepidation that she lifted the receiver to ring the office. Before she'd run through the digits, she slammed it down vowing to write instead. Clare was restless. She'd never realised before just how the grind of work had forcefully filled her mind and time even if she was kicking against it. Rapidly she turned to the Situations Vacant in the paper. It made sad reading, the only need seemed to be for Care Assistants in nursing homes, nothing with animals or on farms. Perhaps Alex would be able to help. Totally on cue, she heard his truck rumble up the lane to the gate. As he pushed open the front door, Clare leapt to her feet, ill at ease and very self-conscious.

'Sylvie rang. She'll be out another six months,' she blurted out before he was fully in the room.

'That's no problem.' He busied himself with the kettle.

'She also said I can stay on as long as I want,' she replied, almost defiantly. Alex swung around. In full daylight, his eyes didn't seem so hooded and were a piercing blue. Clare was subjected to their full glare.

'And you intend to stay on?' he demanded.

'Well, she did say. I'm sorry.' Clare suddenly felt contrite.'Is it going to be a problem?'

'I don't think so, as long as we don't get under each other's feet.' He switched the glare off and Clare felt a blush rising - did he have a girlfriend?

'I won't intrude, I mean, if there's someone coming, I know how to make myself scarce.' It was his turn to be embarrassed.

'No, it's just, well, I'm used to my own company.'

'I won't get in your way.'

To her surprise, he'd made her a coffee, and he handed it to her.

'I'm sorry about last night,' Clare struggled on.

'Forget it,' he said gruffly and turned to the page in the newspaper.

'You looking for a job then?'

'There's nothing there but skivvying for the gentry or looking after the wrinklies. I don't think I could face either of those. Do you know of anything?'

'Don't sneer at those jobs. Someone has to do them. Skivvying as you call it can pay quite well. One family I work for are desperate for a cleaner and would pay £8 an hour!'

Clare nearly choked on her coffee. That was nearly her office rate.

'I wouldn't know what to do!'

'You can hoover and dust can't you?'

Clare bit back a comment on feminism. She wanted to preserve the status quo.

'I suppose so,' she begrudged.

'Well, there can't be much more than that to it.' Alex downed his coffee, picked up a toolbox and left without another word.

The idea of cleaning someone's house, doing as they bid, being a lackey, ruffled something inside Clare. It went directly against all her contemporary thinking and resolves for putting herself first. Modern women didn't need to be serfs anymore, that went out with the Victorian era. But, if no other jobs were going, what could she do? No amount of money was worth having if it meant scraping and bowing. These thoughts and similar spent the next week echoing around in Clare's head, while she searched vainly for a suitable job. All the Pubs and Hotels within reach would be laying off until the 'Season' began again next Easter. There were office jobs in the town further down the railway line, but she had to stick to her vows, there was no going back.

     She did try one rest home, but the sight of a slack-mouthed old lady being bundled into a cardigan by a stern-faced nurse made her feel physically ill. Her imagination scanned all the tasks from feeding to changing incontinence pads, which sent Clare fleeing the Nursing Home before she even got called into the interview. Trudging home in the rain her bleak thoughts turned black. Perhaps it wouldn't hurt to try cleaning. The only other alternative was to claim the dole. Clare remembered the one time she had applied for it. The hours sat on stiff plastic seats with complaining housewives and screeching kids. The form filling had been too personal to be dealt with by an ashen-faced, apathetic woman. Clare had left the buildings smelling of humiliation that came from trying to claim what was a right from a mean organisation. No, she'd have to be desperate to try that again. At her age, there was no excuse for not working. The week of frustration pushed her to the decision. There was nothing to lose by asking Alex if the job was still going.

     Alex. She'd seen precious little of him in the past week. He always left the house before she awoke, and from the supplies in the fridge, she knew he took sandwiches for work. He returned at dusk, while Clare was watching the television. She'd never had time before now so she indiscriminately drank it in like a greedy child until into the early hours.

Clare would hear the clattering and smell of Alex's cooking from the kitchen, but he never joined her afterwards. He would either go up to his room where the stereo would try to decimate the television, or he went out again. The few times their paths had crossed, it had only been to exchange generalities of the weather or to check if the cat had actually been fed or if he was trying it on again. Tigger had become Clare's main companion, warming her lap and purring to the flames. Clare had tried to do her bit around the house - hoovering and dusting. She had even tried to haul in the logs for the burner only to find Alex had brought in a ton and piled it by the fire in her absence. So now it became an act of courage to break through their self-imposed barriers. Surely, he had forgotten that first night, forgiven her for staying? She remembered Phil's grumpiness and how long that could go on for, so she tarred Alex with the same brush. It was with a start she realised she hadn't thought of Phil the whole week and mentally congratulated herself.

That evening she cautiously knocked on the kitchen door, then marched in. Alex looked surprised, sitting behind a mound of spaghetti on toast.

'What can I do for you?' he said with old-world courtesy.

'Well, that job, is it still going?'
He smiled, seemed less fierce.

'As far as I know. Come down off your high horse then? Right, I'll ring them now.' He was gone leaving the spaghetti steaming on the plate. Clare felt flabbergasted at his friendliness - perhaps he had forgiven her and realised they would be able to rub along? She didn't know what to do, so she hopped from foot to foot trying to eavesdrop on the conversation. On his return, he gestured her to sit.

'You're to go over there at 2 pm tomorrow for an interview,' he said with the generosity of a great benefactor.

'Thanks - but where is it?'

'Don't worry, I'll come over and pick you up.' Clare really was startled now.

'I'll be ready. Thank-you. You don't need to put yourself out - I'm sure I'd get over there somehow.'

He shook his head, mouth full, then after swallowing, 'I've got to be over that way then anyway.'

'Thanks. I'll be ready at I.30 then?' He nodded and Clare fled. Perhaps if they kept on keeping out of each other's way things would be Ok. Relieved Clare abandoned herself to yet another game show.

The morning found Clare's room splattered with clothes as she frantically searched for something suitable for an interview with the gentry. For a split second, she regretted the heap of glamour piled on Phil's bed, then resolved that if they didn't take her as she was then she'd have to rethink again. In the end, she ironed the life out of a red pair of corduroys and sponged some smears from a sweatshirt. For the interview's benefit, she released the curls. They combed into some semblance of their original order, but she saw hints of red growing out at the roots.

Alex was punctual and hooted at the gate. Clare now had to take care walking into the lane. She didn't want to smear mud on what no doubt what would be expensive carpets. She was aware of Alex watching her waltz down the path.

'Shouldn't you, well, be in something like a skirt?'

Clare, already on edge snapped, 'This is the best I've got. If they don't like it, that's their problem.'

Sitting in the cab, Clare felt furious with herself for snapping. Had she blown their truce? She looked at Alex, but he was concentrating on driving. He showed no respect for the vehicle and Clare found herself being bumped and thrown until they hit the tarmac. Then they lurched down a maze of lanes, completely losing Clare's orientation, but soon they turned onto another track and the jolting resumed. Ordeal finally over, Clare checked her curls in the driving mirror.

'Will I do?'

'You'll do.' To her relief, he smiled.

The house they'd parked outside was a large Victorian farmhouse that had been tidied, double glazed and landscaped. The few buildings it had been allowed to keep were garages. A wall ran around the courtyard hiding the rest of the property. Clare walked in what she hoped was a sedate manner to the front door and pulled the bell. She saw Alex disappearing through a green door in the wall and she felt very alone. Far away inside the house a bell rang but was instantly answered.

'Miss Brown. How do you do? I'm Mr Harrison.' He extended a hand which Clare took and 'How do you do'ed' back. She followed his tall wiry frame down a long corridor decked on either side by dim portraits, and sideboards groaning with china statues.

They entered what seemed an acre of living-room, all decorated and furnished in shades of grey. A mousey haired woman with bifocals rose and extended her hand in the same manner. Clare was aware she was being scrutinised head to foot and clung to her convictions about trousers.

'Do take a seat,' she gestured. Mr Harrison had vanished from sight.

'Now, Alex, I'm sure has told you we do rather need a cleaner. Someone to get to grips with this 'hise'!'

Clare felt a rise of nervous giggles, the voice was a parody of the false upper-class accents she heard on the telly. It was unbelievable that people actually did speak like that. Yet the look in Mrs Harrison's eyes was friendly. Clare felt the giggles disappear.

'What we need is rooms turning out, some mending. Are you any good at sewing?'

'I have tried making my own clothes.' Clare tried not to see the ragged hems and parting seams of her one effort.

'We have a lot of china which needs cleaning too. All this is on top of day-to-day dusting, floors and things - do you think you can manage that sort of thing?'

Clare began to see the enormity of the task, but she'd seen something of the house and she rather wanted to see it all. She shrugged aside the fib over the sewing, she'd manage.

'I think it'll be a real challenge,' she finally replied.

'Good. Do you have any references?'

'I've got a couple, but they mostly refer to office work.'

'What I need is a character reference.' Clare screwed up her face trying to remember their contents.

'I'm sure they cover that sort of thing.'

'Why did you leave London?'

'I lost the lease on my flat, and I needed a change, so I came down here to try to get a perspective on things,' Clare lied glibly. What else had Alex told them about her? Mrs Harrison was nodding.

'I know, it's so impossible to get a decent place in town. We have got another hise up there. My two sons use that at the moment. We just go up for visits and shopping.' She stood up abruptly as if to change the subject.

'Come and see around the place.' The dining-room was opposite the sitting-room and looked over the courtyard. A huge mahogany table dwarfed the room. Clare inwardly quailed at the thought of polishing it. The sideboard was laden with silver candlesticks and trays. A door at the far end led to a small study, which gave Clare the sense that this was the room they lived in. It was lined floor to ceiling with books. Squashed comfortable chairs were grouped around the fireplace and a television. Through another door, Clare found herself in the kitchen. This was done out in ultra modern units and the worktops were littered with every cooking aid Clare had ever seen. In the middle was an old oak table, and once again Clare felt this room was lived in.

'I do rather enjoy cooking,' was Mrs Harrison's comment. 'You probably won't have to do much in here! Through there is a utility room. This house is rather jolly, all the rooms lead into one another. The children used to run around in circles through the house on wet days. Now upstairs.'

There were five bedrooms, each with their own bathroom. Apart from the master bedroom, they were all dusty with the air of long disuse. Each was decorated with a special colour scheme. Clare felt she was living in a book, the Red room, the Yellow room and wanted to laugh as she followed Mrs Harrison downstairs.

'Now do you think you can take it on?' Clare was surprised so asked - shouldn't Mrs Harrison be saying they'd think about it. They must be desperate but perhaps there was a crunch to it. She was right.

'We'll pay £6 for the first month, then £8 if we suit each other.'

'How many days?' asked Clare, feeling disappointed.

'Monday, Wednesday and Friday, 9.30 am. - 4 pm. Bring your own sandwiches, but I'll supply coffee!' Mrs Harrison said magnanimously. Some of the things Clare had seen around the house were lovely. She hated seeing the place so dusty and uncared for. She'd never been in a house such as this before, but Clare had ideas on how it should be and she would have to be the one to do it, as Mrs Harrison seemed to be incapable.

'Yes, I think I can take the challenge,' Clare stated firmly.

'Wonderful.' Mrs Harrison rose and held out her hand again.

'We'll see you on Monday then.' Her tone was dismissive now the deal was settled making Clare want to tell her to stuff the job, but she didn't. She found herself on the porch, blinking in strong sunlight. Alex was waiting in the truck.

'You taking it then?'

'Yes. it will be quite a task to put it to rights,' Clare clapped her hand to her brow. 'How on earth do I get here?'

'There's an old bike in the shed. I'll oil it for you. But you can have a lift on your first day, as I'm here on Monday.' After thanking him, the conversation seemed at an end. Alex was concentrating on driving. As she jolted, Clare tried to imagine herself working - spending all day cleaning and prayed it wouldn't be boring in spite of her earlier conviction.

The truck ground to a halt outside the cottage and Clare jumped out. To her surprise, as she slammed the door, Alex revved the engine and drove off in a cloud of smoke, without even a casual wave goodbye.

TOM
1988

The room was dark, warm and humid. In one corner the red and green lights of a stereo blinked and whirled to muffled music. Tom on the bed had his eyes fiercely closed, the row in the headphones as loud as could humanely be born, yet still, he sensed another rhythm and hated it with a fury equal to the crescendo in his ears. The music stopped. The other rhythm continued, now animated with voices from the black void. Tom threw the headphones at the stereo and charged out of the room, the noise propelling him into his mother's bedroom.

  'Stop it, stop it NOW!' His screams filled the room, and he sank to the floor, weeping in relief at the silence. The sound of bedclothes being yanked and pulled preceded the light going on, then the room was stage lit over the bed. His mother was sitting up, defensively holding the sheets under her chin, her face white with fear; dismay etched in the bleared lines of her make-up. The dark haired man wasn't so concerned. Bare-chested he reached for cigarettes, lit two and handed one into the woman's trembling hand. He drew hard then looked at the other two with an amused expression. Bold in his relief, Tom demanded, 'Don't hit her. Will you leave us alone now?' Astonishingly, the man laughed with a bull-like roar his head tipping right back. Tom felt it was as bad as the previous shuddering.

'Did you really think I didn't know about you? You two must be thick.' His look turned to one of mild disgust.

'But you hate kids,' said a faltering voice.

'Only my own. Here nipper.' He threw the cigarettes at Tom. 'Go and watch the telly, you won't hear us down there.' He gestured dismissively towards the door. Obedient in his surprise, Tom backed out, cigarettes in hand and shut the door on the conversation that sprung up. By the time he'd reached the foot of the stairs, the roaring laughter was echoing around the house again.

Automatically he turned the telly on. All the cold nights on the streets, all the evenings hiding in the dark, not even daring to go to the loo, the insults, the teasing at school, pure misery for this! Even the beatings he'd received had never felt as bad as this. A casual dismissal. It had all been for nothing. He wanted to cry, hit something, smash it. He thumped the settee until clouds of dust rose, choking him. Temporarily drained of emotion, he watched the dust settle in a layer on the table. Idly, he drew a swirling figure. A slow smile began to spread across his face. Tomorrow he'd tell Douggie, he always knew what to do. After that, they'd have tea together, and they'd make a plan. They'd get their revenge on the Bull. Tom sat down and concentrated on the telly.

The secretive smile stayed on his face all through his mother's apologies and new plans for the future, she thought he was happy now all was resolved. She didn't realise his thoughts were dark.

CLARE
1993

Clare filled the evening writing a long letter to Sylvie, pouring out all the events and decisions of the past few weeks. By the time she scrawled her name at the end, she felt relieved from many unnecessary burdens. Although the cottage had been silent all evening, it wasn't until she saw the pile of unwashed crockery in the kitchen that she realised Alex hadn't returned. Where was he? He'd never been away this late in the evening, and she needed her lift in the morning. He'd be back sometime soon she convinced herself as she closed the bedroom curtains, but when she opened them in the dim morning light, the truck wasn't there.

What on earth was she going to do? Clare's stomach lurched, the mild exhilaration she'd felt on opening her eyes turning to dread. She couldn't lose a job before she'd even started it! Damn Alex and his strange moods. How far was the Harrison's place? It was difficult to calculate because the lanes had twisted and turned so many times. The bedroom clock read 7.30 am., so she'd have to hurry; whatever the distance it would be a long walk. Walk? Hadn't Alex mentioned a bike? Clare dressed rapidly and sped down the stairs.

The shed was jammed by a buckled door but when it finally wrenched open, Clare saw the bike waiting inside. Despite being covered in mildew and grime the tyres were firm. Grudgingly, she pushed it out into the garden. The seat was only just within reaching distance for her legs, but she hoisted herself up and squeaked and wobbled down the path. Satisfied, she leant back against the shed. Her watch revealed how the time had seeped away and her stomach was rumbling angrily. In the kitchen, Clare assembled clumsy doorstep sandwiches and gulped down sickly sweet coffee. Grimly she tucked her socks into her jeans and set out.

As the gate swung shut behind her, a familiar rumble started up the lane. Alex's truck ground to a halt inches short of her front tyre.

'What the hell are you doing. I said I'd be here!'

Alex swung out of the truck, his face haggard, eyes bleary, and a growth of stubble making his face seem more surly than ever.

'I'm sorry when the truck wasn't there, I thought, that well...' Clare realised she hadn't given a single thought to Alex's welfare, only the importance of getting herself to work. Guilt swamped her not only for her lack of concern but her lack of trust. Clare blushed. Alex strode past her towards the cottage.

'You've plenty of time. Put that thing away and come on,' he muttered. Humiliated, Clare pushed the bike back to the shed. She didn't want to go in and face him but there didn't seem to be any choice. Alex was hacking away at a loaf of bread. Clare noticed his hands were shaking, and the slices were crooked. She seized a chance to make amends.

'I'll do them if you want to go and have a shave.' He dropped the knife and thundered upstairs. By the time Clare was jamming the lid on his plastic box, Alex returned, looking fresher but no less tired.

'I must make some things clear,' he stated. 'If I say I'll do something, I do it. I don't let people down. But I only offered you the lift today because I happen to be going there. Don't expect any more favours, I'm on my own, a free agent. I don't want to be tied to anything. Just because we share the place doesn't mean you have to start worrying about when I'm in or out.'

'I had already gathered that, thank you. I can still perfectly well take the bike if it's such a burden to have to take me,' Clare snapped, guilt rapidly dimming. Alex brought any further comments to a halt by glaring at the clock.

'Now it is time to go.' He strode out of the house. Clare followed him, sandwiches firmly tucked under her arm. Inwardly she was seething. This time she was prepared for the jolting and hung on grimly, returning to her earlier thoughts. As soon as she had some money aside she was off. There was no need to live with Alex's grumpiness any second longer than necessary. When they stopped, she leapt from the cab without a word.

The house looked welcoming in the grey December morning, a whirl of leaves blew across the yard as Clare crossed it to the front door. This time there was no rapid answer to her ring, and she shivered in the cold wind. She was just about to ring again when she heard the bolts being drawn. It was Mr Harrison, dressed in country corduroys and a less cordial expression.

'There's a side door we use most of the time,' he stated and pointed around the corner. 'I'm off to get the papers. Mrs Harrison said there's some washing-up to do to get you started. The machine's packed up,' and he stood aside to let her through. Once again, Clare felt deflated. She was itching to tackle the treasures of the house, not scrub pots and pans. However, she filled the sink and set to. She was drying the last plate when Mrs Harrison sauntered in.

'Good morning! You can clear the breakfast things now, then start on the Study. Pull all the books down and hoover them. There's an attachment. Then do the shelves, wash the china in the utility room, then hoover the house right through. That should do you today. Oh, and here's the cleaning cupboard.' She pulled open a tall door revealing a tangle of cloths, buckets, aerosol cans and a hoover.

'The tray's in the dining-room.' With another vague smile, she was gone. Clare felt like telling her to stick the job right then and there. But what choice was there if she wanted to get away from Alex? She had to give it a fair trial. Just look on it as an office boss asking for letters typed, ignore the patronising tone of voice. So Clare trotted off obediently to the dining-room. As she loaded the tray, she noticed that just one end of the table was cleared of dust. Had they eaten in there for her benefit or because they wouldn't have to lug it all back again?

The second bout of washing-up completed, Clare staggered to the study laden with hoover, cloths and an assortment of polishes. She surveyed the three walls of books, ceiling to floor, ranging from great leather-bound tomes of Dickens to Dick Francis paperbacks. Hoover the books! Alright to say if you weren't actually going to do it! Clare pulled over a stool and carefully cleared the top shelf. Down with the books fell an ancient birthday card, a pink picture of a coy little girl who was six. She couldn't resist reading the inscription. Darling Helen, lots of love, Mummy, Daddy and the boys! Clare was puzzled, she was certain Mrs Harrison had spoken only of her sons. Clare threw the card in the bin and soldiered on. The drone of the hoover was hypnotic, but the occasional scan of an interesting book relieved the monotone. As she slipped the last book back onto the shelf, she realised it was 12.30. Her back was aching, her ears ringing, and she was starving. Clare made her way eagerly to the kitchen. Mrs Harrison was in there, sporting a designer apron, stir-frying something indescribable.

'You forgot your coffee,' she indicated a congealing cup.' Never mind, make yourself another and have your lunch.' Clare ate in silence because Mrs Harrison pointedly switched the radio on too loud for any conversation. Clare had been quite looking forward to a chat after the mornings grind, so felt huffy. Now she knew what it felt like to be a serf, and she began to think communistic thoughts. The trilling of the phone sent Mrs Harrison clattering out of the kitchen. Through the thin partition wall, Clare heard bits of the conversation despite the radio.

'My dear, we did have a super time with you and Bill. Did Harry get home Ok?... lovely... Oh yes, we finally got one. It's early days yet, but I think I've found a treasure; toiled all morning without demanding coffee or a fag. No, I won't give her your number!' She shrieked with laughter, 'See you on Saturday, Bye!'

Clare felt slightly mollified, at least she was approved of. Perhaps it wouldn't be so bad after all. She threw her bread wrapper in the bin and returned to the study. Mrs Harrison was holding the birthday card, a horrified expression on her face.

'I found that on the top shelf. I didn't realise you had a daughter too,' Clare said conversationally. Mrs Harrison jumped, then looked at Clare with a blank look on her face.

'The vegetables!' she yelped and tore out of the room, card falling to the floor. Clare picked it up and followed her. Mrs Harrison was frantically stirring.

'Put that in the bin,' she ordered, her back turned, 'I've no idea where it came from. I've managed to save the lunch. I think the bit of caramelisation will set the hearts off a treat. Offal is so good for you!' Clare began to feel sorry for Mr Harrison, the cooking smelt horrible.

The one o'clock news came on, and Mrs Harrison glanced pointedly at the clock. Clare washed her cup and returned to her duties. At last, she could bring the china back to life. She gathered an armful and took them to the utility room. In the hot sudsy water, dainty, befrilled ladies, and blue Copenhagen birds changed from dull, drab monuments to pieces of art, filled with colour and life.

In the distance, Clare overheard the Harrison's at lunch. The deep boom of Mr Harrison carried down the corridor although she couldn't pick out the words. Suddenly the voices sprang into a heated argument. In spite of their breeding, the couple sounded like a pair of fish wives. It ended up with Mr Harrison shouting, 'You stupid cow!' and footsteps pounding upstairs. Clare was shocked, she'd somehow imagined them above such things. Cautiously, she made her way back to the study, cradling her sparkling figurines. Through the door she saw the dining-room, now empty, plates of half finished food left for her to clear. She polished the bureaux then set the collection in a conversational group. That was what it was all about, Clare told herself and returned to washing-up with equanimity.

The rest of the afternoon was spent hoovering through the house, negotiating all the bumps and crannies where the ancient floors sagged. As Clare lugged her tools back to the cupboard, she looked out through the sitting-room window and saw the Harrison's, obviously reconciled, walking arm in arm around the garden. Clare felt overwhelmingly tired. The work was so different from anything within her experience that it generated its own sort of weariness. It was refreshing to get out into the clear air after being stuck indoors for so long. Mrs Harrison appeared around the corner as Clare shut the back door.

'You off already? It's not time, surely?' But a glance at her watch confirmed it.

'Very well then,' she said begrudgingly.'I'll see you on Wednesday. Alex is around in the vegetable garden.'

The door in the wall revealed a large well-maintained garden, the black rows of earth dotted with plants of vibrant green. In spite of the rapidly fading light, Alex was digging beside the greenhouse. The sweat on his still bronzed back, shone as he moved, he looked leaner and fitter than when clad in his uniform of jumpers and jeans. At last, he caught sight of Clare and grabbed his shirt from an idle fork as she walked over. Clare pretended she hadn't seen.

'I won't be long,' Alex gruffly stated. 'Fetch my bag from the greenhouse.' Clare entered the still humid house, which was filled with yellowing worn out tomato plants. The smell from the leaves filled the air. Clare backed out from the stench.

'Never have liked that smell,' she said conversationally.

'Can't say I've ever given it a thought,' he muttered as he took the bag. Once seated in the truck, Clare had to tell him about her day - she had no-one else.

'I'm surprised it went so well. It's really quite rewarding when you can see some results from your work. Do they have a daughter? I found an old birthday card and Mrs Harrison went totally peculiar. Have you heard them argue? I didn't think people like that would fight!'

'Don't think they're immune, just because they've got cash. No, I don't know about a daughter. Will you stick at the job then?'

'You know, I think I will!' Clare saw the hint of a smile about Alex's face as they jolted home.

Clare stood on the steps of the bank in Chardminster, blinking in the strong sunlight. Her visit the Bank had not only supplied her with a cheque book and card but also the knowledge that she was slightly better off than expected. She'd completely forgotten her fortnight worked in hand, so her last pay from the office had been generously large. Clare paused, pulling on gloves. The fierce frost of the previous night had left its remnants in the air as heavily clad shoppers fought their way along leaving trails of steaming breath behind them. The streets were festooned with gaily coloured lights, and for a moment Clare couldn't understand why then a sense of gloom filled her, Christmas was coming. Each shop window was filled with fat Father Christmas's and brightly coloured wrapped empty boxes. Even the bank had gone the whole hog, enticing people to take on that extra debt, so that those very few days would be the most wonderful ever, never mind the fact that the repayments would cripple them for the rest of the year. Clare snorted. Didn't they see the con? The sheer waste of time and money? For the first time in her life, she was glad of her grim childhood, its bleak Christmas's served as a strong warning against all the commercialism. As for all the religious stuff that was hurled about at this time...

Clare swung out onto the pavement and into the throng of shoppers and was carried along with the tide. Despite her smugness, it was very difficult to resist the temptations within the shops, but Clare grimly stuck to her guns and bought only the items on her list. There would be time enough for luxuries when she was financially secure. As she left the last shop her eyes were caught by a familiar mop of hair amongst the shoppers. Clare involuntarily took a step back onto someone's toe. After she had apologised, she took stock of her reaction. Was she scared of Alex? Was he such a monster that she had to cringe at the sight of him? Maybe it was his unpredictable nature. Clare had never been scared of anyone in her life, and she wasn't going to start now. Forcefully she dodged her way through the shoppers but lost him.

The Town Hall clock striking twelve showed her there was no time for her pursuit, she had an appointment to keep. The previous night's paper had held an interesting advertisement which said; GIRL FRIDAY needed for busy Business man. 07423392 Marsh Lane.

While the Harrisons job was well paid, she wanted more money, to give her some sort of financial safety. The lane in question was only a short distance from the cottage. Her phone call had yielded an answer-phone, so Clare had had to grit her teeth and leave a message. The reply was unexpectedly prompt that evening. The man, naming himself Chris Rowan invited her in a soft Scots accent to present herself at 2.00 pm. for an interview.

The cottage was down an undistinguished gravel lane, one of a pair of Victorian Villas, quite out of place in their country setting. One was occupied by a large family because Clare saw volumes of washing hanging on the line. So she shook the rope of a cowbell hanging by the front door of the other. To her surprise, the door was answered by a stunning looking redhead. She looked inquiringly down her nose at Clare who suddenly became aware of her wind swept hair and muddy jeans.

'Clare Brown. About the job.' The woman's face cleared and as she strode off down the path she said, 'go straight into the kitchen.' A secretary wondered Clare mischievously. She almost collided with a tall man who was thundering down the stairs.

'Chris,' he said without preamble and firmly shook her hand.

'Clare,' she stated and followed him to what must be the kitchen. To say it was a mess was an understatement; it was awash with disorder and grime made and Alex seem neat and tidy. In the stark electric light, Clare felt shocked by the look of the man. The designer stubble was alright, but the dark hollows under his eyes and the gaunt cheekbones gave him a haunted look. His dark hair was going liberally grey at the temples and his clothes hung loosely on him as if he'd recently lost a lot of weight. Yet he spoke cheerfully enough.

'Yes, it is rather a mess. I don't major on the domestic side. Can you cope with this sort of carnage?'

'Is the rest of the house like it?' Clare wanted to bite back the words, they seemed so cheeky, but Chris didn't seem to mind.

'Fraid so. You'd better come and look.'

He led her into the sitting-room which was also overflowing with clutter. The bedrooms looked like the aftermath of a jumble sale and the bathroom as if a team of rugby players had popped in for a wash. Chris chatted all the way round.

'I'm working a lot in the states at the moment, so I don't get the time for this. I need it cleaned and serviced regularly when I'm here, and just kept tidy when I'm away! If it would be possible, I'd need you to check the Ansaphone and get in groceries when I'm due back.' They passed outside a locked door. 'Don't worry about this room, it's full of boxes and junk, so I don't use it.' Once they returned to the kitchen, Chris gave the ultimatum.

'Well, can you face it?'
Clare had seen that once the mess was cleared, underneath was quite a neat little house. Chris misunderstood her hesitation.

'I'd pay £6 an hour and say - a set £25 a week when I'm not here.'
Clare gulped, he must be loaded.

'Yes, I think that's er, well fine. When would you like me to start?'

'Tomorrow?'

'No - I'm working elsewhere. You didn't say what hours?'

'Well, I think it will take a day or two to sort it. Why don't you come in and clear it through, then we'll sort out a weekly number of hours.'

'That's fine.' Clare felt the real professional.

'You have done this sort of thing before?' Chris asked.

'I work for the Harrison's,' Clare bluffed glibly.

'Don't know them, but the name rings a bell. 9.30 on Thursday then?' They shook hands and Clare left. On the slow wander home, Clare totted up the earning potential of the job and began to plan her new flat and car. The air was chilling rapidly with the approaching frost, so Clare was glad to bask in the cottage's warmth once she returned. The radio was blaring from the kitchen, and Clare remembered her earlier resolve not to be intimidated by Alex. He was stirring something on the stove.

'Did I see you in Chardminster the other day?' Clare asked to start the conversation. Alex looked surprised.

'Yes, I needed to get some tools.'

'Not Christmas shopping?' Clare wished she'd never mentioned it because he immediately looked cross.

'I don't hold with all that stuff! It's just a waste of money.' He glared at her as if daring her to defy him. He couldn't know her views.

'Actually, I agree with you.'

'So you won't be wanting to deck this place out like a fairy grotto?'

'Good grief, no. Do you go and see your family or anything?' A strange look passed across his face. 'Haven't got any. You?' He muttered.

'Made a complete break a long time ago.' An idea struck Clare. 'Seeing as neither of us holds with all this stuff, shall we declare this place a no Christmas zone?'

'What, just treat it like an ordinary day?'

'Yes, just forget about the whole thing.'

'Suits me fine.'

At last, they seemed to be in agreement on something.

'There's something for you, out the back.' Clare went to look out the window. Leaning against the shed was the bike, but even in the dim light, Clare saw it was polished and oiled, the seat lowered.

'Thanks Alex. Look you must let me cook you a meal sometime as a thank-you. Everything seems to be falling into place. I got another job today, as a girl Friday to a bloke down Marsh Lane.'

'What sort of bloke is he?'

'A business man.'

'That doesn't mean anything. You just watch yourself.'

Clare had to provoke him.

'From what?'

'Well, you know,' said Alex awkwardly. 'Men on their own - well, might be dangerous.'

'Good grief Alex, the Victorian era passed a long time ago, I can look after myself.'

'Well, just be careful then!' he snapped.

'What happened to being free agents then? I'm a modern woman, I can cope!' Clare couldn't take the doubtful look on Alex's face and slouched out. By the time she'd reached the top of the stairs, she was cursing herself for once again ruining the status quo.

TOM
1989

'It's all clear - I'm going Douggie,' Tom
gesticulated behind him. In the stillness of early
morning he leapt, antelope-like across the road,
between the cars to the terraced house.
Carefully, he raised the letterbox and slid the
envelope through. It plopped satisfyingly onto the
floor inside. Once again, he leapt across the
street to the hiding place in the alley. He wanted
to giggle, shriek, hit something. It had all been so
easy. As Douggie had said, the years of
concocting the plan had been fun, but this was
the icing on the cake. So often they'd imagined
the Bull's wife reading the letter telling her of the
affair. The anger, the fright, one of them leaving,
it was incredible to think of it all actually
happening, today. The yellow sun began to tip
over the rooftops, it was time to go. They'd
wanted to hear the furore from the safety of the
hiding place, but the family just hadn't woken in
time. Regretfully, they ran down the alley to the
main street where they broke into exuberant
shrieks and yells.
     'She'll kill him!'
     'That'll wipe that smirk off his face.'
     'Imagine him crying.'
     'He should have left my mother alone in
the first place!'
     Such blissful ideas kept them going until
they turned a familiar corner. Caution was now
needed. People must think He had already left
home if the master plan was to succeed.
Stealthily they crept around the back of the
house through the yard, into the kitchen. Shutting
the door they heard the water running in the

bathroom above. The conspirators grinned, it was so so ridiculously easy, every step was happening just as they'd planned. They crept upstairs to the bathroom where she lay in the sudsy bath, idly rinsing her hair with an old cup, humming to the tune on the radio.

One whack of the cricket bat sent her body to the bottom of the bath, water cascading over the edges, cup skidding across the lino. All that was needed to finish the job was to tip in the radio she'd so carefully wired through to the bathroom. One flash, an electrical zap, and she lay in the pink water, eyes accusing, deep red hair billowing as if in a delicate breeze. Tom's shocked mind photographed the scene in minute detail, to be recalled throughout his life. The bat was quickly and obviously hidden in the back of the wardrobe, wrapped in an old T-shirt of the Bull's. Tom collected his bag, planted his farewell note, carefully dated the previous week in a prominent position in his bedroom. He then sauntered out of the house into the still yellow sun, and waited cautiously at the back of number 32, in case he was spotted while Doggie collected his bag. He waited.

The sun dipped over the houses and he shivered in the shade. Cold spread from his knees, throughout his body and he began to shake. The light in the alley seemed to be growing darker and colder than was right for midsummer. A blast of winter seared through him. There would be no Douggie. His own hands had just brutally murdered his mother. Chilled to the marrow, he turned and slunk down the street. He couldn't go to the police, point a finger and say Douggie made me do it. Because Douggie had never been there.

CLARE
1993

Mrs Harrison, her face flushed with excitement, was waiting in the kitchen for Clare. She barely had time to hang up her coat before she was hustled upstairs.

'The boys are on their way down, they're coming for Christmas after all! We must crack on and get the rooms ready,' said Mrs Harrison as she led the way upstairs. They paused to collect piles of crisp white linen and towels from a lavender smelling cupboard on the landing. The first room they entered was decorated in pastel shades of green, all the furniture and curtains echoing the colour of the walls.

'This has been Duncan's room since he was a baby. I can still see that collection of plastic aeroplanes hanging from the ceiling.' Mrs Harrison sighed and peeled back the covers on the bed with childish enthusiasm. Then she began to make the bed with a matron like efficiency. Clare had never seen her so animated and found herself fumbling with the stiff sheets, as she tried to copy Mrs Harrison's expert folding. Yet all her corners ended up floppy and loose. Fortunately, Mrs Harrison didn't seem to notice because she was busy feeding Clare snippets of information about her sons.

'Duncan's a stock-broker, doing very well in the business and he's only 28. Quite a one for the girls.' At this, she smiled at Clare rakishly or was it a warning Clare wondered.

'Sometimes I wish he'd settle down though. I can't keep up with all the names and they somehow all seem to look alike. It seems only yesterday he was throwing mud at the village girls, and some of the scrapes nanny had to extract him from... He takes after his father in a lot of ways.' At this, she threw the bedspread back over and lead the way through an adjoining door to the next bedroom. This room was done out in pastel yellows and seemed warmer, more cheerful than the other.

'Make sure Peter has plenty of towels.' Mrs Harrison ordered, 'He seems to live in the bath. Now he's just landed a rather good contract with an Advertising Agency, he's a Graphic artist. He's definitely the brainy one, but he could do with being more like his brother. The girls he does bring home are few and far between, and highly unsuitable. It's about time one of them delivered some grandchildren!'

The second bed was made with more efficiency on Clare's part and together they smoothed down its cover. Clare was shocked at the sudden intimacy because now she'd have to look both men in the eye. By the time Clare had scrubbed and polished the bathroom, Mrs Harrison had put welcoming touches to the rooms. Glossy magazines and paperbacks for Duncan, a pile of The Field and a vase of glowing chrysanthemums for Peter. Clare smiled at the simple touches. Mrs Harrison loved her children in the same way as any other mother and trekked downstairs and fetched the hoover. She had become engrossed in cleaning Duncan's room when she became aware of the tingling sensation due to being watched. Clare span around to meet the amused stare of a broad blonde man who was idly leaning against the door frame.

'Service isn't too good here,' he said. 'I've had to carry my own bags.' They burst out laughing and he stretched a hand out in greeting.

'Duncan. I hear you're Clare and a treasure! Don't let it go to your head and don't let them overwork you.'

Clare saw the arrogance in his casually swept back hair and sharp features. He had something of Phil's demeanour about him as he slung his bags onto the bed and clicked them open. Clare realised she was dismissed, so she took the hoover to the next room. She'd been beaten to it. Peter wasn't present but his clothes were strewn all over the bed. A crumpled dinner suit hung crookedly from a curtain rail. From the bathroom came the sound of running water. Suppressing a giggle Clare hoovered the worst of the fluff from the carpet, hoping she'd be done before he came out. Behind the chair, the hoover met a metal object. Clare pulled out a bin, filled with crushed chrysanthemums. She quickly put them back and left the room. The afternoon was spent sorting out the utility room. Clare was putting the last shining vase back onto the shelf when Mrs Harrison popped her head around the door.

'I know it's Christmas Eve tomorrow, but is there any chance you would you be a lamb and come and wash up for a dinner party? We're having just a few of the neighbours around, but with all the work on Christmas Day...'
Clare hadn't realised Christmas was so soon. Somehow she'd lost track of the days, but she couldn't think of any reason not to help. It was all extra money.

'What time would you like me?' Mrs Harrison honoured her with one of her broad grins.

'About 7.30, then you should be away by 10. I'll make sure it's worth your while,' she ended with the now familiar drawl. The afternoon was growing prematurely dark. Heavy rain clouds were skidding across the sky.

'Why don't you press on now before it pours down?' offered Mrs Harrison with magnanimity. Clare readily agreed and was soon pushing her bike out into the wind, pondering on how long it would take her to get used to being patronised. The threatened deluge arrived before she'd reached the end of the drive. Clare's hands began to freeze in the icy bombardment, and she had to keep on stopping to wipe her face dry. To compound her misery the going became very rough. Clare ground to a halt, her suspicions confirmed. The front tyre was flat.

'Stupid bloody bicycle!' She aimed a kick at the ancient frame. Even if it was blown, she was going to ride it anyway, it had to be quicker than walking. Clare pulled her hood higher around her face and began to remount. A familiar roar bellowed through the rain. Clare's heart leapt in relief - deliverance. She leapt up in excitement, only to see the truck plough on, regardless.

'Alex!' she screamed in vain. Now not only was she soaked but also angry. Why didn't he stop, the selfish pig? Clare turned back to the bike.

'Got a flat tyre?' Clare hadn't heard the purring MG following the truck. Duncan's blonde hair was turning brown in the rain dripping from its roof.
'Dump the bike in the field and I'll give you a lift.' The window rolled back up. Clare obeyed with alacrity and slid into the warm cocoon of the car.

'Where to, wet person?' he grinned.

'Harefield Cottages - about a mile the other side of the station.' The car slid on, oblivious of the rutted road, its sophisticated suspension absorbing all the bumps. Clare became aware of the pool she was leaving on the seats and tried to aim the drips onto the floor. It seemed only a matter of seconds and they were outside the cottage. Duncan stared at it, through the blanket of rain.

'Sylvie Mathews place - whatever are you doing here?' Duncan demanded.

'I live there. Sylvie's out in Australia, working on a paper.'

'Well, I never. We used to play together as kids, even went to the same school until we were whipped away to Boarding School. Do tell me when she returns - catch up on old times and all that.' He leant across to open the door. Clare was aware of the assured, masculinity of his movements.

'Thank-you so much. You really saved me.' Clare lurched out. It was difficult climbing up out of a car when you were used to getting down.

'No probs,' he replied, and the car disappeared away into the rain.

Clare felt unexpectedly cheerful. She might even forgive Alex for not seeing her. She ran a boiling hot bath and wallowed until thawed. Providing the rain lifted, she could walk to Chris in the morning, then pick up the bike on the way home and fix it in time for her evening's work. Clare began to sing.

Clare misjudged the timing of her walk to Chris and arrived at 9.15. She was just deciding whether to lurk in the shadow of the hedge when someone slammed the front door and trotted down the path on stiletto heels. Clare pretended she'd just arrived and walked to the gate. This time, the woman was tall, blonde and casually dressed in jeans and a jumper. She looked blankly at Clare, got into her car and sped away.

Another woman? Clare's imagination ran riot, perhaps there was a grain of truth in Alex's warning. The door had slammed itself open, so she knocked and walked in. She found Chris in the kitchen, shaving to his reflection in the cooker hood.

'I'm a bit early, I'm afraid.'
He jumped with an 'ouch' and turned the razor off. Putting on a pair of thin rimmed glasses, he turned to face Clare. His eyes looked overlarge and owlish behind the frames.

'I'm afraid I completely forgot it's Christmas Eve. Jet lag and so on from the States. Do you want to forget it until after the festivities? I'm off to London this afternoon, anyway.' Clare wanted the money.

'Well, what if I do just the morning? I've got to pick up my bike this afternoon and get it back for repair. It had a flat tyre in the middle of nowhere' she explained.

'Oh,' he seemed perplexed for a moment, 'Well I suppose you can attack the fridge and cooker. I'm sure there was something alive under the milk this morning. Then I can be sure I won't poison myself when I get back.' He smiled and his face didn't seem so gaunt. 'I'm going to tinker with Flossie,' and he was gone. Clare set to and was horrified to find that indeed the fridge was alive. How could someone buy such expensive food - then let it rot? Clare threw out half a bag of smoked salmon. Perhaps he was an anorexic and one of his women was tempting him to eat. Do men get anorexia? Clare shrugged mentally and ploughed on. The clock was turning 12 as she slid the racks back into the cooker. The food had been so baked on she'd been able to do nothing more than remove the top layer. Chris' women were obviously not the domestic type. How many did he have running after him? Chris appeared, his thin arms black with engine oil. Not wanting her clean sink to be desecrated, Clare ran the taps for him, his arms appeared unmercifully white when stripped of the oil.

'Flossie needs a run. Can I pick up your bike for you?' Clare hesitated but anything was better than a long walk.

'Thank-you. That's very kind. Who's Flossie?'

'You'll see. Get your coat on, you'll need it.' Clare followed him out of the house to a garage she hadn't noticed before. Outside it stood a pale green Land Rover. It was polished to a satin veneer, without a spot of mud on it. A bright yellow roll bar domed the open cab. Inside were bucket seats, with strong looking seat belts.

'Isn't she a beauty?' Chris demanded, great pride in his voice.

'Well, I don't think I've ever seen one so clean. Do you take it to Vintage rallies or something?' Chris gave a snort of disgust and leapt over the welded shut doors into the driving seat. He reached forward and fired the engine.

'Call this vintage?' the engine burst into life with the power of 8 cylinders tuned to perfection, 'come on, get in!' Clare climbed awkwardly in and sank into the bucket seat. Before she had secured the belt, they accelerated out of the drive with a spray of gravel. The suspension was no better than Alex's truck, but Chris coaxed and wound the vehicle between the puddles with such dexterity that they didn't drop speed. Clare felt the engine wanting to pull away like an impatient horse.

'Why's the exhaust pipe up in the air - and what's the fan doing at the back?' Clare shouted once she got her bearings.

'To keep the water out,' was the enigmatic reply. 'Where's the bike then?' Clare hollered directions. Quite suddenly, they met the road and Clare was thrust back against the seat as Chris stabbed his foot to the floor and they tore off down the lane. Clare was overwhelmed with exhilaration and didn't care that she was freezing and her eyes were watering in the cold. She wanted to go faster and faster. For several minutes she was taken up in the new sensations until she realised that they were heading in quite the wrong direction. Her joy turned to panic - was he some sort of sex maniac taking her to some forsaken spot? What should she do? Try to grab the wheel, shout for help? Now the speed was wild and threatening. She glanced at Chris, he looked almost demonic, a lurking grin, eyes attached to the road, hands teasing and coaxing the wheel.

'We're taking the scenic route,' he shouted with a childish chuckle and looked at Clare for the first time. He rammed the brakes on, bringing Flossie to a furious halt.

'Are you alright - you're as white as a sheet?' Clare was lost for words, not knowing whether to trust him or not.

'I'm sorry, I didn't mean to scare you. I thought you were enjoying it. I do get a bit carried away when I'm showing off, I'll slow down now.' Clare at last found words.

'No, the Land Rover didn't scare me, you did. We're miles away from the bike and I didn't know where you were taking me.' Chris looked at her blankly for a second, then the penny dropped, and he muttered something under his breath before he said,

'Good grief - what do you take me for? No, you're quite right. I suppose it wasn't really in order to take the domestic for a spin. You'd know about these things.'

Clare now felt foolish, her fears were totally ridiculous.

'Let's forget it. I let my imagination run riot. I was really enjoying it until I panicked, but can we turn back now?' Chris let in the clutch and they pulled away at a more decorous pace. Clare felt she had to make some sort of amend.

'I apologise for my remark about vintage rallies - what do you do with her then?'

'Off roading trials, rallying' he replied. It was a strange language to Clare.

'Rallying? I've never seen one of these on the television.'

'Well, it's not quite that sort of thing. We have short courses, some of which are timed, some you just have to do without hitting markers or breaking the Land Rovers. I belong to a Club and take Flossie when I'm here. Why don't you come along one day - if that's permissible of course?'

'I may well. Thank you.' Chris pulled up at a familiar looking gate. Clare climbed out and searched around, but there was no bike. She even climbed the gate into the field to see if the farmer had pushed it out of the way of a tractor. There was nothing. No, telltale tyre marks, only mud and grass.

'What on earth am I going to do for work tonight?' Clare wailed as she got back into the cab.

'Work? Tonight? But it's Christmas eve!'

'Oh, I don't hold with all that, and anyway it's only washing up for a dinner party.' Chris still looked shocked.

'Well, why don't you ring and ask them for a lift, if they're so desperate.'

'You know, I think I will. Thanks, er Chris.' It was a short ride home. To Clare's surprise, Alex's truck was parked by the gate with Alex lifting her bike from the back.

'So that's what's happened!' Clare sighed with relief and began to climb out.

'Hang on,' Chris reached in hispockets and brought out his wallet.

'Here's for this morning and a Christmas tip. I'll be in London until the New Year. I'll give you a call when I return.' Clare felt awkward at taking the money from Chris right in front of Alex who was watching with ill concealed interest.

'Thank you. I'm sorry for the wasted trip.'

'Not at all. Flossie enjoyed the run. Happy Christmas!' Chris nodded at Alex and drove off.

'Thanks for getting the bike how - did you know?'

'That your Boss then?' avoided Alex. 'You want to watch those boy racers. They just buy the vehicle for a pose. Land Rovers are for working in, not playing.'

'Well, I'm sure Chris does a lot of work himself, the garage was full of tools.' Clare was stung by the tone of Alex's voice.

'How did you know about the bike?' she repeated.

'Saw it as I drove past,' he finally answered.

'Shame you didn't see me yesterday then! I yelled, and you went straight past.

Duncan gave me a lift in the end.' Alex swung around.

'Duncan Harrison?'

Clare nodded.

'Steer clear of him too, he's real trouble!'

'Good grief Alex, what are you, my protector? What happened to being free agents?'

'You're new to the area and don't know people.'

'Alex, I can run my own life. Now I must ring the Harrison's for a lift tonight. Chris suggested it, rather than cycle all the way in the dark.

'Don't bother, I'll take you.'

'There's no need.'

'I'll take you.' They stood, glaring at each other.

'Alex, there's no need for you to be protective. You're worse than a big brother. I can look after myself.' She tried not to remember the state in which she'd arrived at the cottage. She took the bike from Alex and began pushing it up the path.

'What time do you want to leave?!'

Clare gave up.

'7.15, prompt.' She pushed the bike into the shed and slammed the door.

When Alex and Clare arrived at the house that evening, a transformation had taken place. It was festooned with gaily coloured Christmas lights. Clare winced at its garishness. She hadn't imagined the Harrison's could show such bad taste. Then again, she realised the cynical part of her mind had labelled the Harrison's into a stereotype but maybe the Harrison's were going to shatter these expectations quite quickly. Carefully, to avoid touching the expensive looking cars parked in the drive, Clare made her way swiftly to the kitchen. The crockery was already piled up but the hubbub of conversation from the dining room hinted of people waiting for their first course. Mrs Harrison swept into the kitchen in a blaze of pink silk.

'I've forgotten the lemons - quick cut some!' She slung a bag in Clare's direction. From the fridge came a tray of delicate blue glasses, filled with prawns and lettuce. Frantically Mrs Harrison dumped the lemons on top and flew into the front room. For a while the conversations dimmed, then rose again, punctuated by shrieks of polite laughter. The reek of alcohol from the cocktail glasses Clare was washing made her wish for a small glass herself. Then she had no time to reflect because the work took off, punctuated by an influx of panic for each course. The main course was an enormous, pink joint of lamb, with a seemingly endless variety of baby vegetables. When it came back, Clare couldn't resist pinching a few of the scraps, just to taste. She was surreptitiously wiping her mouth when Duncan breezed in. He wore the uniform, crisp black dinner suit, his cheeks flush and hair gelled back. He looked wonderfully alien, a model from a magazine, but oh, so sexy. Clare was shocked at the way her insides leapt at the sight of him. Clare blushed.

'A drink for the worker,' he proclaimed and handed her a brimming glass of red wine. 'Mother says, get the pudding out of the fridge to take the chill off.' Duncan whisked away, leaving a trail of aftershave so heavy with masculinity that Clare just stood and sniffed, with her eyes shut. Guiltily, she opened them and went to search for the pudding. The mousse was heavy with the rich strawberry smell of summer. Suddenly Clare's own life seemed so meagre, the dull cottage, the lack of money, the lack of glamour. Oh, to be in their world of elegance, parties, laughter, large bank accounts.

Not the second-rate city world she'd once inhabited, but this rich world. Clare knew she'd never be able to enter their orbit, such a veneer was given at birth, it couldn't be bought. Even if she tried, they'd never accept her. Clare jumped as Mr Harrison came in to collect the dish. He carried it away awkwardly, and Clare realised he was drunk. It was a small chip at the world she envied, but it helped to bring them back onto her level. The next interruption came from Peter, so Clare got her first good look at him. He was opposite to Duncan in colouring and stature but carried the same sharp features. Somehow he lacked the animal glamour, for his suit was ill fitting, his tie askew, and a tuft of hair was sticking up at the back of his head. When he asked for the kettle to be put on for coffee, his voice was softer than Duncan's, with the hard edges of the accent somehow rubbed off. Clare felt no answering leap inside at his presence. She toiled on, wiping the grease and stains from the delicate porcelain. The last plate was piled when Duncan entered the kitchen. To her surprise, he handed her an envelope.

'We can just about manage the coffee cups. This is from mother, she says see you on Monday, and this is from me. Happy Christmas!' He kissed her firmly on the lips. For a second she held the glamour of him but the second passed too quickly and she wanted to snatch him back to do it properly. He was out of reach, fetching her coat. Clare was startled for words, dug the envelope deep into a pocket, and whirled out into the cold night. Her senses were in total disarray, nothing had prepared her for the shock of that casual kiss. The courtyard was dimly lit by the strings of bulbs, but Clare saw Alex's truck parked at the far end. She slammed the door behind her and reached for the belt before the reek of whiskey hit her. Alex looked at her and she saw from the staring expression he was very drunk.

'Shall I drive?'

'Not bloody likely. What do you think I am, incapable?' he snarled. He turned on the engine and they lurched away. Alex seemed to be wrestling with the wheel more than usual. They were zigzagging down the lane.

'Alex, for heaven's sake, you've got only the sidelights on!' Clare leaned over and flicked the switch. Alex roared incoherently at her and went to snatch her hand away. He lost his grip on the wheel and the truck lurched violently to one side. Already too close to the ditch, the wheels teetered over the edge, it fell onto one side and wedged at an extreme angle, the engine racing on to nowhere. Clare fell heavily onto the door, and Alex onto her. It was a couple of minutes before she came to her senses. Alex's weight was numbing her, his seat belt wasn't done up. Clare managed to wrestle an arm free, and release her belt, but it only sent them both slumping harder against the side of the cab. Alex was out cold. She couldn't tell whether it was from the whiskey or a bump to the head, his breath spread the fumes into Clare's face and she wanted to retch.

'Alex, wake up, wake up!' she repeated over and over again, until at last, he showed some signs of animation, mumbling incoherent words. Clare kept on until his eyes opened. For the first time, they were eye to eye. Clare found herself transfixed by his bleary gaze and she had the sensation that he was seeing right inside her.

'Oh Clare,' he murmured and shifted his weight. Clare expecting to be freed found herself in an amorous grip, and he was kissing her, gently, then more roughly, their teeth catching as Clare tried to breathe and stop him. It was only with a herculean heave she stopped him and slid away to one side.

'Pack it in Alex! Come to your senses,' she slapped his face and at finally he did.

'What happened?' His voice was strong again.

'You put us in the ditch because you've been drinking. Now get off me and get out the vehicle.' He obeyed, turning the engine off as he did so. Out in the fresh air, he just stood by the said vehicle. Clare followed him, and they both stood silently for some minutes in the moonlight.

'I'm sorry, I'll never do anything like that again.' Clare realised he'd sobered up in those few short minutes.

'I'll move back to the cabin and leave you in peace,' he continued. 'I know you can't stand the sight of me, but even if you did care, I can't have a relationship with you. I'm better off being away.' It was one thing to vow not to have any relationships, but to have someone say he fancied her, then couldn't do anything about it, piqued Clare. She had to be the one doing the rejecting. Her words came tumbling out.

'You don't need to do that. Perhaps we made a bad start, perhaps we might try on a new footing.' What am I saying she said to herself. The last person in the world she wanted to go out with was Alex. In the dim light, she saw he was shaking from head to foot.

'This is ridiculous - let's get home and forget this stupid conversation, we're both in shock. Clare grabbed Alex's arm and began to tow him slowly home. She felt unharmed by the accident, just shaken and scared, but Alex's shaking seemed to be getting worse by the minute. Several times he lurched and Clare had to take the brunt of his weight. Although the night stayed dry, they were soon soaked to the knees from the puddles. Every now and then Alex started to say something, but he hesitated and lapsed into mumbling beneath his breath. It seemed like hours before they turned up the familiar path. The lights were blazing in the cottage, no doubt left on by Alex, Clare surmised. When she tried to push open the front door, there was something blocking its passage, so she shoved harder. The hall was revealed, scattered with suitcases. The sitting room door opened and a short blonde girl appeared, cuddling the cat.

'Sylvie!' Clare shrieked and leapt to embrace her friend.

TOM
1991

Once again, the red hair billowed in the bath, her
blank eyes still accused. He had to turn and run
from their glare, shout it wasn't me, it was him,
but he was slipping, falling into the bath too. He
braced himself for the heat and the splash. The
bath became a hard bench that dug into every
muscle of his back. Tom sat up, smelling the
damp reek of his clothes and his feet began to
throb again, relics from years of pounding the
pavements. Perhaps now he'd get pneumonia
and die. The thought was pleasant enough to
make him look up and take on his surroundings.
The Playground was empty of children, though a
red painted swing rocked in the rain laden
breeze.

An eerie sense of being watched
triggered him to run again, but something in the
huddled shape on the opposite bench stilled him
to see just what it was. Hunger clutched his
insides, so he groped in his pockets for some
sweets. As he peeled the tatty wrapper from the
chocolate, the heap of clothes showed signs of
animation, and a face peered through a moth-
eaten hat, eyes bloodshot, staring hard as he put
the sweet to his mouth.

A glint of light showed on the stranger's
cheek, and to Tom's surprise, it trickled down to
the chin. The heap moved again, and he saw
something clutched in dirty hands. It was half an
empty burger carton, stained and rubbed as if it
had been held for a long time. Inside sat a small
crust of bread. The watcher's attention had never
been on Tom. Something in the look of the face
reminded Tom of the ever starving ducks at

home to whom he'd fed his leftover chips. Instinctively, he got up and handed over the unbitten bar. Grubby hands grabbed, and it was wolfed down, swallowed almost at the point of choking, the paper checked and picked for any crumbs.

She looked up at Tom with spaniel like gratitude, while he stood, transfixed. In all his years of running, he'd never been in this state, reduced to famine and filth. He'd always found work, but that was because he was a man. A woman couldn't work building sites, there were few options for easy cash, apart from the lure of the Pimp. She must have resisted this. Suddenly, he began to feel strong, like a knight in white armour. It was a new, all consuming, and above all, very pleasant feeling. He wanted to go on feeding her because he didn't want the sensation to go away. He threw all his inane caution to the winds, surely after all these years, and so many changes of home and work he must have shrugged off the police by now.

'I'll buy you a meal,' he gruffly stated and set off towards the shops. He knew she'd follow like a donkey to his carrot. Tom's nose led them to a steamy cafe, pungent in cooking smells and cigarette smoke. With the air of a great benefactor, he let the woman slide onto the bench first, then without glancing at the menu, he ordered two large fried breakfasts, two mugs of coffee and double toast. He gazed steadily out of the window as she began to peel off layers of clothes. Perhaps 'someone' was giving him a new start. He could take her right away from this town, somewhere safe, just the two of them. He would feed her, buy her new clothes then the food arrived.

Sitting in front of someone who is starving, and just wants to get food inside by the quickest means possible is not a pleasant sight, so Tom paid attention to his own hunger. It was only a matter of minutes before both plates were cleared.

'Thank-you,' she stated, in a clear, quiet voice and Tom looked at her fully. A gaunt, drawn face, over-large eyes, wispy, cropped blonde hair and hands with thin bitten nailed fingers clutched the still warm mug. It dawned on him that he'd never been looked at so closely before, and he shuffled uneasily on the bench.

'I'll get us away from here, get a job, somewhere in the country...' He offered.

'Oh, will you? Do you think that after buying a meal, you own me? What else do you expect, payment? I'm not that kind of person,' she began to get up, a desperate look in her eyes.

'No!' he shouted and grabbed her hand. The people in the cafe stared, so she sank back down.

'Not like that I promise. I just want to feed you, give you somewhere to live.' Tom was amazed at how strongly he felt about what he was saying, and how he could actually say it out loud.

'Why?' Her voice was incredulous. Tom felt a clutch of the old fear, the enormity of the risk he was taking suddenly hit him. To be near another person meant he might inadvertently spill the beans, and the police would be called, or Doggie would find him. No, he wasn't going to relinquish one ray of hope. He'd been careful so far, he'd go on being so. He didn't want to go back.

'I, er just want to.'

'OK. My name's Sue.' Tom now felt uneasy at the matter being so easily solved, then he saw her wiping the last smears of food from her plate and understood. Tom looked at her face, to his horror it had gone a nasty shade of green, sweat trickled down her brow. The woman's hand went to her mouth.

'You're not going to be sick,' he stated firmly, and picked up the coats and led her into the fresh air. The young lad coming to clear the table watched them go. A right pair of nutters he thought. For some unknown reason, his Sunday School lessons, buried a long time ago, came flooding back. Cain - yeah, he'd had a mark on him so no-one killed him. Those two looked marked like that. He shivered and got on with stacking the plates. Now, where had that burger carton come from?

A few weeks later, Tom dumped his dinner box with satisfaction on the grass and stretched his arms luxuriantly. He smiled at the park, the daffodils, the kids playing. He'd always liked Parks. The duck busy water glinted in the sun while the soft wind danced the bright green leaves on the trees. He closed his eyes enjoying the glare and the replete feeling from a large dinner.

'Well, long time, no see!' Tom jumped. A thin man was silhouetted in the yellow light.

'Douggie.' Tom strained back, arms instinctively crossing his chest. His legs were paralysed, when he wanted to run. The day grew cold and dark and strange noises hummed in the breeze.

'Thought I'd catch up with you sooner or later. What have you been up to? Seems like only last week, we were up to our tricks. Our plans were brilliant. They all worked. The fuzz got the Bull. He's still inside,' Douggie chuckled. Overwhelming relief swamped Tom. They weren't searching for him. He relaxed his arms a bit and began to feel warmer.

'So why didn't you come with me? Where were you? Why did you leave me alone after all we'd done?' Tom saw Douggie's face almost clearly now, the years didn't seem to have changed him at all.

'I decided it was safer to stay. They looked for you, so I backed up the story. I enjoyed lying to the pigs, it was fun,' he chuckled. In spite of his relief, Tom felt confused. In a crystal clear memory, he still couldn't tell whose hand had held the bat.

'So you were there, and you did hit her?'

'We both did it,' Douggie stated in his old vehement way. Tom knew the subject was closed for now. He shoved his apprehension aside. It was alright. It didn't matter. The Bull was inside. He was in the clear, they were in the clear and life was good. Tom even began to feel regret for the unnecessary years spent running. He had to share his good news with Douggie.

'I've got a girl! We've got a flat.' Tom boasted, and leapt to his feet, 'Come and meet her - we'll have a drink and a chat - there's so much to catch up on.' To his surprise, Douggie looked cross.

'Aw Tom, you always were a burk! Women are trouble, just look at your mother.'

'She's different. She's OK. Come on, when you meet her you'll see,' Tom pleaded.

'Oh alright. But they're trouble, Tom. You can't trust them.' He followed Tom home, through the busy town streets, his comments eating into Tom's newfound confidence. Tom began to wish he'd never suggested it. Why did Douggie have to come and spoil things? From the street, Tom saw the light on in the basement and knew all was fine, she was there like he'd said. He turned and grinned to Douggie.

'See, Sue's there, come on!' He bounded down the stairs into the humid kitchen.

'Hi Ya!' he yelled and sent his dinner box skidding across the table. She was sitting, as usual, reading in the soft chair next to the heater. She looked up and smiled, bemused at leaving the world of her novel.

'I've just met an old mate. Oh, Sue, I've so much to tell you.' He stood aside to let Douggie see her. Sue stood up, expectantly.

'Where is he then?' She asked. Tom thought she was joking and pushed Douggie gently forward. Then Tom saw Sue's face was drained of colour and she looked scared.

'Tom, there's no-one there.' Tom looked. Douggie had gone, vanished. He turned and ran up the stairs, the road outside was deserted, the sky was hinting storms in a red sky. When he returned, she was still stood by the chair.

'Tom, there was no-one there.'

'There was!' he bellowed. 'We met in the Park. We talked. HE WAS HERE!' He strode to her and grabbed her shoulders. His rising panic made him reckless and cruel.

'No-one.' she screamed. 'You're some sort of maniac. Let me go. I should have known better.'

Tom shook her again and again, shouting all the time, he was here. Sue went limp and fell out of his grasp. Tom's mind couldn't believe that she had told the truth, and again he ran to the street, hollering, 'Douggie, come back.' He ran back in. She'd made him run away, she must've said something and scared him away. In the dull yellow kitchen, Sue was filling carrier bags with her clothes.

'Get out you cow. He was right, you women always spoil things. GET OUT!' He raised his fist. In a terrified frenzy she grabbed the bags and ran past him into the street, Tom heard her sobs as she ran away. He reached for the whiskey bottle hidden at the back of the cupboard and drank huge scorching, exploding gulps until a warm glow began to spread right through him. Now he saw clearly, Douggie had been in the Park. Douggie had killed his mother. Sue had scared him away. No, Douggie had come back to scare Sue away, he didn't want Tom to be happy. Douggie was real. Tom had killed his mother. No, Douggie's hand held the bat. Tom drank on. Slowly, another thought came through.

He didn't want any more of this. He didn't want to run, he'd wanted Sue, and she'd gone. Douggie was real and imagined, Tom couldn't stand anymore, he wanted peace. At last, he had the courage for the act he'd yearned to do for years. Still swigging, he went to the bathroom and reached for the container he'd kept as an insurance, so little had he trusted his luck. He swallowed every capsule, then discovered the whiskey was finished. He wouldn't stay here, he had to go to the Park, near the swings, the only place he'd ever been happy. He almost felt his father's loving hands on his back, and he had to hurry before the pills began to work. Tom ran like an exhausted marathon runner through the busy streets, knocking people aside. He was so tired. He catapulted through the gate into the play area, and slipped, falling heavily, his head hitting the closing gate.

Home at last, Tom struck the ground. The mothers were aghast as the drunk collapsed. They clutched at panicking children and stood frozen as the blood trickled onto the tarmac. When he lay still, their wits returned and one rang for an ambulance.

In the empty flat, the front door banged shut in the impish spring breeze. The old partitions rocked in the aftershock and in the bathroom, an empty vitamin pill container rolled off the sink and fell with a clunk to the floor.

CLARE
1993

Once they'd calmed down, Sylvie and Clare remembered Alex. To their horror, he was slumped, shaking against the door, his face ashen sweating.

'He'd been drinking and put the truck in the ditch on the way home - the idiot,' Clare explained. 'He's not injured because he fell on me!'

'We'd better get him into the front room,' said Sylvie. Between them, they bundled a muttering Alex through the narrow door and sat him as close to the woodburner as possible. The mumbling continued, and he seemed unaware of his surroundings.

'His face is like ice,' Sylvie exclaimed. 'You fetch a quilt and I'll fill some hot water bottles.' On their return, they struggled to get his boots and coat off. Once they'd succeeded, they shoved the bottles under his jumper and wrapped the quilt firmly around him.

'Should we get the doctor?' Clare asked.

'No doctors!' Alex came out of his trance and shouted. 'No doctors. I'm just cold. Get me some paracetamol and coffee!' He began to struggle with his wraps.

'OK, OK. No doctors.' The girls agreed, and he sank back under the covers and continued the muttering, which became more audible.

'I'm sorry. No, I didn't mean it. I didn't want it to happen again. I'm sorry. Don't leave me,' over and over again. Sylvie got the paracetamol, and a mug of something steaming.

'No whiskey in it,' Clare warned. 'He'll be roaring drunk again.'

'No, it's milk. Alex - take these and drink this or I will call the Doctor.'

He obeyed, his hands shaking so much he nearly spilt the drink, but he swallowed it all and returned the cup.

'I'm going to sleep,' he stated, and rolled over, turning his back on them. In a matter of moments, his breathing deepened into a snore, and the shivers visibly lessened. Clare and Sylvie exchanged glances and fled to the kitchen.

'Do you think he's OK - should we call the doctor anyway? One minute he's alright, the next he's rambling?' asked Clare.

'No, I think he's best left to sleep it off,' stated Sylvie, and put the kettle on to boil.

'Come on then, spill the beans. What happened to bring you back so soon?' demanded Clare.

'Christmas,' said Sylvie but realised Clare knew her too well to be fooled.

'Something happened out there, which changed me, and I just couldn't go on with things as they were.'

Clare looked expectantly, so Sylvie sighed and plunged on.

'My first job on the Herald was to cover a Church Mission week in a small part of the suburbs. I must admit, I was pretty fed up. This was cub reporter stuff, and I'd just been covering the Iron Maiden tour. I expected to be covering murders and political stuff, not some wishy-washy church thing. So, I went along, determined to drag the waters and expose them all for the bunch of frauds I knew them to be - that would show the Editor!'

'The first event I covered was what they called a healing service. Some bloke was at the front, telling them about how Jesus can heal you from everything, sickness, demons, your past and so on. When he finished, they sang a few catchy songs. I expected him to whip them up into some sort of religious fervour, but they all stayed quite calm. He then made a call for people to come forward for healing. Now, I was looking for the wheelchair and crutch brigade to come rushing forward and to pretend to leap out of their chairs and walk.'

Clare grinned. She knew exactly what Sylvie meant.

'To my surprise, a healthy looking woman went forward. This is ridiculous, I thought, did they expect people to swallow someone healthy being healed? Anyway, she chatted with the bloke, he nodded and began to pray for her. I moved forward to see what was going to happen. The preacher placed his hands over her head and she keeled over; he didn't even touch her. One of his cronies caught her and lay her to the ground. I'd never seen anything like it. The ridiculous thing was when I looked at her, she was lying there, eyes wide open with this idiotic grin on her face. After a couple of minutes, she got up, trotted back to her seat and sat back down with her friend.'

'The preacher was making another plea when there was an uproar at the back. A middle-aged man and woman were frog-marching a young lad in. He was quiet when they entered but as they got closer to the front, he began to swear and struggle. You can't imagine the abuse that came out. Words even I'd never heard. The preacher marched forward to meet him, with a stern expression on his face. Both parents were now having a real fight to keep him there. It seemed the preacher had had enough, because he halted right in front of the boy, and said,

'In the name of Jesus Christ, Satan, I rebuke you out of this child. I rebuke you lust. I rebuke you Obscenity. I rebuke you, greed. In the name of Jesus Christ, come out! The lad seemed to go through some of convulsion, he stopped swearing, and just stood there. His parents let go. Holy Spirit, please enter in this child,' he went on. 'I pray self-control, purity and morality. We ask this in the name of Jesus Christ.'

'He said a lot more, but that was the gist of it. The boy seemed utterly quiet now, he was handed a Bible and sat down at the front. Everyone else then stood up, sang a song and began to leave. Well, I must admit it had been a spectacular show - it could convince someone slightly less cynical than me. So I went to dig the dirt. I checked out the preacher first. The thing that niggled me, was he had the most direct, honest eyes I'd ever seen, he didn't seem like a trick showman.'

She fell in love with the preacher thought Clare.

'He seemed to know what I was going to ask. He told me the woman had had back pain for years, but now the pain was receding rapidly. Well, that's a difficult one to prove, it's one person's word against another. So I asked about the lad. He explained that the lad had been possessed by demons of lust, obscenity and greed and in the name of Jesus, he had cast them out. I then said that spiritualists do the same thing. He shook his head and said that spiritualism is all a sham played by the devil. I dropped that tack and asked if I could talk to the boy and his parents. He gave me their address, followed by a load of the usual stuff about Jesus loving me and waiting for me to turn to Him.'

'So what did you find out?' demanded Clare eagerly, waiting for the denunciation.

'Well, I thought there was no point in asking them first, as they were deep in it with the preacher. So I did some investigating. The lad had been up on a charge of rape a few months previously but escaped on a technicality. I talked to his parents in the end and discovered they had kept him under house arrest ever since. Neither of them were regular Church goers, so I began to think perhaps it wasn't quite the set up I'd expected, but I couldn't fathom it at all. Still feeling puzzled, I went to the next service. I knew there must be a way of finding the chink in their armour. I constantly reminded myself to be clear headed. The songs seemed familiar and even quite enjoyable once you're used to that sort of thing. The Church was crowded, so I stayed at the back and kept a low profile. When the sermon began, I began to feel uneasy.'

'It was a woman speaking this time, but she had the same sort of authority as the other Preacher. She spoke about our lives today and the junk we fill them with. Money, sex, work, travel, and how we endlessly search for that further satisfaction through them, in the belief that each step will finally fulfil us. In fact, all we do is fill the space inside us, which is meant for God, with this junk, so we can never be truly fulfilled. If we clear the mess out and let God in, we'll find the peace, forgiveness, contentment and all we've been so searching for fruitlessly. I wanted to bolt out of the door then because she was talking about me. She explained it was not a soft option for a safe ride through life, but the answer, to all our needs, a lifelong security, with better to come after death.'

'I was thinking through all my arguments to what she was saying, but they all seemed to fly out the window and become meaningless. Then she made a call for people to go up to the front and give their lives to Jesus. I gathered up my notebook and bag before they brainwashed me as well. To my surprise, I found myself at the front of the room, and not heading for the car park. Two old ladies came up, and without speaking to me apart from asking my name, sat me down and began to pray for me. Something snapped inside me and I cried like a child. I knew I wanted all the dross out of my life, and Jesus in. I was going to turn right around from all that I knew, but had never admitted was wrong in my life.'

Then the woman and a bloke - her husband I suppose, came up and asked me if I believed in Jesus, repented from my sins, and wanted to let Holy Spirit into my life. I found I did. I wanted it so much, I wanted to reach out and grab it. They prayed for me and placed hands over me. Do you know, it was an outpouring of the sweetest sensation I'd ever felt in my life, that went from top to toe, setting me tingling.'
Sylvie shamelessly ignored Clare's now disgusted expression.

'I felt so calm, so serene, but bereft when it faded. I wanted to thank Jesus, but the words didn't come. I was gaping like a goldfish, then suddenly words came. Now, this is the really amazing bit! It wasn't English, it was another language complete with syntax and sentences. It just flooded out, for a couple of minutes then slowed to a trickle then stopped. But wow - I just can't explain to you how I felt, it was too amazing. Do you know, I've learnt since, I've been Baptised in the Spirit, and I was speaking in tongues as they did at Pentecost. Clare, He exists, He's there it's all here!'

Clare was now, not only disgusted but alarmed. Which crazy bunch of fanatics had Sylvie got herself roped into?

'I've been through all this church business. I've had it forced down my throat throughout my childhood. I know it's all just hysterical claptrap. What you've seen is just the latest trick to get people in. I thought you were too intelligent to be caught out by them. It's not for me, don't start Bible bashing to me, I know all the arguments and they just don't wash!'

'You know I would never do that Clare. What I've found is God's pure love, and love never forces itself, it waits patiently. You're right, if it's forced, it is wrong.'

'Well, you'll have a bloody long wait for me. We'll just have to agree to differ on this - you keep your ideas to yourself, and I'll keep mine to myself OK?'

Sylvie agreed, feeling a great sadness. If God could break down her cynicism, why shouldn't it crack Clare's? Awkwardly, she went to peer in at Alex. To her horror, he was gone, the quilt thrown dangerously near the boiler. His boots and coat were nowhere in sight. Frantically, they searched the cottage, but Alex had disappeared into the still quietness of Christmas morning. For a few seconds, they were too stunned to think coherently.

'He's in no fit state to go anywhere. We have to look for him,' stated Sylvie.

'He can't be far,' mused Clare. 'It would take another vehicle to pull the truck out of the ditch.' Clare ransacked her mind, only to find she knew none of his haunts. Then she remembered. 'The cabin - he mentioned returning to a cabin.' Clare swung round to face Sylvie, who was looking horrified.

'But that's miles away in the marshes,' she exclaimed. They looked up into the star-laden sky and were filled with the chill of frost.

'It's a long walk, Clare. We'll have to wrap up.'

'Can't we leave it until the light now we know where he is?' She was exhausted and thought longingly of her bed. She didn't want yet another tramp along the wet lanes.

'He's in no fit state to be anywhere on his own. What if he's lying half drowned in a ditch right now?'

'Shouldn't we call the police or something?'

'Good grief Clare, he needs our help, whatever the matter is with him, he needs us, not arresting. It is Christmas after all.'
Clare said nothing, but, unwillingly turned back into the cottage to don layers of warm clothing.

'Just what do you propose to do when we get there - he may not even let us in!'
Sylvie waved a claw hammer at her. 'That'll see to the door, it's only thin wood!'

They set off into the freezing night. The very air numbed their nostrils, so they pulled their scarves up until it was nearly impossible to see. The powerful torch shone the way for them, and they plunged on in silence. Each sweep of the torch revealed an empty lane, no crumpled body. Everything around them seemed frozen, not only the puddles but sound too, the crash of their feet seemed to fill the night in an almost hypnotic rhythm.

Clare's bleary mind filled with resentment. Not only at Alex's drunkenness, and accident, but all his addle pated behaviour with this escapade as its crowning glory. How anyone in their right mind take off into the freezing night was a mystery. The worst part of it was that she was having to follow him into it when he obviously didn't want rescuing. What was the point, he wasn't worth getting cross about. Clare was exhausted. As soon as they got him back, she was going to crawl into bed and sleep forever. It was Sylvie's turn deal with his tantrums now.

'Sylvie - just how do you propose to get him back to the cottage?' There was a pause.

'To tell you the honest truth, I haven't got that far yet. Let's just concentrate on finding him first.'

Clare now had visions of another freezing trek - and this time towing an unwilling Alex. Did she have a mouthful to give to give him when they did find him! Clare had sense enough not to follow this line too far, so contented herself with remembering Duncan's brief kiss, and her gut wrenching reaction. Now here was someone she could fancy. She Shrank at the word but she'd never reacted to anyone that way before, even the first time Phil had kissed her. Was Duncan worth throwing over her vows about involvement? Considering her reactions, yes he was, Clare decided. He'd overturned all her feelings in one swift kiss, so there must be more to love. She must just have picked the wrong people. Clare began to cheer up. The going was getting boggier. The crackle of frost under their feet was now turning to the squelch of water-soaked earth. Clare saw the hedges were now replaced with tall banks of sedges.

'Is it far now?' Clare demanded, trying not to sound cross anymore.

'About a mile. Just keep to the track, it seems the tide's out, so we won't have to wade.'

'Wade!' exclaimed Clare. 'Just where are we?'

'The salt marshes behind Haydens Beach. You know I told you we used to swim there as kids.'

'How on earth can Alex live in a place like this? How could he get the truck down here?'

'Oh, there's a tarmac road on the other side. His cabin is in a small grove of pines just behind the beach. I think it was once a summer house. This is the quicker way!'

Clare didn't dare answer. For a while, the path did seem to become more water than firm, but quite suddenly they were on firm, dry grass. In the distance, Clare saw an uncanny orange glow.

'He's there,' Sylvie exclaimed with relief in her voice. 'I think we ought to approach cautiously. We don't want him bolting again!' She turned the torch down to the ground so that its beam picked out only their footsteps. Once at the door, Sylvie knocked with conviction. 'Alex. Let us in. We know you're in there.'

'Go away!' he bellowed, but at least his voice sounded sober.

'Alex, you're in shock. You can't stay here on your own, you need help.'

'I'm perfectly OK. I told Clare I was coming back here, and I'll not be in the way now.'

'Alex - don't argue - you are coming back to the cottage. We want you. It is Christmas day after all.' shouted Sylvie. Various expletives followed that along with references to Christ's parentage. Clare saw Sylvie as she took the hammer from her pocket and put it against the door. It took but one savage heave and they were in the cabin. It was lit with one small hurricane light. In the corner, a paraffin stove was belching out heat and fumes. The few pieces of furniture were worn and tatty. Alex was sat on a chair, still clad in coat and boots warming himself by the heater. He was no longer shaking and held himself erect.

'Go away,' he said.

'No, we're not going to, you're coming back,' stated Sylvie, calmly pushing the door shut behind her.

'I told you no. I had to go.'

'Pull yourself together, we've walked bloody miles. We're cold and frozen; all for your sake you obstinate pig.' Clare yelled at him, anger boiling over. Sylvie yanked her arm.

'Shut up Clare,' she hissed, 'that way won't get us anywhere.' Clare slunk over to the table and thumped herself down on the chair, glowering. Sylvie crouched down beside Alex. 'Alex, give us a sane, sensible reason, and we'll leave you alone. I'll make a deal. You tell us what this is all about, and if we agree, we really will go. We'll even help you move your stuff back down here.'

'You mean it?'

Sylvie and Clare nodded vehemently.

'I suppose so then - but you'll keep this all in confidence.' He now looked over at Clare, who had pricked up her ears.

'We will,' both girls stated. Alex sighed, rubbed his hands over his face and stated.

'My life began two years ago, on the morning I woke up in a hospital bed with a bad head wound.' He lifted his shaggy hair and in the dim light, they saw a livid red mark.

'I had total amnesia, and I've never recalled a thing since.'

'Haven't you tried to find out?' Alex stilled Clare.

'Let me go on. As the days passed, and I became better, they began counselling me, trying to get me to remember, but I came up against a total brick wall. Utterly, utterly blank. They even offered to take me back to where I'd been found. There was nothing in my pockets except a Mars bar, and some money, no documents, nothing. Then they tried a new drug on me and I went into some sort of deep sleep. I can remember nothing of the dreams. When I woke up, I had this conviction that I had done something that was evil, so utterly evil that my memory blackout was a way of stopping it. Whatever had caused my head wound had buried it all. I felt such a revulsion that I stopped everything they were trying to do for me. The police had no records, so whatever I had done wrong I hadn't been caught for it. Once the stitches were out, I packed my carrier bag and hit the road. I ended up here by chance, found a sense of peace in these marshes and decided to stay put. I take each day at a time now...'

'Some things have come back. I can drive and through a casual job, found I have a knowledge of plants and gardening. It was Joe who I worked with that found this place for me when we did a planting job at Heathfield. So I go on. One day at a time, no ties, no involvements.'

Alex looked meaningfully at Clare. 'I've got such a sense of danger in my past that I daren't get close to anyone. Does that explain my behaviour to you?'

Clare nodded, it did all make sense now, and she felt an overwhelming pity for Alex and his lonely path.

'But, what if you had a wife, kids, family?' interjected Sylvie.

'There would have been a record of me as a missing person. Now you don't need me and my problems cluttering up your lives.'

'Alex, I can see your reasons, but there's no need to set yourself up in this glorious isolation. We don't care about your past. It obviously is well and truly hidden, or it would have returned after two years. Maybe you're wrong, perhaps it was just the side effect of that drug making you feel this evil. Come back to the cottage, we won't make any demands on you.' Sylvie looked ashamed at Clare.

'We'll just let you get on with your own thing. You can't stay here in the middle of winter, you'll get pneumonia.' Clare saw damp oozing down one wall.

'Whatever happened in the truck, can be forgotten too,' she added generously.

'I don't know whether I can.'

'Oh Alex. Perhaps if we were friends, we might get on, something may develop. But you won't find it out, sitting here in the back of beyond.' Clare found herself quailing inside, what on earth was she letting herself in for?

'But I can't, because of my past!'

'Oh for heaven's sake,' said Clare, getting exasperated. 'If it is all hidden, and you've been given a new start, you must seize it with both hands.' Clare knew all about second chances.

'Come on,' pleaded Sylvie. 'Just try it, say for a month and if it's impossible, we'll help you find some new digs.'

There was silence for a couple of minutes. Alex stared into the flames of the heater, decision making. 'I'll come, on one condition,' he stated at last. 'Sylvie, you must promise that as a reporter you'll not leak this to a paper or try to track me down.'

'You have my word.'

'That's not a lot from the press.'

'Alex, I've become a Christian, I keep my word.'

He didn't look any more convinced. 'All right, but only on a month's trial.'

Sylvie could have shouted with pleasure, but instead got up and peered out the window. There was no welcoming light of dawn.' Do we walk or wait till light?' she asked. Clare had begun to drowse, head propped in hand, everything blotted out in a soporific haze.

'Let's go now,' decided Alex, and rose to his feet.

Clare jumped. 'Aw no, I don't want to go out, I want to go to sleep.'

'Come on, it won't seem so bad with a bed at the end of it.'

Sheer force of will propelled Clare out into the night where she began to wake up. They trudged back in silence, all overwhelmingly tired. It was enough to follow the torch beam, let alone think. After an eternity they reached the cottage, and leaving a heap of coats strewn in the hall, fell into their separate beds. Slumber gripped the house well into Christmas afternoon.

Clare was the first to wake, and jogged down to the kitchen, gripped by a fierce hunger. After the initial shock of seeing the time, she felt justified in having an enormous fry-up. She had at least two meals to catch up on. She was just heaping the bacon onto her plate when Alex poked his head around the door.

'Any spare? I smelt it in my room.' Remembering the new ground rules, Clare managed a faint smile and leapt up to pile some more bacon in the pan.

'Do you feel alright now, you were in a state of shock last night?'

'Absolutely fine, just a bit hungover. I had to pick up the coats to get to the front room. This fell out of your pocket.'

Clare looked blankly at the envelope, then remembered her wages. She ripped it open to find a cheque for £50.

'They certainly can be generous,' she said in amazement and waved it under Alex's nose.

'Not really, you worked two whole days and an evening!' It did look less generous. Still, now things were sorted, and Sylvie was home there wasn't such a need to rush off to find a flat. Clare went to put the envelope in the bin when some writing on the reverse caught her eye.

'Join me for a meal on Boxing Night. Will ring, 'signed Duncan, with a sprawled x connected to the N. Clare felt one of her blushes rising, so she hastily screwed the paper up and shoved it in a pocket. Alex and Clare ate in a comparable silence until their plates were cleared.

'I'll fix the bike for you tonight,' Alex offered.

'Thanks,' Clare found it easy to smile at him now she understood. She looked at him anew and decided he wasn't as gloomy looking as she'd originally thought. Yet they became steadily more ill at ease. Friendship was going to be no easier than their armed truce. Sylvie broke the tension by clattering down the stairs and into the kitchen. She wrinkled her nose at the bacon and opted for cereal. Between mouthfuls, she said, 'I'm going to the evening service at the parish church. Either of you coming?'

Alex and Clare exchanged conspiratorial looks, and both said no. Sylvie looked disappointed but said nothing. She glared at the clock, downed her coffee and rushed out.

'Do you think she's going to be heavy on the religion now?' Alex asked.

'No, I've told her my views, and I'm sure she'll respect them. But I suppose we'll have to moderate the swearing and the late night orgies!' Alex didn't respond to the joke.

'Christmas has one thing in its favour!' He now looked at Clare quizzically.

'There are loads of things on the telly. If you make another coffee, I've got some chocolate biscuits in the cupboard.' So they sat for the next couple of hours, silently demolishing a large packet of biscuits, the television saving them any difficult conversation. The calmness was shattered by the return of Sylvie. To their surprise, she was laden with shopping bags which she dumped on the floor in front of the television. Like a long-married couple, Alex and Clare shifted to peer around Sylvie at the comedy show.

'Come on you two, it's Christmas day. I met Max Smith at Church and he let me into his shop to stock up. I've even got a small chicken.'

'Well, we had agreed to give Christmas a miss, seeing as neither of us believes in it. We felt it...' A new idea struck Clare, 'it far less hypocritical.'

Sylvie had to acknowledge their stand. 'Come on,' she almost whined. 'All I've got is a load of food, a few bits of tinsel and a bottle of plonk. Look at it as a welcome home party then, a new start. Whatever, it's all something to celebrate. Don't be such stick in the muds!'

Suddenly aware that this was Sylvie's house, after all, Clare begrudgingly shifted off the settee and peered into one of the bags. All sorts of delicacies, gold covered crackers and Turkish delight tumbled out. Clare couldn't resist the lure and picked up two of the bags.

'No Alex, you stay there, I'm sure you're still feeling a bit under the weather,' said Sylvie.

'I was there too,' grumbled Clare, but followed Sylvie into the kitchen.

Clare felt a childish delight in unpacking the bags, there seemed to be enough to feed an army. One bottle of brown liquid puzzled her, what use was glow-on for food?

'Clare, you look stupid with blonde hair!' Clare was stung, as much as she hated her tresses, she didn't like someone criticising them.

'I found that in the shop,' continued Sylvie. 'Dye it back to red again, it won't take long!'

'Why didn't I think of it before?' Clare grabbed the bottle and sped upstairs leaving Sylvie to the cooking which was what she'd planned in the first place. It took a good hour to complete the process, and mop up the iridescent spills, but the fruits of the labour were good. Although the tone wasn't quite the same as her original deep auburn, it was a deep glorious red once again. The dye seemed to have knocked the stuffing out of the perm because Clare's hair now moderated itself into gentle waves. Thrilled, Clare leapt back downstairs.

'Dah daah!' Clare did a theatrical flounce into the kitchen.

'You just don't know how much better you look. I suppose it was Phil's idea in the first place?'

'Yes, I don't know how he talked me into it to this, he had me completely under his thumb.' Clare proceeded to tell Sylvie the whole sorry tale.

'You got out not a moment too soon. I think your action with the LP's was a bit naughty, though. Have you seen him since?'

'Not flipping likely. I hope I covered my trails. The thought of him turning up here in a rage makes my blood run cold, but it's been several weeks since I left and there's no sign of him.'

'You didn't seem too happy with Alex last night?'

'We didn't strike it off very well. He's been so moody, in fact, a real misery. I don't like him. In fact, I was making plans to move on as soon as possible. Now everything's in the open, maybe he'll be different. Do you think he really is some sort of lunatic?'

'No, they wouldn't have let him out. What happened in the truck?'

'After he'd put us in the ditch, he fell on me, kissed me and tried to declare his undying passion. It was revolting.'

'Clare, you should have explained. Perhaps it would have been better to find some other place...'

'I think he'll be OK, he was quite pally this afternoon. I think he's got over it.'

'Tread carefully, he's not the person to toy with for a quick fling.'

'I know, I know,' said Clare impatiently. 'Actually, I have met someone.'
Sylvie looked askance.

'I think you know him. Duncan Harrison.'

Sylvie looked aghast.

'Clare, he's a total womaniser. There are mountains of women he's used and discarded. Don't get involved.'

'It's been bad enough with Alex warning me off without you coming on the mother hen. I can handle it, I've wised up since Phil. I can stand on my own two feet!' snapped Clare.

'Well, don't come crying to me.'

'He asked after you!'

'He would. He was my first boyfriend years ago. No sooner had he deflowered me than he moved on to Liza Collins, and then on through all the village girls. He's almost like some feudal lord, taking just what he fancies.' Clare changed the subject.

'Well, perhaps you can answer this. I've got a job cleaning at the Harrison's place.' Sylvie took one look and burst out laughing.

'Don't mock, it's the only job I could find' said Clare crossly. 'Do they have a daughter as well as the boys?' Mrs Harrison never mentioned her, and when I found an old card, she went peculiar.'

'Of course, they do. Helen. She's Peter's twin. Are you quite sure?'

'Oh yes. So why should they pretend she doesn't exist?'

'She must have ruined the family name! I'll look into it. My reporter's nose is twitching.'

The phone rang and Clare dashed out to answer, her stomach lurching as she recognised the voice. She answered to his arrangements in monosyllables, then put the receiver down in a daze. He'd been so caring, interested. He wanted to take her out, after such a brief meeting. This must be different for him too, this sudden, almost electrical attraction. Clare began to imagine kissing him and felt a little giddy, she floated into the kitchen, but swiftly came to the ground when she saw Sylvie's disapproving face. Clare felt it appropriate to once again change the subject. 'You never finished telling me about why you came home.'

Sylvie finished bashing the potatoes and said, 'You lay the table and I'll tell you. I came back from the mission on a spiritual high. I wanted to tell everyone about Jesus and all the wonderful things He can do. I even told my landlady, who informed me she was a Jehovah's Witness and very nearly chucked me out. I also told a couple of reporters from the paper who told me to knock it off in no uncertain terms.' Clare grinned.

'Then I goofed. When I handed in the report to the editor. He scanned it and blew a fuse. It turned out he had wanted an expose and not a glowing report. Instant sacking to put it mildly. So I took a week's holiday then came home. It's going to be difficult to get a job now, all my ethics have changed,' Sylvie sighed. 'I'm sure the Lord has something in mind for me!'

Clare cringed. 'Shall I fetch Alex?' She made her way to the sitting room completely forgetting her altered appearance. Alex was engrossed by the television and found himself accosted by a total stranger telling him to come and eat. Clare flicked on the light to see his horrified expression.

'We can't have two blondes in one house!' she said gaily, and the penny dropped.

'What on earth have you done?' he demanded.

'This is my natural colour. I've just speeded nature up a bit!'

Alex followed Clare to the kitchen, her new hair was bouncy and had a glorious sheen to it, so why did it make him feel so uneasy?

CLARE
1993

Why do appearances have to matter so? Clare frowned at the small array of clothes in the wardrobe. It couldn't be too casual in case Duncan took her to a terribly expensive restaurant, but not too upmarket for a small pub. As she went through possible combinations of colour, the familiarity of the sensation took her breath away. All those evenings searching for just the right thing to catch Phil's eye, something to impress him. Was she going to follow the same path with Duncan, trying to make herself into something she wasn't? No, she muttered grimly and sought the cords she'd worn to the interview. There was a tap at the door and Sylvie marched in.

'I still think you're a stupid fool, but would you like to borrow these?' Draped over her arm were a pair of black trousers and a deep red blouse embroidered with flowers. Clare held the blouse up.

'I'll take the blouse, I don't have the courage for those slim tight things. Thanks.' Indeed, the red ensemble set off the colour of her hair.

'You'll take care won't you?' Sylvie asked anxiously.

Clare sighed with impatience and glared. Sylvie left her to get on. Clare stared at herself in the mirror and was glad she'd thrown away all her make-up, any attempt she did make would no doubt get smudged before long. She contented herself with brushing her hair until it billowed with static, clipping on earrings and liberally spraying her best perfume.

'Go for it girl, but keep your head on!' said her inner voice.

Clare's stomach lurched when she saw the time. Ten minutes to go. What would they talk about? Would she show a lack of worldliness? How would she cope with a table laid with mountains of silver? Her quandary was broken by an imperious honk from the lane. Clare tore out of her room and nearly collided with Alex. Somehow Clare hadn't wanted him to know about her date, let alone see her go. He'd spent most of the day getting the truck towed out of the ditch and repairing it, so she'd been able to avoid him. He looked at her, said nothing and disappeared into his room. Clare dithered for a moment, feeling as if she had something she must say to him, but another honk from the lane sent her speeding out into the night. The MG was a warm cocoon, filled with fumes of the intoxicating aftershave.

'What the dickens have you done?' was Duncan's startled greeting. Clare had completely forgotten about her hair. They accelerated down the lane, but there was little sensation of movement inside the cockpit. Clare saw Duncan's smile in the glow of the headlights and was paralysed. His beauty was something she'd never expected in a man. She felt so drawn to him that the sight of the hairs on the back of his hands sent a tantalising glow through her body.

'Where are we going?' was the best she could manage.

'A rather nice little place I know, near Horden Bridge. They have a rather good cellar.'

It seemed just a matter of moments, but already they were arriving outside a thatch-roofed restaurant, decorated with glowing beads of white light. Clare sighed, this was far more enchanting than any gaudy display she'd seen so far. The door was opened for her, Duncan held his hand out to help her up. Clare felt like royalty as she was led in.

'We're a little on the early side, shall we have a drink first?'

Clare was glad to let him take control and followed him to the bar. It was dimly lit, the walls festooned with Victorian prints. The small tables were lit by candles set in old wine bottles. The whole feeling was of warm intimacy. Duncan took Clare's coat and ushered her to a seat.

'What would you like to drink?'

'Gin and tonic, please.' Clare sat, soaking in the atmosphere, while he fetched the drinks. Everything compounded in Clare to give her a sense of glorious anticipation. Duncan returned with drinks and menu. Clare began to scrutinise the list, thankful for Phil's thorough grounding in French restaurants.

'Shall I order for you? It's all a little complicated.' Duncan was flicking a finger to a hovering waiter.

'Two Number Threes, two number Fours, with salad and a number 33 from the wine List.' He ordered before Clare replied. For a moment Clare was cross then realised he was trying to spare her embarrassment. The trouble was, he'd ordered by numbers so she couldn't really be impressed. Perhaps his accent wasn't too good. Clare smiled.

'What did you do yesterday then? Stuff yourself as we did then sit in front of the box?'

'No, I slept most of it, I had a rather late night.' Memories of torchlight flickering across the sedges sprang to mind.

'So what made you come to this part of the world then?'

Duncan's gaze was fixed firmly upon Clare, making her feel vulnerable and special. She found herself telling a much-modified tale of her decision to leave the town and make a new start. Though Duncan appeared attentive, the occasional flicker of his eyes gave Clare the sensation that he wasn't really listening and the knowledge made her wonder if she was boring him. Her words ground to a halt, so she changed the subject, it was a useful tactic.

'What do you do for a living then?' she asked.

'Stock Market and so on. Deadly boring. Do tell more about yourself.' Clare had shut like a clam, but the waiter saved the day, by calling them to their table.

The restaurant was also dimly lit, this time all the candles and dripped wax were a dull red. Once they were seated, the silent waiter approached with a bottle of wine. Clare sat and watched as the two men went through the pantomime of wine tasting. She found it difficult not to snigger at the reverential nod of satisfaction and gurgle of filling glasses. Clare sipped the deep red wine and joined in with her own courteous nod. The plates arrived with the first course, heavy with the smell of garlic, small pieces of meat lay in a sauce of tomatoes and peppers. Clare was thrilled and set too thoroughly enjoying the delicate flavour of the meat. She began to accumulate a pile of bones at the side of her dish. Duncan's pile seemed much smaller, and she looked up to see an amused look on his face, which broke into a shout of laughter.

'Enjoying your chicken?'

'No, I love frogs legs, we used to have them quite often at Pierre's in Mayfair.'

Duncan stopped laughing and looked disappointed.

'I suppose you're now going to tell me they're your favourite entrée?'

'Yes along with squid!'

They continued in silence. Clare was glad to concentrate on the food, she hated it interrupted by small talk.

'That was a wonderful surprise, thank-you,' she said after wiping her mouth.

Duncan's good humour had reappeared.

'You're the first one not to be caught out for a long time. You're not at all what I expected you to be.'

The wine had evaporated Clare's earlier awe of Duncan, she felt equal to everything in him, except his sexuality, so she asked,

'Well, just what did you expect?'

He looked uncomfortable. 'Well, just different. Certainly not a food expert,' he conceded. They both laughed and proceeded to do justice to Steak Au Poivre and Baked Alaska.

Replete, they lingered over coffee. Clare felt deep anticipation, the thought of him just touching her hand sent a fission of excitement through her. Their conversation ranged over many subjects, but finding little common ground, so different were their backgrounds and experiences. Clare felt they were just skirting around the all-important, personal. If they weren't bound by this mutual attraction, there would never be anything to link them together. Was he as nervous as she was that the feeling wasn't mutual? Clare tried hard to keep eye contact, there had to be some way of making that bridge. Clare saw a chance and leapt in.

'Sylvie's back from Australia, I told her you'd asked after her.'

'What did she say?'

'I don't think you really want to hear.'

At last, he looked straight into her eyes, and Clare was hypnotised.

'Sylvie and I go back a long time. I've changed at lot since then.'

Clare had to believe him. His hand reached across the table and took hers. The small touch seemed to reach all of her body, and they stared in silence. Good grief this is pure Mills and Boon thought Clare and took her hand away to take a gulp of coffee.

'I think it's time for us to move on.' Duncan signalled to the waiter. Clare had visions of a night club or another romantic bar, where perhaps, at last, they'd open up to each other. Don't rush it, she warned herself and felt relieved that Sylvie had been so wrong. Once again they sped off into the night. Clare was glad of the music in the car, its sensual undertones were soothing to her rising excitement. Too soon they ground to a halt. Clare peered out and saw they were parked outside a small Hotel, its neon sign, gaudy and cheap. This time when Duncan helped her out, he held on to her hand and swung her close to him. Clare knew what was coming and reached up eagerly for his kisses. The sensation was too much to pinpoint, so she swam in it, until she became aware of his hand inside her coat, slipping under her blouse and upwards.

'Duncan, isn't it all a bit soon for that?' Clare exclaimed.

'Alright, I'll wait until we get up to the room!' He was still holding her tight leaning her on to the car.

'What room?'

His head was coming closer, and she had to dodge to miss his kiss, he nuzzled her neck instead. 'The room where we'll get to know each other better, where we're going to share a little Christmas cheer!'

'Duncan, I'm not going to bed with you, I hardly know you.' She'd never imagined this.

'Come on, it's the best way to break the ice. You've wanted me ever since you first clapped eyes on me!'

Sylvie's warnings began to reverberate in Clare's head. Duncan had changed, he was worse.

'I may have been attracted to you, but I don't leap into bed with everyone I meet.'

Clare tried to struggle free of his arms, but he was pinning her against the car.

'I think you're just protesting too hard.' His hand began to search again.

'Duncan, I'm not a serving wench. Get off me.' The harder she struggled, the tighter he gripped and pressed. The part of Clare's mind which wasn't panicking told her to bide her time, she'd be able to get away. So, she ceased struggling, Duncan gave an almost animal grunt of pleasure.

'See, I knew you'd change your mind!'

He relaxed and moved away from Clare so she took her chance. Her right knee came up with the adroitness of fear and accurately crunched home. Duncan crumpled with a savage groan. 'You bitch!' was all he could bleat.

Clare ran into the safety of the Hotel. The Night Porter stared blearily at her.

'You alright Miss?'

'Yes, just a misunderstanding. Where's the phone?' Clare began to shake as she lifted the receiver. She didn't have a penny on her so had to go through the operator. For a minute she didn't remember the number. Sylvie answer, she prayed, but her luck was out. Alex answered and now Clare felt dirty and humiliated.

'Alex, can you come and pick me up? I'm at the Horton Heath Hotel and I haven't got any money.'

'I'm on the way,' was his only comment before he rang off.

As Clare replaced the receiver, Duncan hobbled in.

'You bitch, you'll suffer for this. I'll see you don't work again.'

To her surprise, the Porter came to her rescue.

'Now Sir, I don't think this will help matters. Why don't you go on home and sleep it off? Things will seem different in the morning.' The Porter stood a good foot taller than Duncan, so he turned on his heel and left, slamming the door.

'Thank you,' said Clare and sank onto a sofa by the desk.

You stupid, stupid twit, was all she could think. You thought you knew everything, then you let yourself be carried away on an emotion which was no stronger than a crush. You were dazzled by glamour and an overpowering aftershave. Her thoughts spiralled downwards into a deep pit of self-pity.

'Clare.'

All her hurt was suddenly cradled in a pair of gentle arms, and Clare began to cry.

'Alex, I've been a real wally,' she said and took a grubby hanky from him to mop her face. 'I always seem to be crying in front of you. I'm not normally like this.'

'Don't worry, I'm not going to say I told you so,' Alex said softly as he led her out to the truck. They climbed into the warm cab. Alex hesitated before starting the engine.

'Clare, you know I feel something for you. In a way, I'm glad this has happened.' She looked at him in disbelief.

'I couldn't have stayed at the cottage with things as they were, despite Sylvie's assurances. Also, I know this is the wrong time because you're upset and tired, but Clare, can we try some sort of relationship? Nothing heavy, just going out every now and then, be a little more than house-mates? I know you may not want to risk it if it's because of my past, and I've been moody but that's been partly because of you. Sylvie's right, if I have been given a new chance, I must take it. I mustn't let bygones hold me back.'

Clare understood just how he was feeling.

'Will you go out with me, no ties, no problems. I know you don't feel anything much towards me – can we give it a try?'

Clare listened to him with a surprising feeling of calmness. She didn't really want another relationship, let alone with Alex. But, she'd just made a complete fool of herself. It seemed as far as following her nose over men went, she had no sense. She knew after Duncan there was a need inside her for some sort of relationship, however much she tried to deny it. Perhaps it would be different to be the one sought after, to let someone else do the running so that she could call the tune for once. She wouldn't have to compromise because she'd have the upper hand, the control over everything. He'd have to take her warts and all. Sleepiness overwhelmed Clare, she now had no will to even think of arguments against his proposals. 'All right, but no pressure!' she said, trying not to sound begrudging. Clare saw Alex's face lit up in a radiant smile, making him look different, no longer ugly.

'You need to get to your bed.'

Clare jumped because for a moment she thought he was meaning together. Then she realised her stupidity, so she grinned at him.

'I am a bit tired.'

They drove home in companiable silence, Clare's eyelids drooping. Once home, at the foot of the stairs, Alex turned and said, with a new temerity in his voice,

'May I kiss you goodnight?'

'Yes.' Clare lifted her head but found a firm kiss planted on her forehead. Bemused, she clattered up the stairs. In spite of her weariness, sleep didn't come easily. Her thoughts were haunted by memories of Duncan's behaviour. He'd fallen completely off his pedestal. How would she ever look any of the Harrison's in the eye again? Had he been serious in his threat of stopping her working? She had visions of Mr and Mrs Harrison as judge and jury and no doubt they would come down on the side of their son. Hadn't Mrs Harrison been almost proud of his exploits the other day? It would all escalate and no one in the area would employ her because of the old boy network, even Chris would hear and sack her - or maybe he'd think her a prime candidate for his harem. Finally, Clare realised there was nothing to be done in the middle of the night, all she could do is turn up for work as usual, and be ready to plead her case. Perhaps Sylvie would use it as a story. Innocent Domestic sacked because she said no! Clare felt a giggle rise and relaxed a bit.

She turned her musings towards Alex. She held to the convictions she'd had in the truck; it would be nice to have the upper hand. All her feelings about him until now had consisted of dislike, distrust and anger. Should she wipe these out and start afresh? She admitted to herself that she had enjoyed their afternoon watching the television and conspiring against Sylvie's Christmas with him, so maybe it would all develop into a calm feeling, of good friends without all the emotional peaks and troughs which caused her so much trouble. She had control over the relationship. If it went too far, she could simply stop it. Clare knew only too well that Alex was not someone to mess about with. His feelings were probably running deep, his moodiness had shown that. A shiver ran down Clare's back because she saw it with dead certainty that her small commitment would be matched by a mountain on his side and it was already too late to back track. He had kissed her once, and all she had felt was revulsion. What if she felt the same the next time?

Her troubled mind eventually switched off, and she slept a deep, dreamless sleep until daylight. The weather had swung around again and was dull, matching Clare's feelings. She returned the blouse and told Sylvie the edited highlights of the previous evening and that did nothing to dispel Clare's glum mood. Sylvie didn't spare her any of the 'I told you so's' and on hearing about the tentative relationship between Alex and Clare, nearly exploded.

'How can you? After all, you've said about him. You can't turn to someone as complex as he is, on the rebound. Talk about playing with fire. Clare you can't go running from man to man like this. If you're searching for some sort of solace, I can tell you the right place to find it.'

Clare already on the defensive, because of the truths Sylvie was speaking, retorted, 'Don't you start bringing religion into it!' she shouted and walked out. She wished she had a dog to walk so that she had the excuse to get out of the house to get away from everything. Clare paced around the sitting room, nothing on the bookshelves caught her attention and the television was all geared to children. Above her head, she heard Alex's heavy footsteps go across the landing and down the stairs. Her stomach turned because she just didn't know how to face him, what to say. Would he see the revulsion she suspected was lurking inside?

To her surprise, his footsteps proceeded along the hall, out the door and down the path... Shortly afterwards, she heard the truck growl away. Clare heaved a sigh, then laughed at herself. Not so long ago, the thought of even going out with Alex would have been laughable, and now she was piqued because he wasn't acting like a lovesick swain and following her about. Clare changed the channels on the television to a black and white film. When Sylvie came in, she was quite engrossed.

'I'm sorry Clare. I was only trying to help. I'll be here whenever you need. Our friendship is stronger than this little upset isn't it?' Sylvie placated.

'Yes, I'm sorry too. Let's forget it.' Clare wanted to get back to the film. Sylvie left the house with an enormous slam of the door but feeling at peace with her friend. The film was reaching a climax when Alex returned. Clare was so immersed that for a moment she didn't understand what he was saying.

'Come out with me, there's something I want to show you.'

'Oh what?' said Clare in genuine annoyance.

Alex glared at the television.

'The wife did it. Now come on and fetch your wellies.' Cross that he'd spoilt the film, Clare followed him and tried to change her humour.

'What is it?' Clare quizzed him all the way, but he wouldn't give in, a mischievous grin that seemed almost unreal playing on his face.

The truck plunged off the gravel and into a farmyard, pitted and soggy with mud. Rusting machinery and a thin, whining Collie gave the whole place a feeling of sadness. Clare felt chilled, it reminded her of home. Alex, however, was bounding through the mud and pulling open the doors of the barn. They stuck and squelched until with a giant heave, they groaned open wide enough for Clare to see what was inside. She ploughed through the mud to see in. With the air of a conjurer, Alex waved his hands and exclaimed,

'Wheels!' Inside stood a very beaten Land Rover, its roof torn, and bumper hanging at an angle.

'You can't be serious.' stated Clare and peered into the cab. Despite a rip on the seats, the cab seemed quite tidy. Speechless, Clare tugged the door open and hoisted herself up onto the seat. The keys were waiting, but first Clare ran through the gears, each one seemed miles apart and needed a real heave to drive them home.

'Go on. Take her for a run.' Alex sat next to her in the cab, Clare began to be infected by his mood, so gingerly she turned the key. The engine eventually hiccupped into life, not the throaty roar of Chris' V8, but an uneven asthmatic growl. It belched out smoke which even seemed to be coming inside. Clare let in the clutch which seemed to take ages to bite, then, at last, she began to roll forward, only to jump about and stop. Clare had forgotten the handbrake. Trying not to get flustered, she tried to release it; in the end, it took two hands. The last person who had parked the Land Rover had really wanted it to stay put. Her second attempt was successful, and they rolled out into the yard. The huge steering wheel had enormous play in it, and the whole vehicle seemed to be shaking. Clare crunched her way through the gears until she reached 25 mph. It took all of her concentration to keep in a straight line, but Clare felt a rising excitement. This was real driving, not operating like in a modern car. Clare stopped at the edge of a small wood. Impulsively she leant across the cab and enveloped Alex in a bear hug. 'It's brilliant, wonderful, how did you know I hankered after one?'

Alex's reply was to turn and kiss her fully on the lips, gently and reverential. At first, Clare was overwhelmed with relief because rather than revulsion, she felt nothing. Then she felt a sort of sadness because of her lack of reaction, his kiss didn't even raise her heartbeat. Well perhaps it was the best she could hope for at the moment, it was a good base to start from, this nothing.

'I've been wanting to do that for a long time,' said Alex as he released her.

Clare couldn't think of any reply to that so smiled straight at him. She'd never looked at him closely before, and now he looked like a stranger. His eyes were a startling blue, the dark eyelashes emphasising them. His face seemed to have an air of nobility about it, but there was a hint of worry in the deep lines about his eyes and on his forehead. A smile didn't come naturally to such a face. Clare snapped out of her musings.

'How did you find out about her?'

'One hears a lot of things down the pub!'

'How much?

Alex shook his head vehemently. 'It's a gift.'

'Alex, there's no need. I can run to this.'

'Please, no. Let me enjoy giving, it's a new feeling.'

Clare conceded, bowing to the need he felt. 'What about the documents? Does she need any work done?'

Alex nearly laughed.' Nothing apart from a new engine, chassis, gearbox and bodywork! But she does have six months MOT and Tax. We can work on her if you want, or just sell her for scrap.'

Clare felt hurt, she was already becoming attached to her gift.

'You'll have to drive me back to the farm now, then make your own way home alone. Can you manage?' stated Alex.

Clare gave him what she hoped was a disgusted look and started the engine. It took a ten-point turn to reverse the vehicle in the lane, so poor was the lock. On the way, Alex explained about the high and low ratio gears, but Clare was too excited to take it all in. 'Will that make her go any faster?' she demanded, they were now flat out at 30 mph.

'No, they'll make her go slower! You might get another l0 mph out of her downhill, with a following wind, but you don't need great speeds for these lanes.'

'We can always put a V8 in her like in Chris' Landy.'

Clare knew immediately she'd said the wrong thing, for on glancing at Alex his face had resumed its familiar stern expression and he was silent the rest of the way back. They stopped at the farm, Clare felt she had to make amends.

'Shall we go down the pub when we get back?' Clare saw Alex visibly relax from the posture of his back.

'I'd be honoured. I'll wait for you at the cottage.'

Clare realised she would have much rather spent the morning driving around and looking over the vehicle. She had played right into Alex's hands. This was no way to keep her distance, to call the tune, if every time she felt she'd upset him in some small way, she had to make it up to him. That was wrong. No, perhaps it was just her sense of gratitude, and they did need to get to know each other a bit. Clare was resolute, she'd had made an agreement and she couldn't back out now. By the time she reached the cottage, Clare's arms were aching from wrestling with the steering wheel. Alex was waiting, leaning on the truck. Clare found she had to put her back to the door before it would stay shut. What a heap, she thought, but it's mine. On the way to there, Alex handed her a note. The paper was thick and scented, Clare's stomach lurched, was this her dismissal from the Harrisons.

'Dear Clare,' it read. 'We've all gone up to town for a few days. Key is under the stone horse to the left of the door. Use it to turn off the box in the cloakroom on the right. When you leave, do the reverse procedure, you have 30 seconds to shut the door after turning on the alarm. We will be back by the weekend. Please, would you clean all the bedrooms, dust and hoover? Polish all the furniture in the dining room. Wash all china in the hall, polish furniture in the hall.'

There was squiggle at the bottom. Clare felt a great weight lift from her. Duncan must have said nothing to them, she was going to be alright. How silly, she then thought, bothering with a burglar alarm, then leaving the key by the door...The pub Alex had chosen was quite a surprise to Clare. Somehow she'd expected it to be very rural, but this was brand new and on the edge of a housing estate. He led her into its brightly painted lounge, and they sat on a comfortable settee. Clare keenly felt the contrast between these and her last outing. When Alex returned with her drink, Clare found she had the boldness to quiz him, her natural curiosity overcoming any temerity she felt.

'How did you find this place?'

'Quite by chance. It's the friendly atmosphere I like. Perhaps I used to go to one like this before.'

'You seem quite reconciled to your past this morning.'

'I've done a lot of thinking lately. I wish someone like Sylvie had told me to seize every opportunity with both hands sooner. I wouldn't have wasted so much time keeping away from folks.'

From there the conversation seemed to flow. Clare had wondered what they would find to talk about, but Alex had spent the past couple of years reading, watching television, listening to the radio, and she found him very well informed in a lot of the subjects they touched. Clare saw how shallow Duncan's responses had been to the same things. Alex went up in her estimation, he wasn't such a lout after all. Yet Clare couldn't get rid of feeling dumbfounded at his lack of curiosity about his past. When she asked he replied quite gruffly.

'I don't want to talk about it at all, least of all in public.' The lounge had filled up.

'You haven't told me the first thing about yourself,' he continued. Clare knew she had to be honest, she owed him that at least. So she told him her life story, only cutting pieces that embarrassed her to tell him, such as her finding Phil and the girl in her bed. Somehow Clare hadn't even thought of the eventuality of sex with Alex, and she found herself shying away from the idea. It was too soon. If she did hold the upper hand, she would only have to say no. Anyway, Alex didn't strike her as the physical sort, he hadn't touched her once in the pub, not even trying to hold her hand. So maybe the problem would never arise. Eventually, time was called, and they made their way out, Alex gallantly holding the door open for her. Clare wished deep inside that she had some passion for him, but it just wasn't there. All she had was an emptiness. She liked him, was even still a little in awe of him, but no more, and that made Clare a little sad.

CLARE
1993

Spring had come early to the South of England.
The early yellows of the daffodils and primroses
running riot in the new deep green grass. Even
the trees were putting on an early display, the
damsons at the back of Sylvie's cottage were
decked in drifts of snow.

Clare found herself looking at this fecund
show of nature on one of her rare afternoons off.
The lawn was aping a meadow and needed a cut
before it ran totally amok. Clare went to the shed
to find the old push mower, doused it liberally
with Three-in-One and pushed it onto the grass.
Overestimating the force needed, Clare charged
at the green swathe and the mower rolled over it
instead of cutting. She tried again at a more
decorous pace and this time the machine cut a
swathe, cuttings flying everywhere. The grass
hid several large stones, and it wasn't long until
the mower hit one. The jolt hit Clare in the
stomach sending her sprawling onto her back.
Winded, she lay in the warm sun, ignoring the
dampness of the grass. Once her breathing
calmed, Clare decided it was too much effort to
do anymore, she would sprawl and do nothing.
She'd ask Alex to cut the grass that evening!

Life had taken a steadier turn after the
dramatic events of Christmas, had become
routine, even a little dull. Lately, Clare had been
aware of an itch, an irritation; its source
unknown. A sense of restlessness that couldn't
be put down entirely to spring.

Alex was at the centre of her life, living in
the same cottage meant they were always in
each other's company. Today was a rare

moment of being on her own. Was he the source of the irritation? Clare admitted to herself that her feelings had changed over the months. She'd lost all her original fear of him and they did enjoy each other's company. Working on Aggie had broken the ice. Alex proved as inept a mechanic as Clare, and they'd really had to struggle, with the manual in one hand bits in the other as they did repairs. She broke down frequently, much to Clare's embarrassment.

Why hadn't her feelings deepened enough to let him creep under the covers of her heart? He was her best friend, nothing more. Her heart never lurched at the sight of him and his kisses never made her want to invite anything more. Was she being unfair to him? He was so much the gentleman; she would never know the frustrations he held inside. Perhaps she should offer to sleep with him and see if that changed something. But what if it didn't, and she felt the same? It might be that they needed breathing space to sort out just where they were. The whole relationship was treading water, going nowhere. Was Alex aware of her restlessness and felt something of the same? Right at the start, he'd warned her of his bad times which happened occasionally. During them, he would take to his room for up to several days and she'd learnt to stay well away. Quite what he went through or how he got over them she didn't know, he wouldn't tell her anything except to say he was feeling fine now. In the past month, he'd had three of these bad times, but had come through much the same as he went in. It hadn't even been a breathing space for Clare, because they'd still been in the same house.

Sylvie wasn't around to keep her Clare company because she'd taken herself off to

London. After Christmas, she had returned from Chardminster with an armful of Christian magazines. Clare had flicked through them when Sylvie's back was turned to discover they were full of pictures of squeaky clean people, with shallow smiles and stories of what the Lord had done for them. Clare had ignored them from then on. Sylvie, however, read them assiduously, and began to write articles, and apply for jobs with them. It was for an interview with one of them that Sylvie had gone to town.

Clare was still surprised at the change in Sylvie. She had always been the life and soul of the party with an endless succession of men in tow. Now there was only one, a drippy looking individual, in Clare's opinion, called Matthew, who was training for something vague at Bible school. Sylvie had thrown out all the home-made wines and beer from the cupboard under the stairs and swear words had completely left her vocabulary. Several evenings a week, Sylvie and her Christian friends would hold prayer meetings in the cottage which usually sent Clare and Alex bolting for the pub.

The gift of Aggie, or Great Aunt Agatha to give her full name, had transformed Clare's working life. Within a couple of weeks after Christmas, Clare's week was filled, and she was still having to turn people down. Several of the jobs were mucking out (as she termed it) between tenants in let houses or holiday cottages. Sometimes they would leave a tip, or perishable goods, which added a touch of enjoyment. Clare had two favourite clients. The first being an old lady in her nineties, who was still cross at having to give in and let someone else help in her house, which was filled with antiques and china. Clare found it a pleasure to keep them in pristine condition. She soon found that Mrs Lock's bark was worse than her bite, and had lately offered Clare tea from the best china. She found herself enjoying the anecdotes of a life gone by, so it suited her to keep the job, despite the fact Mrs Lock occasionally forgot to pay.

The second was the Croft family. Sheila was very much the earth mother and glorified in it. There were five children, who lived in a noisy existence in the small cottage. It was always so strewn with toys and drawings that Clare often felt it pointless beginning to clear it up. The children who weren't yet at school would follow her about telling her about playschool, their toys or even to show her something disgusting hidden in a drawer. Sheila would chat with Clare over lunch, who supposed it was this chaotic, loving family life which she'd never experienced that so drew her here. She felt included, and deep down longed for it somewhere in her future.

The Harrison's were still Clare's main employers, and the skills she acquired there were those she used in the other houses. There had been some real high points there amidst the ordinary drudge. Mrs Harrison had come back from the January sales, laden with new clothes, and had to clear out her wardrobe to make space. Several of the discarded dresses had fitted Clare, so she now had a cupboard filled with elegant silks and linens. She hadn't yet had a chance to wear them, but she felt proud that she could now look smart when the occasion arose. Clare had learnt her position in the house, and once she'd accepted it, she took the rest in her stride. Like the wall in Shakespeare's play, she heard a lot but wasn't supposed to hear; at times she felt invisible. To cope with the inevitable boredom, she developed the tactic of doing everything as fast as possible, without skimping on the quality then asking for more. This threw the Harrison's so much that on a couple of days she was sent home early but on full pay.

The illusions that Clare held about rich people were constantly being shattered. One weekend, Peter brought home an Asian girl, and the arguments that followed shocked Clare; she thought bigotry had gone out with the Victorian era. It had the knock-on effect of calming her own money hoarding and relaxing her own financial targets; she didn't want to become like the Harrison's. Duncan, she had not seen since Christmas and there was never any reference to their short relationship by the Harrison's.

Chris was still breezing in and out of the country, and Clare saw him only occasionally. Alex had been obviously pleased when she finished the enormous task of cleaning and tidying the Villa. It now took only a couple of hours a week when Chris was home. That Alex did not like Chris, Clare had no doubt. He wouldn't explain or even discuss it; the only thing he would admit to was a fierce desire to protect her which had started from the minute Clare had walked into the cottage.

Clare found herself having to inform Alex endlessly about the women in Chris' life, even though there were only two and he wasn't the lothario she had originally thought. Chris was the only bone of contention between them, and Clare knew that Alex would like her to drop the job. She wouldn't. The hackles of her independence would rise when Alex had that look about him and she always went on the defensive. It didn't help that Chris was interested in Aggie. He'd given her a complete physical and largely agreed with Alex's diagnosis. Clare didn't dare tell Alex that Chris had offered to fit Aggie a new engine. Clare enjoyed Chris' company, he had a way of making jokes about things which had Clare howling with laughter. Alex didn't have much of a sense of humour. Chris was always giving Clare details of the Land Rover club meetings and urging her to come, but when she mentioned it to Alex, as expected, he always had some reason for them not to go, and so Clare would have to make excuses to Chris. On the whole, the difficulty with Chris was a minor detail. Just what was the matter then? Clare had transport, well-paid jobs, somewhere to live and a steady boyfriend. Wasn't that what she'd always wanted? Her bank balance confirmed her success, what more did she need?

Freedom! Clare wanted to laze about, like right now, without someone asking her if she wanted a coffee or a cushion. If she decided to go for a walk, she didn't need an escort. She wanted to carry her own shopping home and chose her favourite brand, not the cheapest. She wanted to rise above cleaning, to do something more. Clare's mind followed that avenue because she didn't see how to get out of the other.

How could she change her cleaning duties, unless she got someone else to do it? That was it! Unemployment was rampant here as in any part of the country. If she got a team together, give them some sort of training and uniform, she could cover no end of jobs, and not have to do any of it herself. She would sit in an office in the high street, and work with phones, faxes and computers. She would eventually reach across the county, advertise in The Lady and The Field. There might be branches into house minding, spring cleaning, even into the realms of interior landscaping. Clare sat up, her ideas rushing about in her head. One thought came along, clamping down all the others. Alex would want to help, go with her to the bank, view places, put his own ideas in. Clare wanted this all to herself. Perhaps it was time to stand up for herself and say no. If he didn't understand, that was his problem. Feeling militant Clare returned to the kitchen to the heap of dirty washing she'd abandoned a couple of hours ago.

Clare strolled into the kitchen, turned the radio on full blast and began to fill the sink with hot water. As she immersed the clothes, a waft of fresh air blew in through the back door, carrying with it the scent of the flowers outside. How many generations of women had stood at this sink, gazing numbly out of the window as they tried to rinse a stain from a loved one's shirt? One of her priorities must be a washing machine.

'Do you really think I'd let you get away with it?' hissed a savage low voice behind her. Before she could spin around to face her attacker, hands grabbed her head and eyes. His body pressed Clare hard into the rim of the sink and he pushed her head down near to the boiling suds.

'You thought you had it all taped. But I'm back now,' he continued.

'Duncan, you can't be still angry. I'm sorry, but I'm not going to bed with you! I'll call the police.'

'Just how do you expect to do that?' he snorted and pushed her head right into the water. Clare had sense enough to hold her breath. The water scorched making her want to

scream in pain, but she couldn't. She heard
obscenities and other things being screamed as
the water filled her ears. Suddenly the grip
lessened, and he pulled her head out. Clare
gasped for precious air, then tried to pull herself
free from his clasp, but his strength was
overwhelming. Clare began to scream but found
herself being pushed back into the water. Again
he released her. 'I haven't even started yet. I'll
pick the right time. I'm going to square the
balance for once and for all. You can't have him
back again, I claimed him back once... and I'll do
it again.'

For the third time, Clare's head was
pushed under the water. His body moved away
from her, but as she flailed about, he gave an
almighty shove knocking Clare off balance,
tipping her head and shoulders sideways into the
deep sink. For an eternity she floundered, hair
tangling in clothes, hands slipping on the wet
draining board as she tried to grip. Clare took a
gulp of soapy water before she finally managed
to get clear. She was too grateful for breath to
look for her assailant and groped around for a
tea towel, to clear her smarting eyes.

Clare collapsed onto a chair and looked
around half expecting to see Duncan standing by
the door leering at her, but the kitchen was
empty. She sat for some time, taking in
shuddering deep breaths. Her clothes became
cold and shaky, but she just sat and sat.
Duncan's words hadn't made sense. Have who
back again, claim what back again? Her only
conclusions was that he must be totally off his
rocker. Should she go to the police? Somehow
she shied away from it, although it was the right
thing to do. After all, she hadn't even seen him.
Duncan did seem the logical conclusion but

where was the proof? She felt foolish now if she'd struggled harder maybe she'd have caught him. Clare heard footsteps pounding up the path and the front door opening. Alex's tall frame filled the front door.

'What on earth have you been doing?'

'Alex, I've just been attacked.'

He marched up to Clare and took her in his arms, holding her so firmly that she couldn't move and the shakes stopped. Huddled into him, she told him all she remembered, and her conclusion it was Duncan.

'Should we call the police?'

'No, I can sort him out,' Alex replied angrily.

'Alex is that wise?'

'I can find him. Will you be alright now?'

Clare looked at Alex who had a strange look in his eye. She began to be worried about just what he was planning to do. He was clearly thinking of Duncan as was Clare.

'Alex, don't put yourself in any danger!'

'There's no need to worry,' he said in a patient voice. 'I'm just going to put a stop to his menacing. Have you any dry clothes?'

Clare shook her head.

'There's a jumper and T-shirt of mine in the landing cupboard. I won't be long.'

'Alex don't do anything silly!'

'Trust me,' he said and was gone.

Clare did as she was told, then mechanically went back to her washing. The smell of the powder engulfed her, but she made herself face it. Once it was all hanging on the line, she made a strong, sweet coffee and opened a packet of biscuits. Where was Alex, what was he doing? The clock was creeping towards five when he returned. Clare saw from the gleam in his eyes that he'd found his quarry. Silently she made him a drink and waited.

'He was down the pub having a joke with the peasants. I'd seen his car parked there on the way here. I asked him to come outside. I think he thought I had a message from his parents. However, when I asked him to leave you alone, he denied ever being near. Instead, he insisted you led him on and anyway wasn't it all a bit late for this. So I asked him point-blank if he'd been here today. He denied it, said he'd been at home with his parents and was only on his first beer. I knew that was a lie, so I broke his nose. He got up, blood everywhere, threatening the police and other things. Then I said, if you behave, I'll not tell the police about the drugs you sell to your mates and keep hidden in the well. He went even whiter and shot away. He'll not bother us again,' Alex ended triumphantly.

'Did you really need to hit him? Wouldn't the threat have been enough?' Clare demanded, feeling chilled at Alex's apparent glee.

'Probably,' he admitted. 'but I wanted to drive the point home.'

Things still nagged at Clare.

'What did he mean about having him back again' and 'squaring the balance'?' she asked.

'I've no idea. The only thing I can think of is that he's been snorting some of that cocaine. You're alright now, so stop worrying, it won't happen again.'

Clare tried to feel totally reassured, but the strange words kept on echoing about her head. Alex took her out for a meal in the evening, to take her mind off things, and Clare told him about the Agency. As she had expected, Alex was all for it, suggesting they extend it to gardens, then he could help to run it. Clare didn't have the courage to tell him she wanted it all to herself, she knew it was cowardice and inwardly cursed herself. She would have to find a way to tell him soon.

Chris was in one of his cheerful moods when Clare arrived at the villa in the morning. He came out of the garage, already covered in grime. Inside she saw the engine swaying in mid-air above the Land Rover. Clare was surprised at how relieved she was that he was in, she hadn't realised how much she was still on edge after the previous day.

'All I've got to do is put the engine back in, then I can run her in the trial tomorrow!' he exclaimed, his Scots accent thicker than ever. 'Why don't you come and see how she goes?'

Clare's sense of rebellion was still simmering away, so she replied,

'Yes, I think I will!'

'8.30 a.m. Pits moor Farm. Bring sandwiches and coffee. Be prepared to get ragged about that heap. Will you bring Alex?'

Clare felt dismayed at how Chris obviously saw him as a permanent fixture. 'I don't know.' was the most honest reply she managed.

'There's not much to do inside, but I suspect the rugby players have been back in the bathroom. I'll see you later.' He dived back into the garage, and Clare went into the house.

Carrying the hoover across the upstairs landing, Clare unintentionally banged the door to the spare room. It swung open revealing not a room filled with boxes, but an immaculate bedroom. An array of perfumes and make-ups was set out with military precision on a dressing table. Beside the bed was a photograph of a plump, brown-haired woman holding a bottle of champagne. The wedding ring was clearly visible on her hand. The double bed was made up but didn't look slept in. There was a bang of a door downstairs, so Clare backed out.

The woman was obviously Chris' wife. Had she left him and he was keeping all this in the hope she'd return? If so, why did he have all the women on the go? Clare felt she should be revolted, but instead she felt sorry for the path Chris was following. No doubt he was so thin because he was burning the candle at both ends while he waited for her. Clare realised she was waiting too, for something to come along and change things because she was powerless herself. She felt a kinship with Chris, they were both in impossible situations, which neither of them knew how to change. Had Chris been trapped by the women's sympathy?

All Clare's feelings for Alex began to twist and turn inside her. She must feel something besides being annoyed by his wanting to be in on the agency idea. The trouble was he was so much the gentleman, that she was overwhelmed with guilt every time she wronged him. He had exploited the time when she was at her most vulnerable. She should have called a halt a long time ago. Her gratitude for Aggie had become a ball and chain.

That Alex loved her, in his own quiet way, Clare had no doubt, but where was the spark to ignite the fire for her? Was there any point in going on when she felt this way? Somehow, Alex overpowered Clare, in spite of his gentleness. When he was starting one of his dark times, she'd even sensed a hint of menace about him. That was ridiculous! Clare pulled herself back together, she was letting her imagination run riot. He would understand if she explained things clearly. Clare realised she needed him in a new way now, as a protector, because she couldn't feel any of Alex's sureness that the situation was dealt with.

Clare was leaning on the bannisters, looking over the stairs to the view across the marshes and sea beyond, the distant blare of a foghorn measuring the pace of her thoughts.

'Penny for them?' Clare jumped and dropped the aerosol can she was holding down the stairs. It fell onto Chris' head with a hollow thud. Clare tore down the stairs.

'I'm sorry. I was daydreaming. Are you alright?'

Chris was nursing his head, oil-smeared hands turning his black hair to rats tails. Clare saw a trickle of blood. She ran downstairs.

'Quick, to the sink, before you fill the cut with muck,' she ordered. In the bathroom, she leant him over the sink and turned the tap on. Under its flow, the trickle of blood soon stopped, and Clare saw it was only a scratch. Gently, she patted his head dry with a towel. Clare saw the beads of his backbone under his T-shirt and shuddered. 'I think you'll live,' she said.

'No thanks to you,' he said grimly, taking the towel.

'Good grief, there's no need to look so distraught.' Chris burst into laughter. 'I've had worse cuts than this shaving.' He studied her face.

'To make up for it, you have to tell me what was such a big problem to put that expression on your face.' Chris sounded genuinely concerned. Clare backed away.

'I don't think I can, it's too personal.'

'Is it Alex?'

'No, not at all,' Clare snapped, forgetting her guilt. 'It's nothing.'

Chris stared out Clare, they stood like a pair of children having a battle of wills. Clare suddenly felt overwhelmingly tired and sat down on the edge of the bath. 'Time for tea,' stated Chris. 'You know I reckon I run partially on tea, I seem to spend my life brewing up.' The bartering tone was back in his voice.

'That's probably why you're so thin!' The remark was out, and Clare knew she'd overstepped the mark. He was her employer, not a friend. 'I should never have said that it's none of my business,' she rapidly apologised. Thankfully Chris didn't look too cross.

'No it isn't, but you're right, I just never seem to get around to cooking.'

Clare wanted to ask about the culinary abilities of his girlfriends but had learnt her lesson. She knew it was time to quit before she made another stupid comment. 'I'll skip the tea if you don't mind. I'll finish hoovering the front room then I'll press on.'

'If that's what you want. But you'll still come to the rally?'

'I'll be there.' Clare was determined to get there, with or without Alex's blessing. She wanted this purely for herself, he could take it or leave it. A small tug at her chains, but she had to start somewhere.

A few days later, Alex and Clare were at loggerheads again.

'Look you said you didn't want me going out on my own because it might be dangerous, so give in with good grace. We do plenty of things you like doing, so put up with this for me!' Clare almost shouted.

Alex's reply was to slam the door of the Land Rover with a sullen bang. Clare had mustered the courage to state she was going to the rally, and would he like to come? To her surprise, he had agreed without all his usual arguments but she knew he wasn't keen which was born out by this sulk. Clare began to plan the right words to tell him about the agency idea, while her bravado lasted.

The farm was only a few miles from the cottage, its entrance marked by small yellow flags. They drove through a neat yard, into what could only be described as a rubbish dump. There were small mountains of topsoil and hardcore, littered with twisted pieces of metal and furniture. A thin pig was trotting about, hunting for breakfast. Clare was surprised that they were by no means too early. A couple of dozen Land Rovers were parked on a flat piece of ground behind the dump. Clare recognised Flossie and parked beside it, then she sat and took in the scene. She had never realised there were so many variations on a theme. Some of the Land Rovers were as beaten and worn as Aggie, others had been cut about, jacked up and painted in vibrant colours. From these vehicles came the throatiest roars, everyone was peering under bonnets, under the chassis, doing all the vital last minute checks.

'So you made it!' Chris stood at her window, dressed in lime green overalls which made him look positively sickly.

'Plenty of rain last night,' he continued. 'You're in for some real fun today!'

Alex and Clare jumped out of the cab, and she formally introduced the two men, who were in turn, formally polite. A short blonde man joined them.

'This is Henry, our Secretary and local nutter.'

'I'm not surprised you hid your wreck by Chris',' Henry said with an ironic grin on his face. 'The two go well together. Shame you're too late for scrutineering, we all need a good laugh, early in the morning!'

'I can see he was picked for charm and tact,' said Clare.

Henry gave them some papers.

'If you're mug enough to join, you can hand me the cash or pay me with your body!'

Despite her guffaw of laughter, Clare heard Alex muttering something under his breath, so she gave him a swift nudge in the ribs. There was a small, awkward pause.

'I must leave you,' said Chris. 'The first section is right over on the other side, so you need to make tracks.'

Alex and Clare climbed over the slippery mud to where they saw a trail of red and white markers laid out. There was a great sound of revving engines and the competitors came tearing over. The section seemed a simple task of driving down a slope, through a pool and out the other side. It wasn't until the first competitor went through that the cunning layout was revealed. The Land Rover stood poised at the top of the hill until the flag was dropped, then he careered down the slope and skidded at the bottom. A few feet over into the pool was a ledge, the Land Rover went over too far, tipped onto its side and lay prone, its engine still running to tumultuous applause from the small crowd. A rescue vehicle appeared from nowhere, a rope was attached to the prone vehicle and it was swiftly towed out to finish the section. The next man through was wiser and tore through, sending muddy water cascading up into the air. Two small boys were literally soaked, but seemed to find it vastly amusing. Clare linked her arm through Alex's and gave him a huge grin. 'Isn't this great - don't you fancy having a go?'

Alex looked non committal, 'Seems a lot of wear and tear for no benefit.'

'Come on - you could say that for any sport,' retorted Clare.

Chris drove into view and adroitly drove the section. Clare noticed the audience took more pleasure in the accidents than the successful runs. He re-appeared with several people in tow, including one of his girlfriends. 'What do you think of it then?' he demanded.

'Fantastic. I'd love to have a go, though I dare say I'd give everyone a good laugh when Aggie falls to pieces half way round!'

Chris beamed straight past Clare to the woman.

'See Jane, another convert! Clare, Alex, this is my mate, Jane. Her husband Bill is just about to drive that monster over the edge.' He pointed to a shining black rebuilt Land Rover driven by a bald man waiting to turn. Clare smiled, but inwardly her mind was travelling overtime. What on earth was going on? Does Bill know about the affair? Was it one of these modern 'ménage à trois'? There must be a logical explanation but she just couldn't see it. They stood as a group to watch the remaining competitors finish the section, then they drifted over to the next one. Clare found herself beside Jane.

'You're Chris' cleaner aren't you? I knew I'd seen you somewhere before,' she said. Much to Clare's relief, she let the subject drop. The next set of flags straddled a five-foot deep ravine. Jane explained the problem,' if they don't hit the ditch at the right angle, they'll jam on the other side, and likewise on the way out. Stand well back!' She was right, because vehicle after vehicle jammed, including Chris who nearly rolled over. The only person who succeeded was Bill. Foot firmly jammed on the accelerator, and fighting fiercely with the steering wheel, he shot through, smoke and mud engulfing the watching crowd, who allowed him a begrudging cheer for spoiling the fun. Clare was totally involved, taking in the differing techniques of drivers and vehicles.

'Tea break!' announced Jane. Guiltily Clare looked at Alex who had a bored expression on his face, but he gave her his arm across the rough bits. Back at the vehicles, thermos flasks and sandwiches were shared around. Bill and Chris joined them, both their vehicles no longer looked sleek, they were liberally covered in dark mud. Once the introductions were over, Bill asked Alex if he was enjoying it.

'Not quite my cup of tea, can't see the point in it.' he replied.

'You're of the working vehicles only school then?' replied Bill cheerfully. 'Don't worry you'll get over it.'

Clare saw the angry look on Alex's face and handed him a sandwich.

'You ought to let me rebuild yours, so you can enter,' continued Bill with supreme lack of tact. 'You know the chassis isn't that bad - can I have a look at the engine?'

Clare raised the bonnet, for Bill to snort with laughter.

'Your head gasket is on the way out, look up.'

Clare had never noticed the oil covering the inside of the bonnet.

'I've got a lovely little V8 looking for a home - cheap too.'

Clare wised up. 'Nice try!'

Bill grinned again.

'Would either of you like to drive the next section with me, Alex?'

'Not bloody likely!' To Clare's surprise, he turned his back on them and picked up the threads of the conversation he'd begun with Jane.

'I'll go,' said Clare, trying not to sound over eager.

Bill rewarded her with a huge grin.

'Got anything you don't mind soaking?'

'All this is old.'

'Right, follow me!'

Bill emptied his cup on the ground and led her to the rebuild. Everyone else was getting back into cabs and revving engines. Clare found herself securely strapped into a bucket seat by Chris.

'Take care of her!' Chris shouted over the roar. Alex was nowhere to be seen. They drove over to the markers. It seemed Bill was the first to go.

'You ready?' He grinned. Clare nodded.

The whole vehicle seemed to tip beneath her, as they drove down an almost perpendicular slope, then they entered the water and drove through a lake. Water spewed everywhere even into the cab. Bill kept a steady roar on the throttle, and then they were out. The vehicle tipped right up as they climbed back out the same slope and ground to a halt at the top. Bill stopped the engine.

'Enjoy that?' Despite her shaking, Clare was thrilled, it was more exciting than the most inventive fairground ride.

'It was amazing - can I have another go?'

'Stay right there!'

Alex appeared and ducked under the roll bar.

'I can see you're hooked,' he said not unkindly.

'You all right?' Clare asked.

'Fine - had quite a chat to Jane about growing onions. You staying in here?'

'If you don't mind?'

'No go ahead. When I get bored I'll listen to the radio in the cab.'

Clare was relieved that at last he seemed to be enjoying himself at last, but also cross because she'd asked his permission to stay. She rode the next few sections with Bill, learning to lean with the vehicle into the angles and to trust that it wouldn't tip over, despite all the indications to the contrary. Clare saw Alex still chatting with Jane, so she relaxed about him. It was a brilliant day.

Disaster struck on the last section. Alex stood on his own, quite close to a very muddy path, which they'd already driven through several times. The first Land Rover through, badly misjudged his exit, skidded, sending a crescent of filth up into the car which fell all over Alex. He stood there dripping. Clare saw the anger and fought to release herself from the belt. Bill reached over and flicked it open.

'Thanks Bill, it's been wonderful, but I feel I may be going home now.'

'I understand.'

Alex seemed calm when she reached him. 'I'm not spending the rest of the day soaked to the bone, looking like a prat while you muck about. We're going now.' He strode off. Clare could do nothing more than follow him. They drove home in silence. Clare was sorry for Alex, but cross that they had to leave. She had to console herself with the thought there'd be plenty more rallies, she fully intended to join up.

'I'm sorry it had to end like this,' Clare ventured, 'I thought you were quite enjoying yourself until then.'

'It wasn't too bad,' he conceded. 'But I had the feeling I'd been set up. Have you been talking to people about me? How did that woman know I'm a gardener?'

'I've no idea, perhaps Chris mentioned it.'

'So you talk to Chris about me do you?' Alex seemed to be trying to fuel his anger.

'Don't be so ridiculous, I may just have mentioned it in passing.'

'Well, don't go spreading things about me to that creep.'

'He's not a creep.'

'Well, you wouldn't think that would you. What do you get up to when you're there?'

'Alex, I don't believe I'm hearing this.'

'Well, I'm saying it now. The guy looks like a weirdo, I don't trust him and I don't like you working there.'

'Well, you'll just have to put up with it. Just who do you think you are saying where and what I can do? You don't own me. What happened to the non-heavy agreement? Every step I take you're right behind me. I can't go anywhere alone. It seems a crime to you to want a bit of peace. I'm not out seeking other people, but you are suffocating me, Alex! Everything I do you want part of it. You're over possessive, jealous and narrow-minded.' Clare looked at Alex. He sat there silently. She waited for an explosion. Instead, he looked her straight in the eye.

'I never guessed you felt like this. I'm sorry. I thought we were happy. I will try to lighten up. It's just that I want to protect you. If you want me to go away, I will. You only have to say.' The sadness in his voice made Clare feel such a heel that she embraced him and let him hold her tightly. Inside a part of her was groaning, nothing's changed.

CLARE
1993

Clare stared at the brown envelope before she tore it open. The postmark was local but she couldn't think of anywhere she owed money. A single type-written sheet fell out, it said;

'I'm still here, waiting.'

Clare read it again and again, with a coldness growing up from her toes throughout her body paralysing every muscle. 'Alex' she called. 'Alex, Alex.' Each time her voice grew shriller and shriller. He came tearing down the stairs and took the letter from her.

'The bastard. I thought I'd sorted him out,' said Alex angrily.

'Alex are you sure you hit the right man?'

He turned to look at her, a disbelieving look on his face. 'Who else could it be?'

'Well, I told you some of the things he said which I didn't understand, about having him back, claiming him back, squaring the balance.' The words were seared into Clare's mind. 'But there is one person who would have a reason to seek revenge on me, even though it doesn't make much more sense of what he said. It's Phil, the man I lived with in London. I did some stupid things when I left, ruined his LPs, chucked away his expensive aftershaves, pocketed the rent money, it was all very satisfying at the time, but in the cold light of day, gives him every reason to want to get his own back. Alex, we've got to go to the police!'

'And how am I going to look when you tell them I punched Duncan? If you're right and it was Phil, I might be had up for assault,' said Alex in a horrified voice.

'I thought you had silenced him with threatening to tell about the drugs.'

'So you're definite it wasn't Duncan?'

'I just feel in my bones it wasn't.' Clare's mind was racing on.

'The mark on the envelope is local; he's in the area. It was only posted yesterday,' she shuddered. 'We've got to get to the root of this. Come with me now?' Clare pleaded. Alex shrugged his submission. Chilled to the bone, Clare found her keys and with Alex's arm protectively around her they walked out to Aggie.

'I'll drive,' Alex stated. 'You look too shaken. Have you got the letter?'

Clare was grateful for his calm strength. The Police Station in the village was no more than a house with an office tacked on. The Sergeant was the archetypal policeman, round and red-cheeked, but his manner was direct and precise.

'These are very serious allegations you're making. You'd better come through and we'll get it all in writing,' was his reply to their story. He led them through to a bare office. Clare gave him a description of her attack and was surprised at the details he expected; such as time, were the doors shut and so on. At the end came the inevitable so why didn't you come to us before? So she had to tell the modified version of Alex's meeting with Duncan.

'You took a big risk, taking matters into your own hands. This Mr Harrison could press charges. You realise I'll have to speak to him to corroborate all this? Now Sir, give me your version of events.' Once again he put a thorough explanation on paper.

'Now you say you feel you were mistaken about Mr Harrison.' He raised an eyebrow at Alex and Clare worried for him. 'So who do you think it might have been?'

'It's possibly an ex-boyfriend of mine, from London. Apart from that, I've absolutely no idea. It's all scared me silly.' Clare to her utter chagrin, burst into tears. Alex moved closer.

'Give him the letter,' he ordered. P.C. Smith read it, checked the envelope, scrutinising closely the postmark and writing. 'It's been done on an older sort of typewriter and that's very easy to prove once the machine is found.'

Clare suddenly had the feeling that deep down P.C. Smith was enjoying himself. It must make a change from scrumping and pub fights.

'He could be in the area, although the postmark is Chard Minster and posted in any of the nearby villages. Now, just think again is there anyone else likely. Really search. What about where you work?'

'I clean in various houses, it's all couples and families.'

'What about Chris?' Clare was horrified at Alex's idea.

'He's alright. He bears no grudge, he's a good employer!'

'There's no knowing what's going on in people's minds.'

Clare remembered the enshrined room. 'Well, I still can't see any reason for it,' she conceded.

'Give me the addresses of these two men, and we'll make some enquiries. There's, of course, no reason why a married man shouldn't do things like this. We'll do it methodically. It's a shame you didn't see him, it would make things a good deal simpler,' he understated.

'By the way Sir - can you vouch where you were during the attack?'

Alex went as white as a sheet. 'Driving home. I walked in on Clare about ten minutes afterwards.'

'Thank you. Now, my dear. if anything happens, just reach for the phone, and we'll be out. If things escalate, you may need protection.'

Clare was now terrified and walked out with Alex's hand in such a tight grip that she saw her fingerprints on his hand when she released it.

'Alex, I'm scared to go out of the house - how can I even go to work when he may be lurking around the corner. What's he going to do next?'

'The police are seeing into it, they've got all the addresses. PC Smith will be on the phone now to the Met. They'll go round, and if he's not there, it'll confirm it must be him. They've got a description and will pick him up in no time. He no doubt thinks you're too scared to go to the police.'

Clare let herself be re-assured by Alex's words. She had no-one else to trust in; she had to throw all her confidence into his strength.

'I'll take you to work and collect you, then I'll be around to keep an eye on things.'

For the first time, Clare was re-assured by his protectiveness.

'Won't that muck you about, we work such different hours. We could have done with Sylvie right now.'

'She'll be back in a couple of days, we can manage until then.'

Clare turned Flossie in the direction of the Croft's house, and they drove along in silence; both deep in their own thoughts. Ivy

Cottage, was at the foot of a steep hill. Clare cruised down and indicated right to pull into the drive. The road was clear; she changed down into second with the usual crunch and braked. Flossie rolled on up the drive, oblivious to everything Clare was doing. Sheila's new Peugeot was parked at the end of the drive, the slight slope kept Flossie's momentum steady. Clare didn't know what to do, all she saw was the red car approaching, and she was totally unable to do anything about it. Clare froze.

'Took that a bit fast, playing at racing?' said Alex cheerfully, then he saw Clare's leg, mechanically treading the brake pedal. With lightning reflexes, Alex jammed on the handbrake and jammed Flossie into reverse. A series of leaping coughs stopped Flossie inches from the Peugeot's bumper. Clare was still treading the pedal, a blank expression on her face.

'Clare, are you alright?' Alex pulled Clare to him, her face was a sickly green.

'I'm going to be sick,' she stated, and was, all over Alex's lap.

'Oh Clare,' Alex took her in his arms and held her, ignoring his damp lap. 'Try not to think of anything for the moment, just get inside. 'He reached over and tooted the horn. Sheila came out, and Alex pushed Clare's door.

'We've just had the brakes fail, can you get Clare indoors and give her a hot drink or something?'

Sheila took Clare's arm and led her indoors. Alex shifted out of the cab and wiped himself down on some rough grass, then he lay down and wriggled beneath Aggie. As he'd expected, the brake pipe was hanging loose. Looking at the broken ends in the dim light, Alex wished he had a torch. He could just see the break which was uneven and corroded, it didn't look cut, obviously, it had been going that way for a long time. Had it snapped of its own accord or had it been helped? Alex struggled out and went indoors.

Clare was sitting in an armchair, a blanket around her shoulders, sipping something steaming from a cup. The events of the past few minutes were replaying over and over again in her mind. She didn't understand what had happened.

'I'm sorry Alex - your trousers...'

'No matter. I've had a look. The brake pipe was broken.'

Clare looked fearfully up at him, the question unformed on her lips but understood.

'Through old age, it was bent and corroded. It was just an unlucky accident,' Alex said with grim vehemence.

Clare slumped back into the chair. 'Thank heavens for that,' and she sipped again at her drink.

Sheila came in with a cup for Alex. 'She doesn't look in any fit state for work. Shall I run her home?' she asked anxiously.

'No. I don't think she'd better be on her own. She had some rather bad news this morning and this trouble hasn't helped. Could she stay here until I get some more brake pipe, fix it then take her home myself?'

They looked at Clare who in the space of a few moments had dozed off, her cup tilting crazily on her lap.

'Perhaps that's the best thing. You'd better have some of Mick's old trousers. You're about the same size, then you must tell just what is going on.'

Alex had to tell Sheila the whole story, then when he'd finished,

'It sounds fantastic. If there's anything we can do to help, perhaps put her up here while the police sort things out. Surely this man won't know she's here?'

'No. She'll be safest where I can keep my eye on her,' stated Alex adamantly. 'I wouldn't want to put your family at any sort of risk. This thing with the brakes, I'm sure is pure coincidence.'

'You must tell the police.'

'Yes, yes' said Alex almost impatiently. 'I'll get off to the garage now.'

Alex left Clare still sleeping and set off on the long walk. It took until early evening to fix the pipe, then they drove slowly up the drive, Sheila and Mick watched them from the front door.

The morning found Clare in a better frame of mind. Alex had given her a hot whiskey toddy, and she'd slept the night through. It was such a beautiful day that Clare couldn't help taking on board Alex's optimism. Even so, the shrilling of the phone made her jump. She hesitated before answering, convincing herself it would be good news. It was PC Smith.

'Just a call to check that things are alright and to bring you some good news. I've interviewed all the people you mentioned locally and they all have stories that check out. Even Mr Harrison had a cast-iron alibi. He wasn't too happy about Mr Jordan's actions, but he doesn't want to press charges, he wants the whole incident forgotten. The best news is that the CID has just informed me that the MET has tracked down your Phil. They've got him giving a statement at the moment, and they sound fairly hopeful it is him. Apparently, he was extremely rude and abusive about you. I'll let you know as soon as there are any developments.'

'Oh thank-you, that's wonderful.' Clare rang off and rushed to tell Alex. A great weight had lifted from her, the relief was overwhelming. Things had been solved so easily.

'Matters back to normal?' demanded Clare, wanting it so as quickly as possible.

'Only if you feel fit.'

'Oh, I'm fine now it's all sorted,' she said airily. 'I'll be off to Chris' in about 10 minutes.'

'Don't tell him too much. We can't be a hundred percent sure yet. I really would rather you stayed at home.'

'Come off it. PC Smith said it was as good as sorted.' Clare felt her old irritation rising. 'I've only to do a couple of hours, then he's away for the next fortnight.' Clare buried her worries with her usual dexterity and waved goodbye to Alex, who was hovering at the door, still looking anxious. Clare sang along to the radio as she drove down the leafy lanes. There was a hint of early Summer, so keen were the trees to burst into leaf, and Summer always made her feel good. Newly fixed Aggie stopped at her every demand and Clare made several extra ones to test her. Chris was waiting by the gate.

'I've had the Police around here, just what's going on?'

'I was attacked in the kitchen the other day,' replied Clare bluntly

'I didn't see who it was. I received a hate letter yesterday, but the Police have sorted it all out, it seems it is someone who I knew in London.' Clare peered up at him, trying to see how angry he was.

'It might have helped if they'd explained, instead of this, and where were you on the night of the l6th Sonny stuff?''

Clare saw the glint of humour in his eyes and relaxed.

'Are you sure you're alright - have they caught this man?'

'They're confirming it later on today.'

Clare avoided the concern in his stare.

'The rally was brilliant. If I can afford the modifications, I might enter Aggie in one of the easier ones before she bursts the last tyre!'

'You really made an impression on Bill. You're the first woman not to scream and run away after the death dive slope.'

Clare felt herself blushing. 'I think I'll need bigger biceps too, to manage the steering.'

'You could always put power steering in! Heavens, I must go. I'm off to the Doctor's. Can you hang out the washing, then tackle pressing my suits? I won't be long. Are you sure you're alright?'

'Yes, yes,' Clare tried not to be impatient.

Chris turned to go and half raised his hand to pat her shoulder, but he stopped, smiled instead and went to the garage. Clare felt strangely intimate as she hung his clothes on the line. They carried the essence of a person as they swung gaily in animated confusion. Life was good again in this sun-filled garden.

Chris drove back up the short drive then blasted the air horns he'd just fitted for a joke. He was itching to try them out on the cattle who always roamed the lanes. He was surprised when Clare didn't come out to see, perhaps even these weren't audible in the house. Chris went in search of her. The house was empty, so he returned to the garden. At first, he thought she'd left a heap of clothes lying on the ground, but then he saw the smears of red. Clare lay in a crumpled heap, her head lying in slowly seeping blood, which came from a wound Chris couldn't see. One arm lay crumpled back beneath her body, she appeared to not be breathing.

'Oh no, not Clare. Oh God, why here? Not again, it's more than I can take!' He leant over and, at last, saw her shallow breathing. Chris dithered, not knowing quite what to do. He knew not to move her so, in the end, he belted into the house to snatch a quilt. Clare lay as she was, no change. At last Chris came to his senses and ran back into the house to dial 999, cursing himself for his stupidity. He returned to sit by Clare, silently holding a pad of lint to her head to stop the flow of blood. He watched her every breath, tears trickling silently down his face. Chris prayed. He prayed to a God who was always turned to in dire straights, but was forgotten in happy times in the desperate hope that He would hear and not be churlish after being ignored for so long. Chris memorised Clare's face. It was totally unlike Pam's but had that same repose, that same peaceful unawareness. Did he deserve it to happen again? What had he done wrong he demanded of the empty blue sky? His train of thought was halted by the arrival of PC Smith. He stooped down, and like Chris reverentially touched her face to feel the pulse.

'Now Sir,' he said in police talk. 'What exactly happened here?'

'I don't know. I left at about 9.30, went to Dr Wisemans then returned straight here. Clare had arrived just as I was leaving. I asked her to hang the washing then do the ironing. I found her here like this. I haven't moved her, just put the blanket around.'

'And how long ago did you return?'

'I don't know.' Chris wiped his face in embarrassment. 'Enough time to walk around the house, find her, fetch a blanket, ring you and the ambulance, - you'll have the time of that won't you?'

The sound of a vehicle coming down the lane alerted them to the arrival of the ambulance. Two men rushed in with a stretcher and examined Clare. Professionally they bound her head, put in a drip, then moved her onto the stretcher. They carried her away to the ambulance taking with them brief details of what had happened. Chris went to follow but found an arm stopping him.

'Let them do their stuff, she's in the best hands. I'll make you a nice cup of tea.'

Chris allowed himself to be led into the house. He was sitting at the kitchen table with his mug of tea, trying to make small talk with PC Smith, when the plainclothes men arrived. They proceeded to go through all the events over and over again until Chris' head began to ring.

'Good grief!' he exploded. 'Can't you leave me alone. I've done nothing. You should be out searching for this maniac, not hounding me!' They eased up the questioning, until a uniformed policeman came in, carrying something wrapped up in a plastic bag. The men poured over it, deliberately excluding Chris. Finally, they turned to him.

'Excuse me Sir - have you ever seen this before?'

Chris looked then sank back onto his chair in disbelief.

'Yes, I have. It's part of an exhaust pipe I took off my Land Rover a couple of weeks ago.' It was covered with blood. Chris wanted to die.

'Well Sir, we're checking up on your story. This was found in a bush near the field gate. From the way it was thrown, you may have actually disturbed the attacker before he could finish the job. For the moment this will be all.'

'Can I go to the Hospital now?'
PC Smith then butted in.

'Sir, you do realise this is Clare Brown, who came and made the complaint yesterday?' The two men exchanged annoyed looks.

'No, we weren't in yesterday, we were in Court. Are you a close friend of Miss Brown?'

'No, she is my girl Friday. She started here just before Christmas.'

'I think perhaps we need to continue this down the Station.' Chris was escorted to the car, behind him he caught snippets of PC Smith telling the men about the previous day's events. There seemed to be a swarm of policemen searching, probing their way around the garden and garage. He'd seen enough television to know they were looking for clues. He was glad the neighbours were away on holiday; he didn't want to be at the centre of a peep show for the children. Chris felt the dead certainty that they thought he had done it. Just as they were about to pull away he was asked if he minded them searching the house. Chris had nothing to hide so agreed. The sight of the station then being led down endless corridors all made Chris feel a deep sense of unreality. He had barely sat down when they demanded his clothes for forensic examination. As he stripped, Chris saw the blood on his hands and felt condemned, When he returned to the room, a grey-haired man was waiting for him, briefcase in hand.

'Arthur Peters. Duty Solicitor. I understand you requested my presence.'
Help at last. With relief, Chris sat back down again. They were allowed a few minutes of privacy.

'You don't think it makes me look guilty asking for you when I'm just 'helping with enquiries?' asked Chris.

Mr Peters hastily assured him it was all quite usual. Chris gave him the whole story.

'They're only doing what they must do because logically you are the nearest suspect. Now I'll advise you when to speak and we'll have you out of here in no time.'

'Is there any news of Clare?'

'Not as far as I know.'

'Shouldn't they be seeing that boyfriend of hers? He always seems on the moody side.'

'We'll bring it to their attention.'
The Policemen returned carrying an old typewriter.

'Is this your property Sir?'
Chris looked.

'Yes, of course.'

'Then can you explain this?'

They showed him the type-written note Clare had received, and one recently written on his machine. They were identical. Chris was cautioned, then charged, and led away to a cell, with the threat hanging over him that if Clare's condition deteriorated, there would be new charges.

Clare inhabited a strange world of grotesque nightmares where familiar faces contorted and mad statements made sense. She was carried away on a stream of mad adventures where the obscene was normal. Clare began to tire of these images. She knew this world wasn't real, was this sleep never going to end? Her will rose up inside, she had to wake up, pull free. She didn't want to stay trapped here forever. Open her eyes, she must open her eyes. Trying brought a new pain, a splitting in her head, a tightness of breath and an iron clamp on her arm. Was it worth it? The other world beckoned her back. No, she didn't want to return there. At last, Clare wrenched her eyes open. All she saw was a strip of fluorescent light and a white wall. She could hardly move for the pain in her head.

'Hello love, how do you feel?' asked a strange voice. Clare twisted her eyes, she just made out the edges of a nurses uniform. The nurse stood up and leant over.

'Is that better?'
Clare saw she was young and pretty.

'Can you give me something for my headache and a drink?' Clare asked with a dry mouth. She was given a cup with a straw and drank gratefully. Her senses were returning, but her priority was this pain in her body. Why was it hurting so? Again she tried to move her head.

'You're hurt there love, don't try to move if it makes the pain worse. You've got a fractured skull. Now you're awake, I'll bleep the Doctor.' Clare felt reassured. The Doctor would take the pain away. When he arrived he was short, bald and bespectacled.

'You gave us a fright!' he said with mechanical jocularity. 'Apart from your skull, a couple of broken ribs, and a broken arm, there's not a lot wrong with you!' He produced a syringe full of painkiller. Clare accepted the scratch with willingness. The problem was, it brought with it a drowsiness. Clare fought it for a while, she didn't want to go back.

'How long have I been here?'

'Since yesterday morning.'

That seemed in order. Clare succumbed but this time the sleep was deep, empty and easy to swan out of. Someone was holding her hand. Clare opened her eyes, just a little in case the pain came back. It seemed Alex was sobbing at her bedside. Why should he do that? She must be dreaming because looked up and started to smile as he wiped his eyes. He then began to snort and chuckle. He looked strange, so maybe it wasn't Alex and this the drugs talking.

'They've got him, they've got him.' He now guffawed. 'They're going to lock him up. We've got someone else to take the blame, it's worked again!' He stopped laughing and looked seriously at her. 'It's a shame we didn't do a thorough job. But it'll do, it'll do.'

Clare wanted to run away but couldn't, so she shut her eyes and thankfully blacked out. She spent the next couple of days drowsing and drinking. Each time she opened her eyes, she peeped at first to see if Alex had returned but he had gone. Clare wasn't entirely sure if he had been a hallucination or real, so she was relieved at his absence. Eventually, she began to get control over the pain and found herself sitting up and taking note of the surrounding life. It wasn't until the policewoman entered the room that Clare ever wondered why she was in hospital. June, as the policewoman insisted on being called, led Clare gently down the tortuous paths of remembering, by going through all the events of the morning of the attack. She visualised taking the basket of washing to the line and saw it waving in the breeze. It all came back, the blow, the kicking, the final twisting throw to the ground, to the sound of air horns. The face of her attacker was bland, all she only remembered the strength and violence of his body.

June was interested in the sound of air horns, but wouldn't explain why. Clare was still following events through and came to the point where she'd found Alex sitting beside the bed. She had to recount exactly what he'd said twice before June seemed satisfied, and left. Clare was relieved the grilling was over, she knew the kindness was superficial. The woman was only doing her job. Even so, Clare couldn't make any sense of the events that had been revealed and dozed off. The door opened and Sylvie came bouncing in, with an armful of magazines and chocolates. Clare had a quick look and was relieved to see no Christian ones, the last thing she needed was a dose of religion. Strangely Sylvie didn't have a lot to say for herself except saying that the interview seemed to have gone well. An awkward silence fell on them, then Clare got the idea.

'Have they told you what not to say?' she demanded.

Sylvie looked bleakly at her then nodded.

'Good grief, if I can handle an interrogation from the fuzz I can handle the truth. Spill the beans,' said Clare with some of her former spark.

'Right. I got back from London to find the old Bill on the doorstep. They treated me like some sort of villain until I got through to them it was my house. Then I was interrogated by some Gestapo trainee. After that, they managed to let me know what was going on. You were beaten up at Chris' on Monday morning and they've charged Chris with it!'

'That's impossible, he was at the Doctors.'

'They charged him and held him until you came around enough to corroborate his story. Something about an air horn?'
Clare understood, a suspicion began to rise but Sylvie was going on.

'It seems a note you received was written on his typewriter.'
Clare laid back and closed her eyes to concentrate better.

'They went back to my place to find Alex. They found him gone, his room looked as though it had been ransacked while he packed in a hurry. On searching the room, they found another note hidden beneath his mattress. So Alex is either your assailant, or he's got someone helping him. He must have broken into Chris' house to use the typewriter although they didn't find his prints on it.'

'Or used my key,' said Clare bleakly.

'They released Chris immediately. Alex is now being searched for.'
Clare heaved a sob of relief for Chris, the injustice feeling worse than Alex actual deceit.

'We did this to Alex, Sylvie.'

'What!'

'If we'd left him alone, we would never have started all this. If we hadn't so blindly dismissed all his past as irrelevant, we would never have caused all these things to happen. If I hadn't fallen into this relationship…'

'Come on, he's a grown man,' replied Sylvie indignantly.'We can't take responsibility for this. You might just as well say I hit myself.

We're not responsible.' Yet Sylvie's face was pale.

'Do the Police know about his amnesia?'

'Yes, it's all true, but they've got nothing on him. They're as puzzled as we are.'

'Sylvie he came here! I told the police. I'm sure I didn't dream it. One minute he was crying, the next gloating. It was horrible.' Clare tried to blot out the memory and felt exhausted.

'I'm sorry Sylvie, I'm worn outcome again tomorrow?' Clare was already asleep when Sylvie closed the door.

Clare's recovery was slow but consistent. Within a couple of weeks, she found herself on a busy women's ward and enjoying the bustle of hospital life. Her arm healed well, and she now breathed without pain. Despite the constant chatter, Clare found time to reflect and try to sort herself out. Her conclusions about her life and its direction had been blown apart, and she had to try to reorganise them. She began by reflecting about her freedom because that at least was positive. The Agency could be started as soon as she was fit. Clare filled several sheets of paper with ideas to be worked on. Costings, visiting the Bank, viewing properties, even the challenge of finding her team, although daunting, were all things to be looked forward to on her release.

Everything else was negative. Sometimes she would see someone of Alex's stature in the distance and would shrink back onto the bed. Clare was scared of him and fully admitted it to herself. All the darkness she'd denied was in him was truly there. Something had triggered its release. Perhaps his memory had come back. To think that it was Alex who'd mugged her in the kitchen, then walked in as bold as brass, and even hit Duncan for it, just didn't make sense. Why did he hate her so, what had she done to deserve this? Was it her fault for stringing him along when she'd known deep down the relationship was doomed? Why did he hate Chris so much that he wanted him imprisoned? What did he mean by it not being a thorough job - that he'd wanted to kill her? Get someone else to take the blame for what? She wanted to know why. The whole situation was so unreal, was Alex mad? It was the only thing that even began to answer her questions. To think she'd spent all those months going out with him and at any time he could have turned on her made her blood run cold.

     Clare realised she shouldn't have let him in when she was so vulnerable. Instead, she should have pulled herself together, rather than fall into another man's arms. Clare tried not to let her regrets engulf her but it wasn't easy. The police were searching for him, but there'd been no sightings since he'd left. The truck had been abandoned at Sylvie's cottage, and, as Clare knew only too well, it was so easy to change your appearance by simply dying your hair. The staff on the ward were on alert for him, so Clare felt a small sense of security.

     The generosity of the people she worked for was overwhelming. Her bed was surrounded by cards and flowers. The largest bouquet was from the Harrisons. All said her jobs were waiting for her return, so Clare knew she had plenty to look forward too. Chris had sent a small posy but no more, and that saddened Clare. He must be justifiably very cross with her. Clare's return to health and her eagerness to leave the hospital proved a problem. The police didn't think it at all safe to return to the cottage, especially as Sylvie was still commuting to London a lot. It would be several weeks before she could return to work, let alone drive.

The Crofts came to Clare's rescue, offering to take her in. One extra was easily absorbed into their family. The doctors were dubious, not sure whether she was ready yet to take the noise and sheer energy of the children. Clare was insistent. The thought of being amongst a normal family was so inviting, she wanted a small share of all she'd missed in her childhood. She pointed out that if it all got too much, she could shut and lock her bedroom door.

Clare found herself being escorted from the ward on one hot May morning. She was surprised at the wrench it was. The nurses and patients felt like a family now, but she knew as soon as she was gone, her bed would be stripped and a newcomer absorbed into the community. To be out in the sunlight sent Clare's senses reeling. She'd forgotten the smell of grass, roses and cars, so immersed had her nose become to antiseptic and medicine. She wanted to skip and whirl but strangely her knees were weak. By the time they reached Ivy Cottage, Clare knew that however well you may feel in hospital, it was not the stamina for facing the world. The children had been warned to keep quiet and away from Clare, but that was impossible. They peeped round the door until Clare ushered them in, fingers to her mouth, joining them in a conspiracy. Sheila looked in the sitting room and was at first horrified to see Clare sat on the settee, the television blaring and all the children sat around her. Then she saw Clare was soundly asleep while Daniel, with his best felt tips, was gently a moustache on her face.

CLARE
1993

Clare was swiftly absorbed into the Croft's routine. The day began early with raucous shrieks from the children followed by groans from Sheila and Mick. It never failed to amaze Clare at the way Sheila could get four children, dressed, washed, fed and into their respective schools and playschools on time. At first, Clare was an amused spectator, but was gradually drawn into helping. The sudden peace which descended as the last child left the car was almost a sadness; she felt bereft of their energy and joy. When Sheila was baking, Clare would sit and chat with her. Clare knew she was casting Sheila in a mother substitute role, and she was just a bit too old for that, but she found it healed some of the damage done in her childhood.

It came as a revelation to find that it was quite acceptable to be scared of the dark and to need a light left on all night. Clare remembered only too well her own night terrors. She found the food she'd hated as a child was universally loathed by children; she hadn't been strange not to love liver. To fight and answer back to a parent wasn't being an agent of Satan, but part of learning about discipline and responsibility for your own actions. Clare wished she could hate her parents for these further faults but somehow, she was simply sorry that they had deprived themselves of all this abundant love.

In return, Clare told Sheila her own life story, which was listened to with sympathetic clucks and no condemnation. From there they moved on to many subjects. Sheila would always give her own well-considered opinion; whether Clare liked it or not. Clare had never talked to another woman like this before and she revelled in it. Sheila insisted that Clare took plenty of rest. At first, she spent most of the time sleeping, then as her energy returned she read and planned.

The Agency only proceeded forward on paper. Clare couldn't drive and wasn't allowed anywhere on her own; the Police had advised it for her own safety. There was no news from the search for Alex. Sheila didn't have the time to accompany Clare on all the necessary interviews and visits, so Clare had to wait.

One thing she had to acknowledge to Alex was thankfulness for pointing her to a whole new realm of books. Clare now eagerly dipped into the Classics and Science Fiction. All her other feelings towards Alex were carefully bottled until he was found, because it made her head swim when she let all the guilt and anger she felt engulf her. Even so, sometimes Clare found herself staring into space and wandering. It was during these times that she began to recognise a loneliness in herself. Although she had the friendship of Sylvie and Sheila, there was still something empty inside her. An understanding began that she had been trying to fill this emptiness with all the men she'd been out with. From her arrival in the city, she'd filled her life with people, places and work. She saw now that these hadn't satisfied either. Was it so wrong to seek that boon companion, to fill this loneliness? Had her search been apparent to all these men, so they'd seen and used her weakness? Perhaps now she had acknowledged this need, it was time to fill this gap herself, with being busy, doing things, being strong. Then if she did ever have another relationship, she would be looked on as a whole person, not a weakling to be used. This self-knowledge would arm her fully before she went chasing after the next man who crossed her path.

Clare became so absorbed into the Croft's life that it came as a surprise to have the plaster cast removed and be cleared for a little light work. Her arm felt strong but didn't have any stamina. Clare spent several days flexing it to renew the muscle tone. Sheila realised Clare's new restlessness and set her to do small tasks. Their completion helped to begin to renew Clare's self-esteem.

Aggie was still parked at Chris's. Several times Clare had gone to ring him and apologise for all he'd been put through, but her contrary spirit nagged her. Don't go running after another man. He's got enough women already, and probably won't even want to re-employ you. He's no doubt got someone else there right now. Get someone else to collect Aggie, let him ring you up and do the sacking. Clare let the days drift by and did nothing.

The convalescence came to an end at last. The Doctor told her to let everyone know she could return to work on the following Monday. Friday found Clare busily weeding Sheila's front garden. From up the hill came a familiar noise, for a moment Clare was unable to pinpoint it, then jumped up in excitement. She ran to the gate and was surprised at her disappointment when she saw it was Sylvie guiding Aggie up the drive.

'Surprise, surprise! I kidnapped her for you. I knew you'd be fretting at the bit, and I found your spare key in the kitchen. Isn't she a swine to drive!'

'Did you see Chris?' asked Clare, finding it difficult to say his name out loud.

'No, when I went around yesterday, there was no one in, so I slipped a note through the door. I'm afraid I had an ulterior motive. I need to get the Intercity from Chardminster this morning, and I'm too skint for a taxi - any chance of a lift?'

Clare was itching to get behind the wheel. Sheila came out to join them.

'Am I allowed to make a return journey on my own?' Clare demanded.

'You're still not supposed to be on your own.' Sheila saw the expression on Clare's face.

'Well, I suppose if you come straight back and you lock all the doors.'

She was already climbing into the cab.

'Ring me from the station,' Sheila yelled over the engine.

Clare found the steering heavy on her weak arm, but she wasn't going to admit it, she was having too much fun. Sylvie was dropped at the station in plenty of time. Clare added ten minutes on her return time when she rang Sheila, then she hit the open road with a chuckle of glee. The scenic route she had chosen passed the turning into Marsh Lane. Impulsively, Clare turned down and pulled up outside Chris's house. Memories of her last visit flooded her, and she looked uneasily about as she walked up the path.

Clare tried to explain to herself why she was here. What on earth was she going to say? Apologise, hand in her notice and go? It was too late to back away, if he was in he'd have seen her. Clare hoped Sylvie was right, and he was abroad. In spite of the brisk morning sunlight, Clare saw every light in the house was on. The effects of an all-night party, or Alex? Clare nearly turned heel and ran away. She heard a radio blaring in the house next door and that helped put things in perspective. The front door was ajar.

'Chris?' called Clare, quietly at first then more loudly. 'Chris are you there?' The door moved open to her tentative touch, so Clare walked in, the scar on her head throbbing as if in a warning. The kitchen was deserted, so she made her way to the front room, still calling. Chris was sat on the settee, staring into thin air, a smashed photograph lying on the table in front of him. He didn't seem to notice Clare enter. She saw the dark shadows beneath his eyes, and the stubble on his face, which seemed leaner and paler than ever.

'Chris,' she said again and at last, he heard. He looked up. Clare felt he didn't recognise her.

'She didn't come last night, I've been on my own all night. I didn't think I could do it.'

'Do what?' Clare sat on the floor to be on a level with him.

'Jane didn't come.'

'I'm sure she will, did she ring?'

'Oh, she rang. Bill's wrenched his arm, and she had to stay and look after the kids. Monica was out too, it wasn't her turn.'

'Her turn for what?'

'To stay with me.'

Clare was unable to grasp the sense of what he was saying. 'But shouldn't these women be with their husbands?' It was out before she could help it. He looked at her again, and at last, realised who it was.

'Clare,' When he said her name, it was like a caress. 'Are you alright now?'

She had a feeling he was going to ask her to stay too. She had to get to the bottom of this.

'I'm fine. Chris just what's going on here? I know I've no right to ask, but you seem in such a state'

Chris took a deep breath.

'Nearly a year ago my wife, Pam, died. In that room upstairs. We knew she hadn't long, we were waiting for a place in the Hospice. In the middle of the night, she left while I snored on. She was alone at the end, and I failed her.'

Clare's heart went out to him and all his pain.

'But you can't blame yourself for that. She could have woken you.'

'People keep on telling me that, but I just can't forgive myself.'

'So you try to ease your grief with other men's wives?'

Chris looked at her, a horrified expression. 'Oh no, that's not what you think is it?'

Clare was unable to answer.

'Jane and Monica are nurses. I pay them to sleep over here so I'm not alone. Bill and Jeff do it occasionally, too, but you must have missed them.'

'Then why don't you leave here? how do you manage in the States?'

'It's not so bad there, in the anonymity of a hotel, it's easy to forget. I can't leave here yet; not until I can get shot of her ghost.'

'You sound as if you don't want to.'

He looked at her again. 'To a certain extent, you're right. I got angry last night. Angry with her for the first time. I actually got fed up.'

Clare was overwhelmed with relief that nothing had been as she'd expected. The clock struck ten, and she yelped.

'I must ring Sheila and tell her where I am. May I use your phone?' He nodded.
Sheila was surprised and a bit cross at Clare's call and made her promise to ring before she left. Chris hadn't moved.

'Why do you need to tell her that?' he asked dully.

'If I'm late, they'll send a search party. I'm not allowed to be on my own in case Alex turns up.'

Chris began to emerge from his trance and rubbed his stubble.

'I came to apologise for all I've put you through. I understand that it wasn't until I came around that they released you.' Clare kept her voice neutral.

'I can't say I want to repeat the experience,' said Chris wryly.'They did apologise profusely, it was all understandable in the circumstances. You certainly are not the one to apologise.'

'And, well, I must hand in my notice. Obviously, you don't want any more trouble.' Clare got it out in a rush. To her surprise, Chris took her hand.

'There's no need. Your coming here has been the best thing that's happened to me since Pam died.'
Clare let him hold her hand for a while then gently moved away.

'Is there anything I can do for you? Tea or something?'

'I could murder a tea!' Chris rose with great stiffness and Clare wondered just how long he'd been sat there.

'My legs are dead,' he moaned and tottered towards the kitchen, Clare hovered anxiously behind him. Chris wouldn't let Clare do anything and gestured her to sit. It was only when he dropped the mug, sending pieces of china cascading over the floor that Clare leapt up and threw her arms around him. Clare had never heard a man cry before and didn't know what to do or say. She stood firm and let him get on with it. Slowly, he stopped. Chris stood a good foot taller than Clare, so the first thing he saw on lifting his head, was the livid scar and bare patch on Clare's head.

'He did that to you!' he exclaimed, now angry. 'I would kill him if that didn't put me on his level.

'The day I found you will be etched forever in my mind. You lay there, just like Pam; the same look on your sleeping face. You have such a joy, an eagerness to try things. I hated to see that blotted out. I prayed that you'd live and be whole again. If you did, I vowed to protect you from any more such harm until my dying day.'

Clare tried to take a step back, but he held on to her. She'd had enough of people trying to protect her.

'That's a bit heavy,' said Clare lightly. 'Chris don't ask anything of me at the moment. I've been burnt in every relationship I've had so far. I think I'm learning a lesson. Thank you, it's lovely to think you do care.'

Chris kissed her. For the first time in her life, Clare felt a kiss that was right. A rightness that went completely through, touched the parts of her that hurt and healed them. When he released her, it was all she could do not to search him blindly out again. Had he seen? Tactfully, Chris turned and plugged the kettle on again. Clare saw his hands were still shaking.

'Let me do it,' she stated. They sat facing each other across the table. Clare avoided his eyes, she was in such a muddle inside. Had she been half aware of his feelings? She wasn't sure and knew it was not the time to rush into another relationship. It was too soon. She needed time to breathe, straighten out what was left of herself.

'Chris, you're going to have to wait.'

'I know. I've all the time in the world.'

Now she met his eyes and was drawn in by the wonder that here was something she hadn't sought; in her shocked state hadn't wanted and was being given when she least deserved it. An awkward silence descended and Clare's head began to throb, the first headache since she'd come out of hospital.

'Chris, I've got to go. I need some painkillers before this gets too bad.' She rubbed her eyes. Chris looked at her in consternation.

'Would I have anything in the cupboard?'

'No, these are on prescription.'

They rose.

'Are you alright now?' Clare asked.

'I'm fine. I've got some hope now.'

Clare wasn't sure if he meant getting through the night or her.

'Will you still come and clean?' His soft Scots accent made the question sound like a plea from the heart.

'I don't know. Can I ring you in the morning?' asked Clare in confusion. Chris looked a little sad but nodded his acquiescence. Clare wanted to leap back into his arms, so she took a fierce hold on herself and got into the cab.

'Lock your doors now,' Chris ordered. 'I'll ring Sheila for you.'

It was only as Clare saw his figure receding in the mirror, that she realised he hadn't cracked a single joke. The headache proved a blinder and Clare was glad to be able to fall into bed for the rest of the day. Sheila clucked around, drawing curtains, putting a flannel on Clare's head, threatening to call the Doctor. Clare insisted all she needed was decent sleep. In fact, she wanted to think about Chris, but when Sheila left her, the drugs took hold and she fell into a deep sleep, which felt as muddled as when she was awake. She drifted in and out of consciousness into the darkness of early evening. At last the headache was beaten and Clare felt saturated with sleep. Sheila poked her head around the door.

'How are you feeling?'

'Better.'

'Are you able to get out of bed?' Clare tried to lift herself up, the pounding returned.

'No.' she stated and sank back down.

'Oh crumbs. Mick's just rung. His car's packed up at the station. It's pouring with rain. Do you think I can risk leaving you for ten minutes while I fetch him? All the children are asleep too.'

'Ten minutes won't matter,' said Clare impatiently. She was fed up with the restrictions. Sheila hovered a while longer.

'Right, well, I'll secure everything, then I'll rush there and back.' She was gone. Clare heard the car revving up the hill and it seemed only a matter of moments before it returned in an equal rush. The house had been silent in the meantime, the only noise had been a door slamming shut. Clare listened to the sounds of their arrival, the meal, television and bed, then she dozed off again.

'Clare, Clare, Clare.' The voice was insistent, not part of her dreams. Clare opened her eyes but still wasn't sure if she was dreaming. The voice kept on, so she turned over to look. Shocked, Clare sat up, there was someone standing at the foot of her bed. Clare pulled the sheets up to protect herself.

'Clare, don't be scared. I'm not the one who's done this to you.'

It was Alex. The light switched on, and Clare blinked in the light. He was dishevelled, sporting a new growth of beard, but the expression in his eyes told her this was her Alex, not the half-crazed maniac who'd visited her in hospital. Somehow, she didn't feel scared.

'How did you get in?'

'That's not a problem. I haven't damaged anything. Clare, I've come to warn you and to ask you to come to a safe place where he won't find us.'

'Who Alex?'

'My past has finally caught up. Clare, I know who I am, and all that's happened. You're in great danger because of me, and I want to help you get away.'

'Alex, you're not making sense.' Clare's head was still fuddled with sleep.

'There's a man, who was a friend in my childhood, but for some reason; I suppose because he's mad, he keeps on catching up on me and spoiling things. He's done it once before, but the girl only got scared, and she escaped but this time I know he's out for blood. Now Chris has been released and they're searching for me again, he's really angry.'
Clare began to shiver.

'He's not far away, we've got to run!'

'I'm not going to come with you Alex. It's not that I don't trust you, but I'm not going out into the middle of a stormy night with you and a nutter on our trail. Why don't we call the police and get them to pick him up?'

'No, there's no time for that now, we must go now!' Alex urged. He came closer and sat on the bed beside her. Clare felt hollow inside when she looked at him and shrank away.

'I'm not coming,' she repeated. 'Alex, whatever we had in the past few months is over, you must understand that. It was wrong, I should have left you alone in that cabin, in a way I led you on. I took you on the rebound and we got in a rut. I don't care what your friend did. Why don't you just find him, tell him it's all over between us, then go somewhere far away? Then we can both begin our lives again.'

'But you're not safe. He will find you!'

'Alex, I'm safe here. There are people all around and the police at the end of the telephone. Let me call them now, and they can catch him.' Clare tried to edge out of the bed.

'No, they won't be able to.'

'Are you scared of him too?'

'Of course, I am. That's why I need you. Together we can get far away. I've even got money for plane tickets, he'll never find us abroad.'

'Alex, if he can find you when you've already changed your identity, he'll find you again. I'm not coming. If I loved you, maybe I would, but I don't. There's someone else.' Clare hated herself for the cruelty and the bleak look that arrived in his eyes.

'I suppose I knew that already. It's Chris isn't it?'

'How did you know!' Had he seen her today?

'The day you leapt out of his Land Rover, when you'd been searching for the bike, I saw something binding you together. It was stronger than anything I hoped to build between us.'

Clare was astonished. 'Then why did you bother with me, put me through all this if you knew it was hopeless?'

'False hope. And I wanted you so much,' Alex ran his hands through his hair, the familiar gesture shook Clare. 'He hadn't found me then, and now he won't believe anything I say.' Alex stood up and went to peer around the curtain into the black night.

'He's getting near. I can sense it.' Clare felt a shiver of fear run down her spine.

'If they had kept Chris in prison, he would have left you alone. Soon as he heard of Chris's release he was after your blood.' Alex stated again.

'Alex, this is just too crazy for words. I'm not running away with you,' said Clare in desperation. 'I'm going to call the police.'

Clare was surprised at the ease with which she was able to dart past Alex, out of the room and into the hall. She'd picked up the receiver before Alex reached her, but it was no good, the line was dead. Alex was beside her, his height and breadth threateningly close.

'I told you, he's not playing games,' he said in a hoarse whisper.

Clare had never felt total fear before and now discovered its paralysing strength.

'If you won't come with me, go to Chris, he'll protect you,' he appealed.

Clare was no longer thinking straight. She forgot the family sleeping unawares all around her. All she could latch on to was getting away from Alex and his friend. Chris seemed the only surety in this nightmare.

'Clare,' Alex was insistent. He caught her arm and dragged her back into the bedroom. 'You must go now. I'll go out, meet him and send him off in the wrong direction.' He kissed Clare on the forehead, in his old generous way and that convinced Clare more than anything that this was a real sane man; it really was his friend causing the problem. She sensed that he hadn't expected her to come. For a moment she hesitated.

'Goodbye Clare. Thank you for the time we had together. I hope for both of our sakes we don't meet again.' His tone was bleak and final then he was gone; noiselessly shutting the door behind him. Outside, the rain pounded on. Clare felt a sense of unreality; of dreaming as she dressed in warm clothes and dug out her wellies. Should she take a bag? No, Chris would be able to come back with her, and they'd collect her stuff. Carefully she crept through the lounge and picked up her keys from the table. She nearly dropped them so numb were her hands. It seemed like an eternity as she crossed the hall and slid back the bolts on the heavy oak door. She shut it, equally carefully, as the rain began to lash her back. It seemed a personal thing, as if it were trying to drive her back into the house. She groped her way blindly down the side of the parked cars and into the road outside. Aggie was parked in the lay-by opposite. Clare swung herself in and bolted the door behind her. She checked everything was shut tight from the inside and then tried the engine. She prayed it wouldn't be one of her arthritic days and refuse to start. The engine roared into grinding life at the second attempt. Clare rolled her way onto the road and into the night. No other cars passed her on the windswept, almost God-forsaken night. Aggie was buffeted and shaken, despite her heavy bulk. It was difficult to see any distance because the old wipers were barely man enough to push against the onslaught. Clare nearly missed several of her turnings, and on one, the end of Aggie flipped into a skid. Clare managed to right her and put her foot down on the gravel track. So close, so near, and she'd be safe. All she thought of was Chris and an end to this nightmare.

Clare pulled to a halt outside the villa; narrowly missing a car parked outside. She didn't recognise the green Fiat, perhaps Chris had given in and got a minder for the night. The lights were still on in the front room and surprisingly the curtains not drawn as a defence on the wicked night. The settee was by the window, and Clare saw Chris's head framed in the light. He appeared to be talking to someone. Clare stood in the rain watching when she should have been running and hammering on the door. Someone came over and sat down on the settee beside him. Clare couldn't make out through the drips who it was, so she wiped her face then looked again. She saw Chris' arm laying on the back of the settee. She saw him bring his arm around the stranger. His fingers reached into her hair. Clare now saw it was long and brown. He gently pulled the woman's head so that she shifted and came to rest against him. He continued gently stroking the hair. The simple love and affection in the gesture went through Clare like a knife. There was nowhere to run to now. No safety. Clare ran back down the path and into Aggie. She wrenched the catch shut as if shielding herself from the outside. Clare jammed her into gear, and sped off, the gravel slipping and cascading into the air. The downpour had slackened enough for Clare to hear the pebbles hitting the bonnet of the Fiat, and was glad.

Driving blindly, she took any turning she saw, sometimes it was another gravel track, sometimes tarmac and for the first time, she cursed Aggie's lack of speed. The rain stopped for a while and Clare took a left turning finding the worst track of all. It was so deeply rutted that Clare heard Aggie's sump hitting and once the wheels slipped. They went through some water and for a second Clare was terrified she'd driven into a river. Some water seeped under the cab doors, then the wheels gripped and she was out and back onto the track. Aggie twisted from side to side, as the ruts grew deeper and deeper. The inevitable happened; with a muffled crunch, Aggie hit something immovable. She lurched on to her side, wheels spinning. Clare knew she was stuck. For a while she sat there, watching the rain make patterns in the headlights. Clare grew tired of that, so she switched off the engine. In the darkness, she began to sob; deep, gut-wrenching sobs from that hurt place inside. There was no one there to give her a hanky. Desolation engulfed her. After a long time, the sobs slowed and then stilled. Clare leant forward onto the steering wheel and fell asleep.

The dawn chorus can be vociferous in June and it was that which woke Clare. Bleary-eyed, she raised an aching neck from the steering wheel and shifted frozen limbs. She knew, exactly how Chris felt when he'd stood up. Chris, oh no, Chris. The feeling of betrayal was familiar to Clare, so she decided she to cope with it. She was even glad that she hadn't made any foolish commitment too soon. It was a shame because she'd been so convinced in her spirit that at last here was something right. He had touched her in a new way, something purer than anything she'd met before. She'd lost it. She'd have to live without it.

Alex. Had he led the danger successfully away or was she still under a real threat from this man? She had no-one to protect her now. Why had she let herself be convinced by Alex that she had to go to Chris and not the Police? How could she have left Sheila and Mick like that? A glance at her watch revealed it earlier than even Peter's waking time. They wouldn't even know. Soon they'd see - find the phone cut, run next door and call the Police. The whole scenario as it played out in her mind's eye was comforting. They would search for her. Clare felt the danger lurking around. Perhaps she should try to find a phone and get help herself.

The morning light was revealing Aggie's predicament. Her bumper had caught on a tree bole which was jutting out into the lane which had caused her to fall against the steep bank. The lane was so narrow that Clare saw no way of turning around. She stepped out of the cab to check the damage. One of the windows was cracked where it had hit a tree, and the bumper was twisted but that seemed all. Clare climbed back in again and started the engine. Aggie wheezed and grunted, but wouldn't go. Clare then realised she was at such an angle that the little petrol she wasn't going to get through. Clare got out again and went to stand on the bonnet. The lane was so deep that she couldn't see further than a few hundred yards. The edges were lined with dog roses, elder and tall oak trees at the top. She was glad of her wellies, the track being nearly a bog. Clare smelt something different from the sweet smell of the roses. She sniffed trying to pinpoint it. The sea, the sea was down the end of the lane! If she walked along the beach, she'd find habitation.

Around the corner, the track came to an abrupt end. A rickety gate enclosed a mature pine wood. Clare pulled the gate open far enough to squeeze through and walked onto the thick bed of needles. Above her head, the tops of the trees swayed in a gentle breeze from the azure sky. Clare plunged eagerly into the green light. When at last she broke through, the sun blinded her. In green depths, the sea stretched calmly to the horizon, but on the beach, it lapped on brown pebbles with a gentle touch. The water was so clear, that Clare felt an almost irresistible urge to skip, jump in and cleanse herself from all the mess in her life. She eyed the water, deciding, no, she'd come back here one day when it was all sorted. The morning had given her a measure of calmness. She strode carefully along the slippery stones. The wood behind her was thinning and soon gave way to half-tamed fields and hedges. In parts the marsh had won and clumps of sedges dotted the grass. There was no sign of a friendly farm so she plunged on.

The beach took a sharp turn, revealing a small cove. It was surrounded by bent oaks and pines. Underneath them nestled a small house. It looked old and worn by the sea, the surrounding garden a tatty mess of rhododendrons. Somehow it was welcoming, like a friend waiting to greet. The faded tiles, and the wood clad porch felt like an invitation to enter, maybe someone still lived here. Clare ran along the short stretch of sand and up the steps onto the grass, and over to knock on the weather-beaten door.

CLARE
Earlier

Sylvie watched Clare drive away then hurried to go onto the platform. It was so hard to understand Clare's opposition to Jesus when He was standing there, waiting to help her out. Sylvie had to keep on remembering her own opposition, double it, then she had some measure of just how difficult it would be to show Clare the light.

On time for once, the train rumbled into the station and Sylvie sank on to a seat in an empty compartment. Out of her holdall, she took out several copies of a Christian magazine. She was seeing the editor of this particular one for yet another interview, so she needed to be boned up before she got there. She soon was engrossed in an article on Baptism and took little notice of someone sitting down opposite.

'Got religion now, have we?' asked a familiar voice, and she jumped. Duncan was sitting there, the familiar arrogant look on his face.

'Do you good to get a bit of it! Might make you clean up your act a bit,' Sylvie snapped. She saw the lump in the middle of his once perfect nose and regretted her indirect responsibility.

'Alright. Maybe I got what I deserved. By the way, have you seen that lout lately? He hasn't turned up for work, Ma and Pa are threatening to get another gardener.'

'Haven't you heard? Chris Rowan was released when Clare came round because she backed up all he said. They're searching for

Alex, but he's done a bunk. It seems he did it. Clare has to tell someone her every move in case he comes back and has another go.'

'I've been in France, so I've missed all this drama. He must be some sort of nutter.' Duncan inadvertently touched his nose.

Sylvie couldn't think of any other explanation and agreed with him.

'So what are you doing going up to town? I thought you'd swallowed the moral idyll and all that,' he asked.

'Searching for a job. I'm having the second interview for this magazine today.' She waved it under his nose.

'Well, if you have no luck, I'm sure I can find you a little something in the office.' He gave her a conspiratorial wink.

'Get knotted Duncan. I know all too well your little ideas. Aren't you ever going to grow out of womanising and settle down?' Sylvie felt like an elderly maiden Aunt.

'Don't think so. It seems to have got in the blood. Then again, if I found the right woman, I'd give it all up and go and live on a remote island. Forget about the world.'

'As long as it had a private jet, a large bar and a swimming pool!'

They both exploded into laughter.

'Sylvie, you're the only one who ever saw right through me, all the rest get stuck at the image. Is it really too late for us?'

Sylvie felt a twist inside which had nothing to do with the motion of the train. 'It was too late when you dumped me for Teresa Smith.'

For once Duncan looked someone fully in the face and felt a new sensation, regret. He rapidly re-armed himself with his old cocksureness. If it was too late, it was back into the old routine.

'Duncan, what's happened to Helen?'

The surprise question put him completely off balance. Sylvie saw him lost for words and as white as a sheet. While he searched for words, Sylvie waited.

'She went off the rails,' he said awkwardly. 'Did a runner. Ma and Pa have disowned her, in fact, they won't even admit to having a daughter.'

That explained the Harrison's reaction to the birthday card, but it was still inexcusable.

'How could they? Where is she now?' asked Sylvie in disgust.

Once again she saw Helen's Heidi-like curls and boyish looks. They'd been friends, meeting after school, sharing Helen's pony, until Helen's new school had started her on the habit of pulling her hair off her face with a scoop of the hand, and the patronising attitude towards anyone who went to another school. The friendship had ceased altogether by the time they were fifteen. Yet Sylvie still treasured her memories of childhood.

'Haven't the faintest idea.' Duncan interrupted her daydream. 'All this happened just over three years ago, and yes, I'm afraid they are totally capable of such cold-bloodedness. Can't let the side down and all that.'

'Didn't Peter keep in contact? I thought they were still close after he left school.'

'It was at his engagement party that it all came to a head. Imagine the scene all these females decked out in their simpering best, tossing about pressies and congratulations. In walks Helen, stoned out of her brain, clad in an old T-shirt and jeans. A path clears its way up to the happy couple. She waltzes up to them and gives them a toaster. Not a new one, but an old one in a carrier with the flex hanging out of a hole. Wishing them every happiness, because she 'ain't had none.' She throws up all over them and passes out. Ma and her army step in then, take the squeaking Rosie away and chuck Helen out - and I mean literally. They just threw her out the door and slammed it with a 'don't darken our doors again.' When I went to look after all the kafuffle had died down she was gone. Peter never married Rosie after that either, it was the beginning of the end being thrown up on.'

'And Peter?'

'Lives in a sulk of thwarted love. Mention Helen to him and he blows a fuse.'

'But surely you all looked for her - through the old boy network and all that?' Duncan now had the grace to look embarrassed.

'I well, er was rather busy at the time, and...'

'You just left it and left it, going on your own sweet way. Duncan, you ought to be ashamed of yourself, she's your sister! She might even be dead.'

Duncan shrugged and turned to look out of the window.

'Duncan, come with me now and find her!'

'What!'

'How can you rest at night not knowing where she is? Come on Duncan, for once in your life, do something you won't have to be ashamed of.'

The buffet trolley came in, giving them both a breathing space. After it had gone, Duncan gripped his coffee.

'Maybe you're right old thing.' Duncan looked pleased with himself. 'For once I will get something right. The old folks seem to be getting more bitter the whole time, Peter's just ambling through life as if he'd lost an arm, but won't admit it. Perhaps it's time to bring her back, have a big bust-up, and put them all straight.'

'Right then. Where shall we start?' That brought them back down again with a start. Three years was a long time to catch up with someone. Duncan moved back into gear.

'Well, I've got to go and collect the heap - having its annual beauty treatment. What time's your interview?'

'10.30.'

'Right, get your job sorted then I'll meet you say - my place at one?'

He saw her warning look.

'Ah, well, ok then, two at Harrods for lunch.'

'Only if you're paying. I can just about manage a burger.'

'No, definitely one on me,' said Duncan hastily. 'I'll do some discreet phoning around, then we'll know where to go.'

For a while, they were immersed in their own thoughts.

The train began its rumbling approach into Waterloo. In a panic, Sylvie gathered up her magazines. The train had now managed to get itself late, so it would have to be a fight for a cab. They went their separate ways with a cheerful wave.

Sylvie knew she didn't give her best at the interview. She prayed as she went in, but the grilling she received was more fitting to an oral exam at University. They still didn't seem too happy with the fact she'd only been a Christian for a few months. What a shame she couldn't lie anymore. She went through the perfunctorily nods and 'we'll let you know' with a real itch to get onto the real problem.

The sheer height of London buildings never failed to dazzle her, and as she worked her way through crowds to Harrods, she became all too aware how one person was an insignificant blot in this miasma. Would they be able to find someone who had been hidden for three years? The choice furnishing of the restaurant seemed overdone and fussy to Sylvie's country orientated eyes. Do people really need all these decorations to enjoy their food? Duncan was waiting, he stood up and pushed her chair in, ever the gentleman.

'Not gone vegetarian or anything?' he demanded.

'No. Actually, I'm not hungry. Might I just have a ham salad and I know about the frog's legs scam!'

Duncan grinned ruefully. 'Looks like you've been briefed by someone about me!'

'Yes and don't forget it. Any progress?'

'Well, most folks who might have helped are out earning a humble crust. But I did find the address of her old flat. That might be a good place to begin. What's that you're saying?'

'I'm saying Grace.'

Duncan hid his smile and got on with his baked trout. He'd resisted the temptation for a bottle of wine, he'd need to be clear headed today; not risk being done for drunken driving again. He found himself enjoying Sylvie's company. It was a novelty not to have to turn on the charm because he knew she'd see straight through it. They finished quickly and set out in the MG. Sylvie loved sleek cars, though it was quite humbling to be sat below the people walking along the streets. She rifled through his cassettes and winced at the choice.

'Vanilla Ice and Sheena Easton - Yuck!' She ferreted around in her holdall and came up with one of her tapes. It was a selection of contemporary choruses sung by a small choir. Sylvie noticed his wincing at some of the honeyed tones, so she pulled the tape out and put the radio on. Soon they were away from the main crowds and heading into Chelsea. They pulled outside a well restored mews. Duncan leapt out to ring the bell.

'I'm sorry to bother you,' he said in the laconic drawl.'

'Sorry mate, no rooms at the moment,' came the woman's sharp reply.

'Actually, we're not looking for accommodation but trying to track someone down. A Helen Harrison, who lived here about three years ago,' The woman peered suspiciously under her permed curls.

'Oh yeah, I remember. Just took off one day. I kept the room till her rent ran out then put her stuff in a box. Still got it I think. Who are you anyway?'

'Her brother.'

'Well, shouldn't you know where she is of all people? Darren!' She yelled into the house. 'Go into the back shed and get that blue leather box for us.'

'Do you remember any of her friends?' Duncan quizzed.

'Right bunch. Into drugs and lah-de-dah accents. No good. They left her when all the cash began to run out.'

A thin lad came out dragging a cobwebbed box behind him. Together they shoved it into the MG; Duncan trying not to see the scratches in the paintwork. It took the two of them to haul the box up the steps to Duncan's house, and into the dining room. The top of the box was jammed with clothes already outdated in three short years. Then came a layer of toiletries, a few books and a battered teddy bear. It seemed precious little to be all that remained of someone's life.

'I wonder how much they helped themselves too? She had quite a large collection of LPs,' said Duncan cynically. Sylvie caught the slight thickness in his voice. Then came the meat. Old letters, an address book, a picture of the family (in a battered frame) with the children in shorts and T-shirts; happier times. Sylvie took the letters and Duncan the address book. The letters proved to be no more than invitations for weekends from school friends, some dating long back to their teenage. Many of the writers left only casual notes, no address. Duncan cross-referenced the address book with his own and found three who were not known to him.

'I reckon we try these first. Our own crowd wouldn't have been able to keep it to themselves if she'd have turned up on their doorstep.' He dialled the first number to find they'd moved on leaving no address. The second was fruitful. They remembered Helen. She'd stayed there a number of times before. Sylvie leaned close to the receiver to hear.

'Freddy took off for Spain. No, she was sure she hadn't gone with him because it was a boys only trip, and they weren't back yet. When had they gone? About two years ago.' That was as much as could be gleaned from the vague answers, so Duncan left his number and tried the last one. To his shock, it turned out to be a

YWCA hostel in Clapham. They suggested he came down and talked to the manager.

The hostel was a resplendent building in new red brick, the floors carpeted. Sylvie took sneaky glances as they followed the manager down the corridor and saw each woman had a snug well-fitted room. Miss Dennis introduced herself with a firm handshake.

'I've only been here six months myself, but I have managed to track down the files of that year but no Helen Harrison.'

'May we look? It may be that one of her friends stayed here,' asked Sylvie.

'I'm afraid that is beyond the rules of confidentiality. Can you give me some names?'

Duncan racked his brains for names of Helen's cronies, but she'd been at the periphery of his social orbit and surnames never stuck.

'We can always ask Jessie,' the woman exclaimed. 'Wait here!'
She returned with a grey-haired woman, who was obviously the cleaner.

'Do you have a photo?' she demanded. Fortunately, Helen's passport had surfaced in one of the envelopes. Jessie took it, and scanned it, even lifting her glasses to get a better look.

'Yes, I remember her, but her name ain't Helen!'

'What was it?'

'Sue. She came in here one night with the shakes. Been sleeping rough under the Embankment. Had had her cards and everything nicked. Said a friend had stayed here, and she knew it was somewhere she could stop. She was a right one. Came in blinding drunk several times so they packed her off to St. Margaret's.'

'St. Margaret's?' Duncan and Sylvie asked in unison.

'The drying out place in Fulham.'

'Yes, we do have a record of her here, and it bears out all Jessie said, dated three years ago last January,' endorsed the Manager.

'It all ties in,' said Duncan. 'Can we have the address of St Margaret's?'

Again they drove into the night, the city now filling up with neon lights and emptying of shoppers. The response at St. Margaret's was no less helpful but led them nowhere. Sue/Helen had been there but had discharged herself after a month. No-one knew where. The trail was dead. There seemed nothing for it but to retire to a wine bar and regroup. As they sat and brooded, a tall lanky man with a decided stagger circumnavigated his way to the bar.

'Perry you old bugger, what the dickens are you doing here?' laughed Duncan. Perry waltzed over and plopped himself down on a stool and leered at Sylvie.

'Bit of this and that you know…'
Duncan had a light bulb moment.

'Listen - now this sounds daft, but have you heard from my batty sister at all recently?' Perry guffawed. 'NoW there's a coincidence! She was up for a bit of you know… dealing some things. I bumped into her of all places, serving in a bleeding MacDonald's in the Bullring in Birmingham! At least she didn't throw up on me! Swore me to secrecy…' He pressed a finger to his lips and looked for a glass to swill. Duncan called the barman and Perry toasted them with a double scotch.

'Do you fancy a drive up north?' Duncan asked Sylvie. They made their excuses to Perry and left as soon as was polite. Sylvie had begun to feel weary with disappointment, but this new trail revived her energy.

'My navigation's not too good,' She admitted as they got in the car.

'Can't really miss Birmingham, it's a bit big. Shall we have something to eat first?' Sylvie sighed realising that Duncan and creature comforts were never far apart, so they bought snacks at a garage, filled the car with petrol and set off. Duncan drove swiftly through the night, asking Sylvie to take over never occurred to him. Eventually, she dozed off. Every now and then, he glanced at her peaceful face and to his horror, a sense of real regret flooded back. Despite the MG's exuberance in breaking the speed limits, it was the early hours of the morning before they reached the outskirts of Birmingham. He drove on through the empty streets until he found a multi-storey car park where he parked. Sylvie slept on, so he covered them with his coat and dozed off himself. The rush of office workers' cars squealing their way in, roused him. Duncan, in pure instinct, reached out to touch Sylvie. There was so often an unfamiliar face beside him when he woke, it was nice to see someone he recognised. Something stopped him from proceeding and waking her with a kiss. He knew too well the feeling of her slap in the face from all those years ago. In the end, he pulled the coat from her and she stirred.

'Morning honey,' he drawled. 'Do you want breakfast in bed or out on the patio?' Sylvie stared at him blankly for a minute.

'No, I think MacDonald's.'

'Let me just freshen up then.' From a compartment, he took a razor and plugged it in.

'Where's the sink hidden?' Sylvie laughed, then they drove out into the morning.

It was a shock to discover just how many MacDonald's there were in the Bull Ring. One breakfast in one was enough and Sylvie had the aftertaste taste of synthetic food all day because it took them hours to track down the branch where Helen worked. Perry's vague description of the Bull Ring was no better than saying Hampshire or Dorset. They struck gold at 3 pm. Yes, she did work there. Yes, she was coming in to work that evening at six. No, they wouldn't give her home address. Swearing the staff to secrecy, claiming it to be a big surprise, they left the shop with a sense of real exhilaration. The three hours seemed an eternity to fill.

'We can always find a motel room,' ventured Duncan. The look in Sylvie's eyes squashed him.' A walk in the park?'

'How about the cinema - we passed one back there?'

And so it was, they spent a thoroughly enjoyable couple of hours until the bit in the film came on with the witch in it. A happy, plump, witch who was just trying to help the poor people in the plot. Sylvie began muttering under her breath until Duncan got fed up.

'Let's go - what's making you so cross?'

Sylvie tried to explain how witchcraft, under whatever guises, was evil and from the devil, and shouldn't be made out good. Duncan didn't see the harm, and they began the sparrings of an argument as they walked back to the MacDonald's.

'Duncan - what the hell are you doing here?'

There stood before them a Helen. Not the Helen they knew, but a plump, red-cheeked woman almost bursting out of her uniform. Duncan's arms rose to greet her but the years of restraint still held him firm.

'Sylvie - you've changed!' she exclaimed at last.

'Well, it has been a few years!'

'I'll get tonight off, we need to talk.' Duncan and Sylvie watched her disappearing back then looked at each other.

'Not what I expected!' Duncan understated then was silent.

They saw her talking with frantic gestures, to the manager who finally appeared to relent. Helen returned, stuffing her tabard in a bag.

'Come back to my place. It's not far to walk.'

'We've got the car, but I suppose it'll be alright where it is.' Helen seemed to be saving herself for when they got to her house because she said little more than give directions as they walked. Finally, they turned a corner into a line of terraced houses. She led them to number five. There was nothing exceptionable to its outside, but inside came as a shock. It was done out very much as a high-class London house, plain but expensive. There was no evidence of poverty in the luxurious fittings. Sylvie felt bewildered, as she sank into a plush settee. Helen bustled about, pouring them a beer then plumped herself down on a chair.

'I want you to hear my story before you say a word. I always vowed if even just one of you bothered to look for me, I would at least give you the courtesy of an explanation before I chuck you out.' Sylvie caught the twinkle in her eye.

'The night I walked in on Peter's party was a turning point in my life. In some ways, my actions were pure jealousy. He'd swum with the stream and seemed to have it all sewn up. Good job, marriage, a new house. There was I with one O level in French, no job, plenty of cash, just drifting. I had already latched on to the drink drug crowd, and that for a while had seemed to be the answer. I filled the days with every vice, and believe me, I trod at the edges of some very dark pits.'

'When I got chucked out and told not to come back, it all came to a head. I drowned it in the biggest bout of drinking I'd ever had. Even today I can't believe just how much I knocked back. It all ended up with my cash card being nicked. The only place I could go was the YCWA. Jessie had stayed there. It didn't help, I just thieved the money for booze and soon enough they caught up on me. I was packed off to St. Margaret's. As soon as the DT's had gone, I got myself out and hitch-hiked my way up here. At least the booze was out of my system, so I stayed clear of that. I found myself in with the other down and outs, begging and stealing. I was the only one who stayed sober, so they started to resent me because I wouldn't join in. It ended up with a row, and them beating me up. It hurts more than your body when you find yourself alone. I took myself onto the streets begging and began to starve.'

'Then I met Tom. I was sat in a park, and he was asleep on a bench. He awoke and proceeded to eat a mars bar. Has the sight of food ever made you want to weep? I couldn't look at anything else. All of a sudden he stood up and handed it to me. I know now what manna from heaven tastes like because that mars bar was it. I've never tasted one like it since. The next thing I knew he led me to a cafe and spread a feast before me. It ended up with him finding us a flat, feeding, clothing and befriending me No word of repayment, no thanks ever received. I still look back at those days, as if I were being guarded and cosseted by an angel. He bought me books, and let me cook for him. Oh maybe it was a strange relationship, it was totally platonic. He didn't take anything from me, he just gave and gave. I dare say it wouldn't have gone on for very much longer like that; no relationship is static for long.'

    'One day he came back early from work. I'd never seen him so animated. He'd met some old friend in the Park, and wanted him to meet me. But he must have lost him somewhere on route, or he bottled out. I don't know. All that is certain is that there was no one with him. When I told him so he flipped. After rushing out to look he came back in and started blaming me for scaring his mate off. He grabbed my shoulders and shook the living daylights out of me. I couldn't take that or the crazy look in his eyes. When he finally released me and ran back outside to look for his friend again, I packed my few things and fled. I sat in our cafe for a couple of hours and thought things through. It became clear that he was as much in need of help as I was, and this was no time to be running. Whatever it was, I had to come alongside him and help him through. I went back. He was gone. I've spent the past few years searching for him, but no sign. He left a mountain of money hidden in the bedroom which I used to buy this place, to make a home for us when I find him. I work in the MacDonald's because that was one of our places and it's a good point to keep a lookout from.'

    She paused to take a long drink. Sylvie had the feeling there was still more to come. Duncan just looked blank, such devotion was totally outside the realms of his experience.

'So why didn't you at least contact us and let us know where you were?'

'Have you looked for me until now?' she countered.

'Touche. Would you at least contact the folks and let them know where you are?'

'No. I'm coming down to see them now. I knew a time would come when quite clearly I would have to face them, and I'd be obedient to that call. It's taken me a long time to forgive them for what they did.'

'Come on, you asked for it at the party.'

'That was a symptom, Duncan, not the cause. I know they're pretty much victims of their class, and they wouldn't see anything wrong in their actions. But to farm their children out on an endless succession of girls, not even a consistent nanny. To just pat the kids on the head and bestow unwanted gifts at Christmas is not any way to bring up stable adults. To split twins up and send them to separate boarding schools at the age of eight is inhumane. Look at yourself To make up for your own hurts, you've adopted the morality of a rabbit and the manners of a rogue. Just examine yourself, Duncan.'

Indeed he was silent for a while. Sylvie had been digesting the facts of the story, from whatever angle you looked at it, it held the touch of the bizarre.

'I feel you've still more to tell us,' she said to break the silence.

'Well, I don't know how you'll receive this either. Someone else was searching in the past couple of years, but for me.'

'I think I know what you're going to say,' butted in Sylvie with a broad grin on her face. 'The Icthus on your jumper has given you away.'

'You too?'

'Me too.'

'Oh no - not another God botherer,' groaned Duncan. 'Now I get this forgiving business. Please, I don't want to hear the details. I'm beginning to feel got at.'

'I don't see why Duncan, no one's sat you down and forced you to look at a Gospel,' said Helen with a grin on her face. 'If you two will wait a minute while I throw some things in a bag, I'll be with you!'

They both looked at her in surprise.

'You're taking me to the grand old reconciliation with Ma and Pa!' Helen laughed and leapt up off the settee.'

'Are you regretting all this now?' demanded Sylvie when Helen had thundered upstairs.

'No, I don't think so. Perhaps we all needed to be stopped in our tracks for a while. Even if she can't get on with the rest of the family, they can't go on disowning her; it's eating them up.'

Before long the MG was threading its way through spaghetti junction and heading south. Sylvie and Helen became engrossed in swapping their Christian experiences and found them both running on similar tracks. Helen had even become a deacon in a local church.

'Can't you two cut the Christian speak for a while. If I hear the expressions 'He spoke to me' and 'I just have to share this' once more, I'm going to embed this car in a concrete pillar!'

Guiltily, Sylvie changed the subject.

'Why do you think you've never tracked this man down?'

'He never spoke of his past and I'm still not entirely sure what he did for work. He always had plenty of money though. Here,' she fumbled about in the bag that was wedging her into the back. 'Someone took this shot of us when we were at a local carnival, and he wasn't too happy about it, but I insisted we kept it because I paid for it.' Helen handed over a tatty Polaroid. Sylvie had to hold it close to the window to get enough light, then she looked, and looked again.

'Duncan, does this vehicle go any faster?'

He looked at her surprised because they'd both ticked him off for going over 70.

'Duncan, Helen's Tom is Alex.'

To Duncan's credit, he didn't swerve too much.

'You're sure - really sure?'

'There's no doubt, he's even wearing that donkey jacket with the tear in.'

'Oh, God. Tell her the story Sylvie, then you two had better do some serious praying for my driving.'

Sylvie told Helen the whole story as they drove into the darkness. Helen listened, the look of radiance at the news rapidly fading to one of grim sorrow. She began to weep.

'Oh, Tom, you need my help more than ever now. I should have searched harder,' she grieved.

'Helen he may not even recognise you. He certainly was clear that he didn't want his past found because he felt the evil in it,' warned Sylvie.

'We must pray for him, and Clare too.'

So they did. Duncan listened to the special tone their voices took, and the different inflation in their language, and at first a hint of a grin played on his mouth at such earnest words. They kept on talking to someone who they presumed was listening, but after a while, he felt a hint of their conviction that all this was doing something. The smile left his face, and he pushed the MG on. It was very late when they scrunched up the drive to the Croft's house. The sight of the Police car parked outside sent a groan up from Sylvie.

'How could we have left her so alone?'

At first, the policeman wasn't going to let them in, he seemed to think they were Press. In the end, they got him to ask Sheila, and they were duly let in. She didn't spare them.

'Clare has disappeared, sometime last night. the Land Rover's gone and they've been searching for her all day.' She burst into tears. 'I left her for ten minutes last night to collect Mick, he must have got in then. Why was I so careless?'

'Don't blame yourself. He would have got there sooner or later, even if you hadn't. Sheila, there's someone here who may be able to sort this all out...' said Sylvie, pushing Helen forward.

CLARE
1993

Clare stood cottage door, her hand poised to knock feeling an absolute fool. It hung at an angle, its hinges long rusted away. The house was derelict and had been for a long time. The early morning was warm and Clare smelt the jasmine growing all over the porch. The temptation was too much, she pushed the door open and walked in. The hall was dark, on Clare's left was an empty room which must have once been a sitting room. It was decorated in a manic dull green. To her right was the kitchen which Clare entered. She visualised the rusty range shining and burbling. The floors and walls re-stained and bundles of herbs hanging from the ceiling to dry. In the corner by the window, she saw Chris sitting in an old rocking chair, reading a magazine. Clare shut the door firmly on that daydream and explored further.

Behind the kitchen was another room, a damp bathroom, an ominous drip coming from somewhere within. Clare turned around, on her right was the front door and before her was the staircase. Clare climbed, each step creaked in protest. Upstairs she found three bedrooms. The front one gave the most spectacular view over the cove and the sea. Clare wanted to live there, wake up every morning to the sea in all its moods. On the days when the sea attacked the shore, on the days when it lapped calmly and she wanted Chris to wake beside her.

It was too late. Clare suppressed the howl that rose and fought to regain her equanimity. She'd been through all this once before and she knew deep down that she would get over it again. Clare wanted to rush back to civilisation, find the owner of the house, and beg, steal or borrow the money to buy it. If she couldn't have Chris, then this would have to do instead. Clare clattered downstairs forgetting their frailty, so one had to break sending her slipping down the last few. Another trip down a flight of stairs suddenly came to her mind. Clare inwardly congratulated herself at how much she'd toughened up since then. Someone was standing at the back door.

'Alex! Did you get away from him?' Clare squawked. 'You see, well, Chris and I weren't about to happen. You were wrong.'

He walked over and she saw the crooked grin on his face.

'I'm not Alex or Tom.' The voice was different, higher, almost that of an adolescent. 'My name is Douggie. Tom is my friend. We always do things together. Whenever he's in a fix, I get him out of it.'

'People always make trouble for him, so I come and help,' he repeated.'We have tea together. I've been away for a while, but now I'm here to put things straight.'

Before Clare moved, he grabbed her arms and pulled her to her feet. Still holding her in a vice-like grip he said,

'I'm sorry I didn't get it right the first time,' Clare cringed at the menace. 'I thought I'd pinned it on that Chris. Now they're after my Tom again. Sometimes he hides from me, but now I'm going to keep with him. Once you're gone, we'll run away and this time I won't leave him in the lurch. He can't manage on his own. Look at the mess he's made now. I always told him women are trouble. We had to show his mother that. Now, where shall I do it?' He looked wildly about.

'Alex, Alex,' Clare screamed into his face. 'You're not Douggie, you're Alex.' It didn't have any effect. He pushed Clare towards a door beneath the stairs she hadn't seen before. He released one hand to open it, so Clare put all her strength into struggling free. It was impossible, however much she flailed about, his grip remained firm. He was indifferent to her blows. At last, he wrenched the door open and looked into the cupboard.

'There, look at the lovely red light in there, it's quite cosy. When you bleed, the blood will make lovely patterns in the air!' He pushed her in and shut the door. 'I won't keep you waiting long.' He laughed as he went away.

Clare fell onto a heap of indescribable objects, and lay still, recovering her breath and trying to calm her panic. She moved carefully, feeling layers of dust grate everywhere her fingers touched. From nowhere came the smell of the friendly honeysuckle, and with it, a hint of light. Clare saw its source and shoved at whatever was blocking it. Several small objects hit the floor. Hope rising, Clare pushed at the light, then tried not to shriek as something ran across her hand. Her fingers found rotten wood, and a few pieces came away, but then they grated on brick, and Clare knew that it was only an air vent, not a way out. She moved several more of the objects, just in case there was another hole but to no avail. The objects were books, so with hopeless curiosity, she pulled one close to the tiny strip of light. It was a Bible. Clare threw it with disgust to the floor. She huddled in her arms and closed her eyes, trying to think of anything but here and now. As she settled and her ears adjusted to the small sounds of her prison, she began to hear voices, somewhere outside. Clare's heart lurched, was help at hand? It appeared to be two men arguing. Slowly she began to pick out what they were saying and her heart sank.

'Douggie, we can't kill another person, it isn't right.'

'You never mentioned that when we did your mother. We can do it again this time, I won't abandon you. It'll be alright.'

'Clare hasn't done anything to harm us!'

'She wanted you then betrayed you to Chris. She never loved you, not the way I do.'

Douggie's voice was wheedling. Clare imagined the two men arguing. Why hadn't Alex's twin found him before? Why did he have two other names? She understood one because of his memory loss, but two?

'I think we should let her go. She's done me no harm, hasn't looked me out or tried to buy me off with another man's cash,' Alex pleaded again.

'She has, she has! She was going to live with that Chris.'

'Then why can't we leave them and run away together as we planned. Oh, why not?' Alex's voice now sounded like a young boy's. 'It will be such fun.'

'She knows too much. You shouldn't have told her about me last night.'

'Douggie, I'm sorry. I didn't try to run away with her. I was trying to keep her safe.' He ended on a sob.

Clare struggled to her feet. If Alex was there, surely the two of them might be able to overpower this Douggie. She picked up the largest book she could find, then stood straight and fell with all her weight onto the door. The damp had made it soft, she stumbled into the hall, choking on the rising dust. Clare rose quickly, weapon in hand.

'Alex, grab him, two of us can beat him!' Then she stopped. There was only one person in the hall. 'Alex, is it you? Where's he gone?' Clare stammered in relief.

The evil smile appeared again and Clare's legs turned to lead. 'You still don't understand do you?' he jigged on the spot like a child. 'He is mine. I am him.'

'You're a schizophrenic.'

'Oh no, we're definitely two people.'

Stealthily he approached Clare and with lightning reflexes, he trapped her again. To her horror, he had found some rope and with a maniacal deftness, tied her arms and legs and dragged her into the kitchen. Clare fainted. When she came to, she kept her eyes firmly shut. The argument was continuing like a pantomime. She heard the two voices going on the same ground over and over again. Clare began to peep through her lashes. What she saw was almost unbelievable. When Alex or Tom or Tom was speaking, he was recognisable, all the familiar gestures were there. As soon as Douggie spoke, Alex's face somehow changed. The expressions and nuances altering so that a completely different identity was imposed on Alex's face, and it was evil. To Clare's horror, it became apparent that Alex was losing, and Douggie began exploring various gruesome schemes for despatching Clare. A violent sneeze began to build inside her, and there was nothing she could do about it, her cover was blown. Douggie was squatting in front of her when she opened her eyes. Frantically, Clare tried to think of something to delay him. She tried meeting Douggie on his own ground.

'So you and-er-Tom have been friends a long time?'

'Oh yeah. We used to play some brilliant games and have tea together.'

'Tell me about them.'

Clare drew out of him many childhood recollections. For a while, Douggie's eyes became dreamy. He obviously enjoyed telling them. The anger returned.

'That bitch. She got rid of his Dad, got in a lover boy, locked Tom out when the Bull was there.' His voice was rising in hysteria.

'We got our own back. The Bull's still in prison for the murder. Serves him right!' He went into peals of childish laughter.

'It was very naughty of me, but I left Tom for a while afterwards. I had other things to do.' Again he grinned.

'But I came back as soon as someone else tried to mess up his life.'

'Me?'

'No. Some drip called Sue. He ran away from her because I did my disappearing act. He forgot all about her afterwards. I made sure of it with a little bump!' The laughter made Clare feel sick.

'He was alright until you came heavy footing it in. I had him alone and miserable, just how I like him. You used him. You must pay the price.' Douggie ended in a scream.

'I didn't mean to Douggie,' Clare adopted his wheedling tone, 'I would rather you and Tom were happy together. I don't want to upset you. Why don't the two of you go off and play like you used to? I'll go away. I promise not to tell a soul.'

'Nice try Missus! You women are never to be trusted. You'll just run to the pigs as soon as you can. Lie there and have a nice rest while Tom and I sort things out.'

Douggie turned his back on Clare and squatting on his haunches, began to rock himself. Every now and then he'd turn to look at her. Clare lay powerless awaiting her fate.

The evening was an endless torture for Clare. At one stage, Douggie came over to her, brandishing a gun, she thought her time had come.

'You're lucky,' he stated. 'He won't let me use the gun. It's dark now, so you're going back into the hidey-hole, ready for the first light. We'll have it all ready for you then.'

Douggie picked Clare up and shoved her back into the cupboard. She heard him propping it shut with some wood. All night long, Clare had to twist and shift, because of the books digging into her back, she felt the bruises forming. Fear, thirst and hunger kept her awake.

The deafening roar of a helicopter sent the house shaking. Douggie came to the door and pulled Clare out. She was surprised to see it was already light.

'You've told them where we are!' He hit her across the face with the back of his hand.

'I told him the planning was taking too long. We're stuck.'

Clare had an idea. With a sandpaper throat, she croaked.

'Instead of talking you can use me as bargaining for a getaway. You can make them leave a boat in the cove for you. I've told you, Douggie, I won't tell, I promise!'

He looked thoughtful for a moment. 'She may be right Tom, what do you think?'

Again he contorted.

'Let her go, don't kill her,' Tom pleaded. Clare wanted to weep at the desolation in his eyes.

'OK then,' Douggie said and threw Clare onto the floor in the kitchen. To her surprise she saw the Bible she'd picked up the previous day. It lay, twisted but open. Seeking diversion, Clare idly read the text. Douggie and Alex were arguing again. The old language in the book was difficult to understand. Clare concentrated her whole being on it, it took her away from this world. Admittedly she wished it could have been another book. The section visible dealt with Jesus rebuking a demon which was in a man. It cried with a loud voice and came out. This is just too weird, thought Clare. Then remembered Sylvie's account of the deliverance in Australia. Was Alex possessed or ill? Would it make any difference to the situation if he was? Having no hope and feeling a little delirious made Clare bold.

'Douggie!' she called. He span round.

'Who or what are you?'

'I'm me, Douggie.'

'But where do you come from?'

'Home.'

'Where's home?'

He looked perplexed.

'Douggie come out of Alex and leave him alone. Jesus tells you!'

He roared with maniacal laughter, then dropped down, coming to rest with his face inches from Clare's. 'Jesus I've heard of, but who are you?' He was about to say something else when there came the unmistakable blare of a loudhailer from outside.

'If there's anyone in there, make your presence known. Come out slowly from the front of the house.'

Douggie's reaction was to jump up, grab the gun, run to the front door and fire out into the garden. Clare struggled while his back was turned, but the knots were too tight.

'Help!' she yelled. 'He's possessed. Help me. He's going to kill me. Get me.' Douggie's hand was clamped around her mouth before she finished.

'It won't do any good. You're our bargaining point. Don't go and louse it up, or I may have to wing you. Slightly damaged goods won't matter.' He dropped her and went to secure both doors with pieces of wood from the broken staircase.

The police had the cottage covered on three sides, with men hiding in the woods. The demand for a boat to get them away in return for Clare's safety was being considered. They were convinced there were two men in the house because of the two voices. One was demanding and threatening, the other pleading them to make a decision quickly. There had been no further sound from Clare and that was a major consideration in their tactics. Approaching the house was also difficult because two men could watch the whole area. The day had started gloomy, heavy clouds threatening more rain, but the weather turned in the police's favour. The slight breeze dropped and a bank of mist came rolling up the coast, clipping the tops of the trees with a shroud of grey.

Two men, in thick jackets and carrying guns, were sent to the wood's edges. Impatiently they watched a slight breeze toy with the mist, then let it go, sending it rolling into the cove. Like hares, the men lithely ran out of the wood, along the high tide mark and up the steps. They veered to the left away from the kitchen windows, and crouched, breathing heavily, waiting to see if they had been detected. From the front of the house came the loudhailer, instructing that the men come to the front door to hear the reply to their demands. The marksmen poised like athletes, listening to the sounds of movement inside. Distantly they heard the catch on the front door being dropped. The first man leapt, smashed the window and leapt into the kitchen. Simultaneously the other put his full weight to the door which fell easily and ran into the corridor.

Everything happened with a frustrating sense of slow motion. Clare tried to shield herself from the flying glass, then the man was nearly on her, his gun at the ready before most of the glass had hit the floor. The second came down on Alex with his full weight, throwing Alex hard against the door. He was then manhandled to the floor and handcuffed in a matter of seconds, a heavy knee pinning him still.

'Where's your mate?'

'He's gone. He promised he wouldn't leave this time, but he's dropped me right in it again. I begged him not to do it.' To the policeman's disgust, the man below him began to weep.

'Is she alright?' he demanded of his partner.

'She's fine, call in the light brigade.'

Alex was dragged away from the door, and the waiting entourage piled in. He was bundled into a van and driven away. A policewoman helped Clare untie herself. To her surprise it was June.

'I'm going to be with you while you sort yourself out. Are you hurt in any way?'
Clare shook her head, she was rubbing her sore wrists and ankles.

'I'm starving, thirsty and filthy, but apart from that, fine, simply relieved it's all over. I'm not going to Hospital. I want to go home. If you think I need a doctor, he can come to me. What will they do to him?'

'Excuse me, Miss.' An enormous Policeman towered over her, 'Just how many men were here?'

'One, Alex or Tom if you want. He also calls himself Douggie. Listen to me, he's ill, very ill. He doesn't need punishment, he needs help.'

'Oh, we know that.'

'Seriously ill. You mustn't lock him up.' Clare didn't trust the man. 'He's got a split personality. He's convinced his friend did all of it. You must help him!'
Clare rose and dragged on the man's arm in desperation.

'Alright, alright,' he said placatingly, releasing himself from her grip.'We know what to do. You get yourself straight and make your statement. You can put it all in that.'

The first thing the crowd at Ivy Cottage heard about Clare's release was Clare herself walking into the house. After they had all embraced, and the children stopped yelling, Clare demanded feeding. She'd had a drink in the police car, but that had only served to make her hungrier. Sheila rapidly cooked an enormous fry-up, which Clare bolted. She followed it with thick slices of dripping toast and mugs of coffee. Replete at last, Clare realised her filthy state. Everyone had been tactfully not asking questions, although she saw they were itching to hear.

'I'm sorry,' she said at last. 'Let me get clean, then I'll tell you everything. I feel barely human.' It was strange to return to her bedroom and see it very much as she'd left it. Even the bottle of pills was still on the cabinet. Maybe she could forget the past 48 hours, pretend it had never happened. In the bathroom, she tipped in bubble bath and salts while the taps roared. The mirror was misting up, so she wiped it clear. Her eyes were heavy-lidded from lack of sleep and her face was noticeably thinner, but she sensed a lightness, it was freedom from fear. Now was time to begin again, on her own. She was so lucky to have been given yet another chance. Clare dived into the steaming suds and luxuriated in the oily caress of the water. It soothed her bruised back. In the hot limbo, Clare went over all the events, making herself face it all from the moment his first blow had knocked her out until the shower of broken glass released her. That she was still in a state of shock never entered her mind. All she sensed was a growing elation. Memories of things Douggie had stated sent her sitting up so quickly that a wave of water crashed over the edge of the bath onto the lino.

'The Bull's still in prison for her murder!'

Alex's mother. A great weight settled on Clare. Things were bad enough for Alex, but to throw in a murder on top? But what about the innocent man still in prison? Half of Clare wanted to protect Alex because she still couldn't totally hate him. He'd been her friend, and she'd seen his torment, but the other recoiled at the waste of a life. It was up to her to put Alex through this or keep silent.

The bath water was cooling, so Clare rapidly washed her hair and got out. She'd always prided herself on her ability to make quick decisions, but even so, she paced up and down the lino. Might she spend her life with the knowledge? Whether Alex was mad or not, everyone had to pay the price for their actions. He'd hardly treated her well. But he did try, said an inner voice. He'd tried to get her to Chris. Once again Clare saw the careless touch, and it hurt more than anything else she'd suffered. All her coiled emotions sprang out and attached themselves to the hurt Chris had dealt her. If only he'd be there when she opened the bathroom door, with a simple explanation and open arms. He wouldn't. Perhaps she should ring Bill and let him know a few home truths about his wife.

'Are you alright in there?' Came with a thump on the door. Clare sniffed and realised tears were coursing down her face, 'I'm coming.' She mopped herself on a towel and set a determined face on the world. The Doctor was waiting to examine her, so she had to strip again. She was passed fit but tired. Clare came out feeling quite smug. The feeling disappeared when she saw the detectives waiting with their notebooks and forms, but Clare felt expert now at giving statements and was able to relate the events of the past few days with surprising calm. She tried to make nothing worse for Alex than necessary, sticking to facts not emotions. She omitted the reference to the murder in a spot of cowardice. It nagged away when they said have you anything else to add. Clare crunched her hands beneath the table, she had to do it.

'He made a reference to a murder.' It was out. Clare felt the weight lift. 'Douggie claimed they had murdered Alex's mother and

got someone called the Bull to take the blame.'
That triggered more questions, but at the end,
Clare had a clear conscience; it was out of her
hands. The relief brought on sleepiness. All she
wanted to do was crawl into a womb of a bed.
Clare made her apologies and like a
sleepwalker, made her way to the bedroom.

Helen was already at Chardminster
Police Station. She'd organised a solicitor for
Alex and placed herself on a seat with no
intention of budging until she found out what was
going to happen. The solicitor was Ted Farmer, a
thin cheerful man with a penchant for brightly
coloured ties. He seemed unperturbed even
when he left the interview room.

'Well, my dear. They may let you see
him. It seems there's now a murder thrown into
this mess. He's totally adamant that none of this
is his doing, all of it is down to his friend
Douggie. Now we've either got a really good liar
on our hands or he's a genuine psychopath. Both
ways it'll mean life imprisonment.' He winced at
Helen's distraught face.

'I'm sorry, but it's best you know all the
facts. I've got to go back in.'

One of the detectives appeared and
ushered Helen into a side room. She was grilled
about Tom's twin but she could tell them nothing.
They'd never spoken to each other about their
past. The only thing she affirmed was the
presence of an imagined friend.

'He remembers you,' said the Detective.
'He admits that Douggie came along when you
were cohabiting, and that's what caused him to
take the overdose and lose his memory. Further
back than that he won't go. He says it's all
irrelevant. Miss Brown has claimed that Douggie
admitted to murdering Tom's mother. We've got

to get to the bottom of this. Somewhere there's an innocent man serving time. If we were to let you see him for a few minutes, it might trigger some memory or something. It's a bit unusual, but it may do the trick.'

'I'll do it,' she stated. Helen found herself lead down a long pungent corridor and into a bare, chilly room. In it were sat Mr Farmer, a uniformed man and the Doctor. Sat huddled at the desk was a dark haired man, head held in his hands, with an air of utter dejection.

'At 14.05 pm, Miss Helen Harrison was brought in to meet Mr O'Neal.' At the sound of her name, Tom looked up, sheer amazement on his face. They searched each other's faces, the years had changed them both.

'Hello Tom,' was all Helen could manage before Tom leapt up and enveloped her in a bear hug. They managed to hang on to each other for a minute before they were gently prised apart. Helen was given a seat opposite him and they were allowed to hold a hand across the table.

'I came back for you, but the flat was empty. I've spent all these years searching for you.'

'It was better you didn't find me. They've told you everything? How did you get here?'

'Duncan and Sylvie turned up on my doorstep and brought me here. I'm Duncan's sister.'

Tom looked at her, searching for the waif he'd rescued. Under her plumpness, he sensed she was still there. 'I never saw the likeness. Helen, you must go away. It isn't safe here.'

'Tom I'm staying. Now I've found you I'm not letting go.'

'Helen, you must go for your own safety!'

He snatched his hand away. To the amazement of all those watching, his face twisted and contorted.

'Yes, Helen. You must run away.' The new voice sounded like a boy's.

'I'm back. You're not having him. He's mine. I'll make sure of it by making them lock him up and throw away the key!'

He broke into a peal of laughter which made everyone cringe. Helen wasn't deterred.

'You don't scare me, you don't exist. You're part of Tom's mind and he can be healed from you!'

'They can try, but they won't succeed. I'm too strong!' he boasted.

'Right then Douggie,' said one of the men. 'If you're determined to have Tom locked up.'

Helen gasped but was silenced by another.

'Drop him right in it. Tell us how he murdered his mother!'

'Not going to tell. He's going to be locked up anyway, and we don't want the Bull out on the streets, pestering innocent women again.' He pouted like a child.

'Did you enjoy the Bull being put away then?'

Once again the laughter made them shudder.

'You won't get it out of me,' Douggie sneered. 'If she goes, I might tell.'

'I don't scare easy,' said Helen before the policemen ushered her out, 'I know who you are!'

Douggie snorted in disgust.

'If we're going to lock Tom away, don't you want to make it as bad as possible so he stays in for a long time?'

'Not going to tell.' Douggie folded his arms and scuffed his feet beneath the table.

'Why did you let Tom run all the way to Birmingham from Coventry on his own then?'

'Stupid man, it was Leeds.'

'Wasn't it rather a daring deed for two schoolboys?'

'Bleeding cheek. We were both l6. Anyway, it wasn't...' Douggie checked himself. 'Won't work,' he stated.

'Oh but you've helped us quite a lot already. We should be able to track down the case now.'

For a second, Douggie looked like a spoilt child, as he realised what he'd given away. Then he screamed, starting off like a childish squawk, then deepening into the bellow of a man in pain. When he stopped, everyone could tell Tom was back.

'Helen, you must go. He's up to no good. He's lurking about, planning to hurt you.' Tom continued as if he'd never been away.

'Alright, I'll go now. If you want me...'

'No go.'

'Tom, as long as you're in here, he can't hurt me. You're possessed.' Tom plainly didn't understand. The dead look in his eyes cut Helen to the quick. When she reached the corridor, she found her knees were shaking. Something evil, horrible was in that room. Mr Farmer followed her out.

'I'm afraid dear, we'll have to plead unfit to testify due to insanity. Two doctors will certify him, the Magistrates Court will put it to the Crown Court and they'll put a hospital order on him.

Someone like him can't be convicted, but he'll be put away because he's a danger to the public.'

'But what if he's cured?'

'I've never seen a case as bad as this, but it's possible. In some ways, he's more hope for freedom this way than if he stands trial. It'll mean the Home Secretary and all that entails. Where will you be so I can keep you informed?'

Helen spent the next few days getting under the feet of everyone in the station. She wasn't allowed to see Tom again and had to rely on reports from Mr Farmer. The search for the Bull was drawing a blank. Tom and Douggie were adamant in not giving the police any more details. Tom from fear. Douggie in defiance. There had been many murders in Leeds in the past twenty years, but finding one which filled the few details they had was a hard task. Prisoners had been released and transferred, none fitted the description of a Bull-like man.

The questioning of Tom continued, with many manifestations of Douggie, who was becoming increasingly violent while Tom was distraught. In the end, Mr Farmer insisted they stopped the questioning on medical grounds. Tom was seen by the two doctors and certified. Until the trial, he was held in the psychiatric department of a local prison. The Crown Court hearing was held, and the court order duly issued. The Police had failed to track down the Bull, so they couldn't even bring murder charges. Their search continued while Tom was sent to a secure unit in the Midlands.

It took a week before the furore of publicity died down enough for Clare to move back to Sylvie's cottage. It was a wrench to leave Sheila, but Clare was itching to get on with life. Lugging her bags up the path almost brought a lump to her throat, so much had happened since that Monday morning. Clare was returning a different person, sadder but probably not wiser. After leaving her bag she looked for the very first time into Alex's room, which he'd never let her in. Clare was surprised at its frugality, apart from the stereo and some books, there was nothing of the man to be seen. Sylvie joined her.

'Feels a bit sad doesn't it? I keep wanting to chuck it all out and re-decorate, but somehow I can't. I feel responsible,' she said.

'You're not the only one. It doesn't bear thinking about that none of this might have happened, if we'd left him alone. Still, he will be helped, he's in the best place possible.'

'Sylvie, have I told you about my plans for the Agency?'

'Several times,' Sylvie replied dryly. 'Who's this?'

A taxi had drawn up outside the gate. Helen laden with suitcases was making her way up the path.

'Oh Clare... I completely forgot to tell you. I gave her an open invitation....'

Clare was watching with interest, the two had yet to meet. She and Sylvie ran downstairs to help her with the bags. When Helen saw Clare she looked worried.

'I'm sorry, I didn't realise you'd be here. I don't want to intrude.'

'Oh you're not,' Clare hastily assured her.

'We were just in Alex Tom's room. I haven't had a chance to clear it.'

'I'm glad you haven't, it'll be nice to be close to him, even in a small way.'

Clare and Sylvie exchanged concerned looks.

'One thing I must ask of you, please don't let my parents know I'm here. I want to wait until things are sorted out with Tom before we stage a grand union. Duncan's been sworn to secrecy too.'

Sylvie and Clare agreed and helped to carry the bags upstairs. Helen surveyed the bare room.

'Is this all he had?'

'He took his clothes, they've not been found, but yes, this is it,' stated Sylvie.

'Clare, well, your relationship with him. Are we going to be in competition?' asked Helen in a rush.

Clare almost laughed. 'No, Helen, he's all yours. It was never a close relationship, and it was drawing to a finish, anyway. I'm looking after number one from now on. There's no reason, is there, why we can't be friends? I expect you'll want to know more about what he's been like.' Helen smiled her acquiescence.

'Let's chat over lunch, I'm starving,' interrupted Sylvie, and they made their way downstairs. Over beans on toast, Clare received quite an interrogation. It proved cathartic, she felt all the load of Alex, his problems and fears, transfer firmly onto Helen's capable shoulders. When she tried to apologise for telling the police about the murder, Helen stilled her.

'It would have come out at some stage,' she said with conviction.

'Tell Helen about the Bible,' interjected Sylvie. Clare scowled at her, she'd told Sylvie in a moment of intimacy because she'd felt so embarrassed by it.

'Well, at one stage, I grabbed this book. It was a Bible and somehow it was also in the kitchen. I must have thrown it I suppose.

Anyway, it was open at a bit about where Jesus cast out a demon. When I accosted Douggie, he said he knew Jesus but not me.' Helen jumped up. 'Tell me all that again.'

Clare blushing furiously did so.

'You don't really think he's inhabited by a demon?' she asked incredulously.

'It confirms things I'd already guessed.' Helen sat down again, still looking excited.

'Oh, you Christians are a bunch of cranks. He's schizophrenic. All that demon stuff went out years ago. Shouldn't you just be glad he's safe?'

They obviously didn't agree so Clare decided it was time to go for a walk. The lane wore a heavy mantle of summer. Late dog roses filled the air with their scent and the elderberries were turning from frothy foam flowers to green clusters of grapes. The grass and cow parsley ran rampant everywhere. Clare kicked at the growth. She felt the whole world was against her. She didn't want to go back to work, but she no longer had an excuse. Saying she needed time to get over the trauma was simply stalling for time. Everyone was waiting patiently, all dying to hear the gruesome details over an intimate coffee and Clare was sick of the whole thing. All the events seemed to be hanging over her like a thick glue. Clare didn't understand Helen's doglike devotion to Tom. She saw the room would become a shrine to him, and Helen would talk about no other subject. How was it possible for Helen cling on to someone who had done such awful things? Clare climbed over a gate and into a meadow. She threw herself down in a shady corner and picked a blade of grass to chew. The very air felt humid and oppressive. Perhaps she ought to make another new start.

No, she was sick of running. Clare wanted continuity, peace. How could she find it with Helen and Sylvie droning on all the time?

Clare remembered the brief peace she'd felt at the beach cottage and the vision of an idyllic life there with Chris. An intolerable ache for him rose up inside, but she thrust it down. He hadn't written or phoned. He must know she'd seen his deception and kept his silence like a coward. It was people who caused her problems. If she could get away from them, then life would be simple. Create a nest. Shut the world out, then perhaps she would find contentment. First of all, she knew she had to go back to the cottage and see if it still felt the same. Clare leapt up.

The afternoon was getting hot and drowsy when Clare finally found the cottage. She knew its rough location from her drive home in the police car. Her night flight in Aggie had taken an indirect route. The entrance was concealed in the yard of a large farm, not even a dog barked as she walked through. Despite the passage of the police vehicles the lane was nearly blocked by the undergrowth. Clare walked beneath an archway of bent oaks, which appeared to protect the cottage from the world. A name-plate was hanging crookedly on the gate post. 'Peacehaven.' Clare smiled at the appropriate name. The house was less weather-beaten on the leeward side. Roses worn out by years of neglect were vainly flowering around the door. Clare tried the front door and found only a gentle push was needed to get in. The smell of damp and rot was familiar, almost welcoming. The police hadn't bothered to clear up. There was still broken glass all over the kitchen floor. Clare pulled open the back door, and an ozone laden breeze filled the house, temporarily banishing the mustiness. The back doorstep invited Clare to sit, so she did, and watched the sun play games with the waves, making them jump to catch its light.

The honeysuckle was recovering from its battering, a few small flowers reaching out through the dead leaves. Clare breathed in deeply. Peace was still here, her trauma hadn't left any marks on the place. She would live here, rest and heal. Opening her eyes, Clare was temporarily blinded by the sun. When they had adjusted, she saw a picture of the grass mown and neat flowers in the beds. A child was climbing up the steps from the beach, wide-legged shorts, sandy feet and a crab dangling from his hand. The triumphant grin on his face belonged to her and Chris. Clare shook her head and stood up. The garden was part of her, but not that child. Carefully she closed the doors and said a mental goodbye for now to the cottage. She wanted no-one else there until she claimed it as hers. It took a long time to raise an answer at the Farm. Clare didn't go into deep explanations, she simply asked who owned the cottage and was it for sale or rent.

'That dump?' said the woman incredulously, looking at Clare as if she was an alien.

'It was his Dads, but he died a few years back. We were going to put the new cowman in there but he wanted the nearer place up the road. I suppose Fred might sell it at the right price. We'd have to have an access agreement. Call about ten tonight, he's out at the moment. After all the kafuffle there the other day he might be glad to be shot of it.' She gave Clare a grubby piece of paper with the number on it and shut the door.

Clare strode off, cock-a-hoop, beginning to plan the restoration. The money would have to come from somewhere, she'd have to crack on with the agency. Her head was so full of ideas that somehow Clare missed her turning. Even climbing to the top of a gate had her perplexed; woods, fields but no landmarks. Clare had gone too far to be able to retrace her steps. Her feet were sore, she was hot and thirsty. Her earlier eagerness evaporated into grumpiness. She walked a bit further then tried another gate. At last, she caught sight of a roof, so she climbed over and began to make her way towards it. Having to shut the edges of the crops made it seem even further than she'd thought. At last, it was only one field away, and she saw two roofs and washing hanging on a line.

It wasn't until Clare was practically on top of the houses that she realised where she was. To turn around was impossible, perhaps she might skirt around without being seen. Why did it have to be his place? Clare's thirst was overwhelming, and the heat was sapping her strength, there was no choice. She very nearly made it. She skirted around the edge of the other villa but the only way past Chris' side was along the track. To cross further up and walk past behind the hedge was out of the question, there were no gates. To make a run for it was the only option, but as she did Clare saw the garage door was open and Chris was working in there from the hammering coming out. Perhaps that would help her. Clare put on a spurt. His shout of 'Hi', gave wings to her feet, and she kept on until her breath was tearing her chest. She'd done it, he hadn't followed. Clare bent to her knees to ease the cramp. Then she heard the familiar growl and knew she was caught. It was time to face him. Maybe it was better to get it all out in the open. Clare stood in resignation. Chris stopped the Land Rover and looked down at her from the cab. She couldn't read his expression behind the sunglasses and oil.

'Who are you running from now Clare?'

'You.'

'Why?' He sounded shocked.

'Because you're a two-faced, lying bastard!'

Chris swung out of the cab and Clare cringed, she almost felt his anger. He stood, took his sunglasses off and wiped the sweat from his face.

'Clare, look at me. I've never lied to you.'

'Oh yes, you have. All that rubbish about women helping you through sleepless nights. I came around on that night and I saw you cuddled up on the sofa with one. How many do you have on your string of sob stories - did you want me dangling at the end?'

'Clare, look at me,' he demanded again. Clare raised her face, but not to meet his eyes.

'You came here on the night you were abducted?'

'You must know I did. I expect you both had a good laugh about it!' Clare said bitterly.

'Wait, a minute. You saw me and another woman?'

'Yes,' snapped Clare, did he want to prolong her agony? She saw once again that soft caress and knew how much she had wanted it for herself.

'Clare, that was my daughter, Tamsin. When I came to see her off, later on, we found stones all over her car as if someone had accelerated away in a hurry. So it was you and not that maniac.'

Clare nodded.

'The police were on my doorstep the next morning. I was there when they bought you and Alex out. You looked straight through me as if I wasn't there.'

'Then why didn't you come and speak to me, tell me the truth, instead of leaving me alone? I was in shock and needed you!' Clare shouted.

'I rang Sheila every day, but she said you never mentioned me. So I presumed all I'd said had meant nothing to you. I promised I'd wait, not force myself.' Chris' explanations came tumbling out.

Clare stood, not knowing what to do. She felt a fool, utterly stupid, with nothing of any sense to say. Clare wanted to crawl into the ditch and stay there. The silence between them stretched out until all she could do was turn and walk rapidly away. With every step, Clare took she was silently screaming if you want me, come and get me, prove it.

Chris watched, not knowing what she wanted. He tensed like an athlete, to sprint and catch her. He knew that if she walked away now, it was the end for them. Too much had been misunderstood. He'd let things ride too long in his fear of overwhelming her. Chris ran.

The pounding of feet made Clare tense all over, she didn't know what to expect. When his arms came around her, her body turned giddy with relief. His embrace was a sweet familiarity, strong and safe. Clare breathed in his aftershave of oil and sweat and felt the thinness of his body through his T-shirt, but it was strong. For a while, she froze, then she pulled away.

'Chris, I can't bear it. I've been through too much. I've been so scared, so alone, beaten and hurt. Every relationship I've had has ended disastrously. Phil swore undying love. Alex always seemed as steady as a rock, but both deserted and betrayed me. I don't want to face the future alone, but I've been preparing for it. Chris, if you take me on, you will have to reassure me constantly, be there when I need you. You're going to have to be strong for me because I'm wrung dry. If you're not up to this, then let me go now. I can't face anymore hurt. I think I'd kill myself first. You've got to be honest, I'd rather face the pain now when I'm half prepared.'

Keeping her distance, Clare anxiously searched his face. She saw nothing but tenderness, but he hesitated to reply. Clare's spirit began to sink.

'I will never let anyone hurt you again.' He'd only been searching for words. 'I told you I'd sworn to protect you and I mean it. I do have the strength, come, let me prove it to you.'

Chris took Clare's hand and lead her back up the lane, forgetting the Land Rover. He led her into the house and up the stairs. He threw open the door to the spare room and went in. The room was empty apart from carpet and curtains.

'I've spent every night this week, here, alone. I can do it Clare, her ghost is gone!'

Clare's response was to tilt her head up to receive his kiss. Once again she was astounded by the perfection of it. The way he healed her hurt. Tears that had been surging upwards swam away.

It was hours later, when the sun was beginning to dip behind the trees, that Chris thought to ask her what she'd been doing in the lane. They were sat in the back garden on a swing seat. Clare's head nestled onto Chris's lap; her still aching feet balanced on the armrest. She had told him all about her life. She wanted him to know everything, no dark secrets to spoil the calm waters she now lay in. Chris had told her of his upbringing in a middle-class area of Glasgow. The almost routine marrying of the girl next door, the challenging job, the move South, the birth of his daughter and the death of his wife. They lay on equal ground, luxuriating in simply being together.

'I'd come to the conclusion that I was meant to be alone. Do you remember the cottage on the beach where Alex found me? Before he arrived, I'd been looking around and had fallen in love with it. Today I decided I was going back to check on my original impressions. On my way home I got lost.'

'A little serendipity never hurt anyone,' quipped Chris. 'Did it still feel right?'

'Oh yes. I sat on the steps and basked in the sun. I don't know whether it's right to say this.'

Chris squeezed her arm to encourage.

'When I opened my eyes, I saw a little boy coming up the steps from the beach. He looked like us and that hurt me so much...'

Chris shifted so that he saw her face.

'Clare, when I said I was going to look after you, I meant it. I love you and will never betray you. The few years difference in our ages means I'm a different generation with perhaps old-fashioned standards. If I make a commitment, it's the full thing, no shacking-up together. It wasn't so with Pam, and it won't be with you.'

Clare felt a genuine pang of regret for the easier course she'd always steered.

'Have I been stupid again?'

'No, never think you're that. I haven't made myself clear.'

'Are you saying you want to marry me?'

'I am.'

Clare was silent for such a long time that Chris became worried.

'It's too much to take in,' she said, at last, the incredulity plain in her voice. 'But I'm going to say yes in case it all disappears.'

'There's no hurry. I'm always going to be around.'

Chris kissed her again, but with a new assurance now she was his. The slow darkness of summer had fallen and a few stars were coming out.

'It's getting late.' Chris shifted again. 'I'm going to take you home now.'

Clare had still imagined they'd be together through the night, despite what he'd said, but then she saw him in a new light. He was indeed far stronger than she'd ever imagined.

'In the morning,' Chris continued.'We've three things to do. First of all, we're going to Chardminster to buy a ring. Then we're going to look at your cottage. Then we're going to rescue Aggie.'

Clare was ashamed to find she'd completely forgotten Alex's gift.

'Poor Alex,' she said.

'Yes, poor Alex, but lucky, lucky for us. By the way, did you ever fill in the form Henry gave you? We could apply for joint membership now!'

Clare replied by chucking a cushion at him. Together they walked around the house and

into the lane where Chris had left his Land Rover
all those hours ago.

TOM
1993

The psychiatric unit was set in the grounds of a
Georgian manor. Built in the seventies, it was an
attempt to bring the faculty into current thinking.
The angular shapes and unusual angles in its
structure echoed the new ideas used to treat the
patients. The strengthened windows were
carefully concealed, along with the high
perimeter fence. The gardens were attended by
some of the more stable patients. Life followed
an orderly pattern as far as was possible in such
a place. This sunny August morning, the whole
unit was in an uproar due to the unannounced
arrival of two uniformed policemen. Several of
the male patients had needed sedation.

Mr Adams, the hospital manager, had
ushered the men as quickly as possible into his
office. He had plied them with coffee until the
furore died down, and he could call several of his
staff to the meeting.

Peter Jones and Jack Byrne came
bustling in with sheaves of notes under their
arms and wearing harassed expressions. The
trouble the police caused didn't make them feel
co-operative. Once their feathers were soothed,
Mr Adams cleared his throat and began.

'Thank you all for being here so quickly,'
he placated. 'Inspectors Rye and Spencer are
here with some news about Tom. However,
before they proceed, they would like a progress
report. Peter, can you give them an idea of how
Tom was when he arrived here?'

Peter wasn't going to stand up and feel like a lemon, so he shuffled the papers and began on the defensive.

'Tom arrived here in a thoroughly bewildered state, after some very heavy questioning while being held in custody. For several days he had to be sedated with chlorpromazine while he calmed down enough to be assessed. We understand that during most of the questioning he was Douggie and at times extremely violent.'

The policemen had enough grace to be shifting uneasily in their seats and so agreed with Peter's statement.

'Once Tom realised the pressure was off, we saw very little of Douggie. Tom felt abandoned and betrayed. In the next few weeks, Tom manifested some typical symptoms of schizophrenia, withdrawing into himself and rejecting offers of friendship. He still had the delusions of influence, i.e. of control, but at times he appeared to be quite a normal, well-balanced man. During these spells, he was willing to socialise when asked. But,' here Peter paused significantly to heap guilt on the police. 'So much damage had to be repaired. We had several calls and letters from his girlfriend and she filled us in a lot about his background. Tom's childhood had always been hidden from Miss Harrison but the one constant theme throughout was Tom's conviction that Douggie did exist, had a separate physical presence and he alone had carried out all the assaults. This meant that Tom functioned on a normal level as long as Douggie wasn't around. He knew that Douggie hated women and resented any in Tom's life; to the point of assaulting them. After the assault on Clare Brown, Tom was totally adamant that the two were separate; hence he refused to take the responsibility. It was all Douggie's doing. Now, this behaviour is unusual but not unheard of.'

'Unfortunately, and Miss Harrison has apologised for this; at one stage she accused Tom of being possessed by a demon. This opened a new corridor of thinking to him. Along with being pressed to reveal his past, he now had to consider he might have done the deeds, possessed or not. This would be devastating to a normal person let alone someone being interrogated. However, Tom began to settle down once we'd decreased his sedation. Please take over here Jack.'

'Tom began to understand that Douggie only existed in his head, and the horror of his actions caused a deep depression for a few months. We led him to evaluate the evidence for his beliefs and found alternative explanations. This is known as cognitive restructuring. He came to terms with his illness and co-operated with all the programmes we introduced.'

'The use of Pimozide has been particularly beneficial in his case. We've started him on self-management procedures; that is ways of blocking the manifestations. We found giving him a Walkman and putting it on full blast helped a great deal. Then we started role-play; particularly with women. At first he had a lot of trouble relating to women his mother's age, but he's progressing. These procedures are all ongoing. Tom is becoming a valued member of the unit. He's certainly a success story. We would like to think that he will one day live again in the community. He still feels deep grief for the harm he's caused and is quite happy to stay here, in case he's still dangerous. However, he has had visits from Miss Harrison, when there were no manifestations and the interview was mentioned. We will encourage these now. Family intervention is one of the best ways of re-integration.'

Mr Adams looked askance at the men. Inspector Ryan coughed and stood up.

'I feel I must let you know about matters in person because of the unusual nature of the case.'

'Guilt, because of their bad handling,' thought Peter.

'Our investigations into the murder of Tom's mother are now concluded. We've tracked down the 'Bull' whose real name is Richard John Marks. This is mostly due to the information you've passed on to us.'

'Mrs O'Neal, died of a stroke last year. She and Mr Marks married about ten years ago and were living in her house. Mr Marks gave us a full account of Tom's childhood. He was a difficult child, a loner who disappeared after informing Mr Mark's first wife about the affair.'

'So there's no murder involved?' butted in Peter.

'It was all in his head. We were trying to prosecute an innocent man. We've had a detailed report from the Crown Prosecution Service. Due to the length of time he's been held, we would not see fit to press charges for all the other offences, and the plaintiff is happy for that too.'

'So he could be a free man?'

'Well-no. Obviously, he's still certifiable and the Court Order still holds. However, if it can be proved he is cured, we will not stand in the way of an application to the Home Secretary for his release!'

The Inspector smiled as if bestowing Christmas gifts and rose to his feet to go. He smartly shook hands with everyone and left with the sensation of a job well done.

Mr Adams ushered the policemen out of the Unit, through the back entrance. Back in the office, the two men grinned at each other.

'Who's going to tell him then?'

'Shall we both?'

They made their way to a small room. Tom was sat on the bed, reading a heavy book. Peter tried not to frown, they hadn't been happy at Helen leaving him a Bible, but he was quietly evaluating it, and not getting any religious delusions. He put the book away and smiled.

'What can I do for you?' His courtesy as ever was impeccable.

'We've got some good news!' said Peter. 'The police have traced your mother. Tom, look me in the eye. Tom, you didn't murder her. You did run away after telling the Bull about the affair, but you never touched your mum. She and Mr Marks married ten years ago, and she died twelve months ago from a stroke.'

Tom's face drained of all colour, he didn't react at all in the way they'd expected. His hand began to shake, and he wept.

'Tom, remember what we've taught you.' Tom clenched his hands to stop the shaking while Peter fetched the Walkman. How his ears stood it they didn't know, the music was so loud. Gradually, under the hypnotic beat, he relaxed. Tom swallowed the pills, then lay down on the bed and fell into a deep sleep.

'Perhaps we should have broken it more gently?' Jack asked.

'No, I genuinely thought he would be pleased. This is most unusual; he'll have to be watched. Get Ken to put the monitor on for 24 hours.'

It wasn't until the next day that they began to understand Tom's reaction. It had been regret for the years spent running, for the harm he'd done in his actions. Tom went into a course of intensive counselling for several weeks before they broached the possibility of release. Tom needed a lot of convincing that he would be safe; he was already becoming institutionalised. It was only after meeting with Helen that he showed any enthusiasm. She brought brochures and spoke of a convalescent hotel in Cornwall, where they would rest and restructure their lives. Helen was Tom's family now. Together they went through lifestyle and social skill training so that Tom might eventually go back to gardening. There came a day when the unit could do no more.

The cogs of government move slowly. It wasn't until 13 months after his arrest that Tom packed his bags, together with his medication and a letter for the local Doctor and set off for Cornwall with Helen; a free man.

It was a real wrench to leave the unit, it had become like a womb to him. All the staff were intimate friends. There had been days out, but there was always his safe room at the end. Now he wasn't coming back, and that scared him. Tom hugged the knowledge that he was allowed to go back if he was unable to cope or had a relapse.

Tom wasn't sure about his feelings towards Helen. She'd been part of the identity of the old Tom. Did he want a relationship, when in so many ways he still didn't know who he was?

He felt he should love her, but it mustn't be out of gratitude. If it wasn't for her, he'd now be transferring to a bleak hostel. Travelling soothed Tom, and with his quandary unsolved, he fell asleep.

Helen stole covert looks at Tom while he slept. The time in hospital had changed him physically, he'd lost his tan and put on weight. When they were out, he had held her hand like a small scared child hanging onto a mother; everything she'd suggested he'd agreed to. She had seen the obvious relief on his return. Was he ready? Inside Tom, she knew there had to be a great strength which he needed to control the illness. He obviously needed space to organise his life, but she just couldn't stay away, her wait had been too long. Abandoning her knight-in-shining-armour when he was wounded was unthinkable.

She was guilty. Guilty of not telling the whole truth about their destination. It was indeed a place particularly suited for convalescence, but nearby was a Church, with a Pastor whose particular Ministry was Deliverance. Helen had been severely taken to task for the accusation of possession she'd thrown at Tom and had to bite her tongue when the idea was ridiculed. It was still a surprise that the Unit had let Tom keep the Bible. Apart from handing it over and saying it might help, she'd left the subject alone.

Helen knew Tom was schizophrenic, he manifested a lot of its symptoms, which the unit had taught him to control. Now, what he needed was deliverance and most of all, healing. Helen knew she was treading on thin ice. She didn't want to slap the face of the medical profession, but Tom was different; they saw only within their recognised parameters. None of the doctors at the Unit had any faith. The casting out of demons had been slung onto the scrap heap along with

Christian belief and morals when psychiatry had increased its knowledge of the working of the brain. Helen wanted a whole Tom, nothing but the best for him, and she knew only Jesus had the answer.

The car scrunched up the drive, and they stopped outside the Hotel. Gently, Helen called Tom to wake up. He stretched and looked about him, she saw it took him a while to find his orientation. Finally, he got out and inspected the Elizabethan facade. Hanging baskets festooned in lobelia and geraniums adding splashes of colour.

'They're going to have a lot of problems with greenfly.' He grinned and came back to help with the bags. Helen heaved a sigh of relief, he was going to be alright. Their rooms overlooked the sea. Although not adjoining, they were only a couple of doors away.

Tom threw open his suitcase and hung his clothes in an orderly precision. He set his washing things exactly on the basin and went to re-arrange them but stopped himself in time. Repetitive behaviour had to be controlled. He opened the windows and leant out to take deep breaths of ozone-laden air. He remembered the months in his little shack on the marshes and was relieved to find the memory held no pain. Far out at sea, a trawler bobbed up and down on the invisible waves. Tom felt like that trawler. He was in a sea with no coastline, and he knew was in for a certain amount of tossing before he found a port. He turned to answer a knock at the door.

'Lunch?' enquired Helen. 'Cor! You've got a better view than me,' she said, coming alongside him. 'I'm at an angle to the sea. At least the beds are younger than the house.'

Gingerly, Tom put an arm around Helen's shoulders. They looked at each other for a moment, each afraid of what the other might or might not feel. Tom's arm dropped - they turned and headed for the dining room. Over a plate of steaming pasties and vegetables, Helen broached the subject of what they would do.

'There's a quaint fishing village nearby with a pub and some shops. There're miles of coastal walks, and Newquay for discos and things.' Helen began suggesting.

Tom paused to reply. There were things he did want and getting himself straight came above all other things. He suspected Helen wouldn't be happy with his ideas.

'I want to read, sleep and walk, and most of all, think. If it means all day in my room, then that's what I want. I know it sounds incredibly selfish, but I need time on my own. There's never space to think things through to the end at the unit. Someone is always organising a meal, counselling or an activity. I know that'll leave you at a loose end, but I need the space.'

'I know. Did you see that cardboard box? I've about 20 books to read and I need time for me too. How about we meet at breakfast, see if our plans coincide and go from there?'

Tom smiled. It had been easy after all. With a clear conscience, he took himself and a book to bed for the afternoon. He moved the bed as close as possible to the window and fell asleep before he'd read a page. Tom slept the rest of the day and right through to the next morning. Helen heard his snores when she called him for supper.

Breakfast found him, refreshed and eager for the new day. The unit seemed miles away, another life. Much to his surprise, he wanted to spend the day with Helen. Tom had a map ready when she joined him.

'How do you fancy a l0 mile stroll to Port Jacob and back?' he said breezily.

'I was planning on going to Church this morning. I can always go this evening instead.' She didn't want to disappoint him.

'I might come with you this evening then.' Helen's jaw nearly dropped in surprise. Tom felt more of a desire to please than any real conviction. He'd read the Bible through, enjoyed its peace and had liked Jesus tremendously, but he saw him as no more than an extremely foolish man. Tom didn't see how a 2000-year-old document would have any bearing on his life today.

Before they reached Port Jacob, they stopped for a rest. The sun was blazing in a clear sky, but the stiff breeze made them feel almost cold. A lee from the wind behind some gorse bushes was found, and they sat on the springy turf. Helen had brought some squash and biscuits in a small haversack. Once the snack was devoured, they lay back in the sunshine and dozed. Helen came to first and watched Tom sleep. His face seemed part of her, she had searched and waited so long that the thought he might want an independent life scared her. She turned and found a small red Gospel in the haversack. Helen was so engrossed that she was surprised to look up and find Tom watching her.

'Can't understand why he let them do it!' Helen couldn't think who Tom meant.

'What sort of father, if Jesus was his son, lets his only child be tortured and executed?'

'He had to, it was why he came. The Father's love is greater than we can imagine. Someone whose son is eternally part of him, but his love for the greater family is as equally important. The Father is so hurt by the disobedience and disloyalty shown by the family that he tries all means to get them to be reconciled to him.'

'Go on.'

'God gave the Jews laws and regulations by which if they committed a crime they paid for it by sacrifice. For example, their best ram lambs or a goat, and the debt was paid. The Jews ignored these rules or twisted them to their own satisfaction. God promised Noah he wouldn't send another flood as a punishment, so he'd run out of ways of well, forcing their love. The regulations in the law are too much for man to bear, they could never get them right. There was always a penalty to bear.'

'God offered the Jews a choice. Jesus came to earth, told everyone the way to Father and then accepted the betrayal by dying on the cross. He was the one last sacrifice. As God's own, he took the rap for all we've done. This repealed all the laws and regulations. It's like a magistrate sentencing someone, then paying the fine himself. When we believe in Jesus, he takes on board all our punishment and sets us free to walk hand in hand with him forever. No more regulations or rituals. It's all there on the Cross. However bad we may feel we are, nothing's too bad for God. He'll clean up and bless the worst person on earth when he comes and says, I'm sorry, I love you. Then we have a true relationship with him, that's just, amazing'

Tom looked at his boots then jumped up.

'Let's see how much further we can get before we need to go back. Does that make sense?' He grinned and grabbed Helen's hand to help her up. They walked in silence, Helen not daring to take the subject further.

The Church was old, matching the village, but inside the pews were new, and the decor fresh. The congregation was small, but even so, Helen and Tom sat at the back. Helen had given Tom ample opportunity to back out, but he seemed determined to keep his side of the bargain. Where had all his fierce opposition gone?

Tom didn't sing, but sat and listened to the modern energetic choruses, tapping the beat on his knee. He seemed quiet while the Pastor prayed. It was only in the second session of singing that Helen noticed his hands were shaking. She remembered her lessons and gave him a pill, which he swallowed but the shaking increased. The Pastor began to preach and Tom started muttering beneath his breath. Helen pulled his arm, but it was like a rock. Helen had merely hoped to introduce Tom to Frank. She'd never expected this. She beckoned to the steward who was sat nearby.

'My friend is ill.' Helen didn't want to say any more at this stage. 'Frank knew we were coming, but I'm worried something may happen. Can you tell him Helen and Tom are here, he'll understand.'

Helen sat down again, being careful not to touch Tom and began to pray. After a couple of minutes, the eruption came. Tom stood up and a stream of blasphemy came pouring from his lips. It was Douggie's voice. He reviled the Church, the Pastor and Jesus, then began taunting them that he was the strongest, none of them could beat him. Several of the congregation left, but Frank came striding down the aisle. He gestured to Helen to let Tom out of the pew.

'In the name of Jesus!' began Frank, but before he got any further, Tom lunged out and hit him squarely in the face. Frank reeled across the pew gasping for breath.

'Help me!' screamed Tom.

'Thought you can stop me, did you preacher man?' said Douggie and lunged again. This time, Frank was ready and leapt over the pew to distance himself.

'In the name of Jesus!' he cried in a gasping voice and ducked a blow. 'I command you, spirits of mental illness, deceit and anger who call themselves Douggie, to come out. You are not to speak any more or to harm Tom.'

While Frank said these words, Tom recoiled, to fall with the force of being thrown to the floor. On the ground he began to writhe about, curling in upon himself until he was in a foetal position. He began to shriek as if to drown Frank's words.

'Go now to the place which has been your destiny since Jesus shed his blood, died on the Cross and rose again, defeating your master Satan. Go in the name of Jesus!'

Frank's voice rose to an authoritative shout. The shriek continued for a while longer then died away as if disappearing down a tunnel. Frank knelt beside Tom.

'Jesus, fill this child with your peace that passes all understanding.'

He began to pray incoherently, and everyone joined in. They prayed for Tom's salvation and for blessings. Tom lay still, then gradually began to uncurl. After ten minutes he sat up and yawned.

'Hello, friend,' said Frank. 'How do you feel?'

'Well, calm. What happened?' Frank looked askance at Helen.

'You had a fit, but Frank has prayed with you, so it won't happen again,' she explained.

'Would you repeat something after me?' asked Frank. 'Say Jesus is Lord, several times until you feel happy with it.'

And Tom did. At first with a real indifference, then a slow smile began to creep across his face and they all heard the wonder in his voice.

'You're right Helen,' he said incredulously. 'He must be because I've never felt this way in my life. I'm warm, and inside is such a feeling of wonder; it's amazing!'

He rose to his feet and saw the people standing about and blushed. Tom had never blushed before and it wasn't unpleasant. Everyone was smiling, and the embarrassment disappeared.

'Would you like to stay for the rest of the service?'

Everyone remembered where they were and returned to their seats. Tom sat clasping Helen's hand with the grip of a bear, an idiot grin on his face. The sermon had gone out the window because they sang and prayed for the next hour. Helen was surprised to find Tom had a good tenor voice. They hung on after the congregation had left, and Frank joined them.

'Are you still feeling amazed?' he asked jovially. It seemed almost a rhetorical question.

'Will you come and see me tomorrow morning? I understand you've been ill, and I'd like to pray with you to make sure you're

completely well, and I'm sure you'll want to ask some questions.' Tom eagerly accepted.
Helen had never seen a grown man skip before, but Tom did, all the way back to the Hotel.

In the morning, they arrived on time at Frank's house. Tom was sat in a position of honour in the study and Frank's wife joined them. Frank, sporting a black eye subjected him to an intense scrutiny, and then prayed quietly for him. Tom stayed put, the smile still on his face.

'Helen, Sue, with Tom's permission, I would like to lay on hands for the baptism of the Holy Spirit and healing.'
Tom grinned, 'I feel fine, but if you think it'll get any better, I'm all for it.'

They prayed around Tom, their hands gently resting on his head.
Quite suddenly he slumped and Helen had to prop him up. Everyone continued praying until his eyes opened and joy lit his face.

'You are now filled with the Holy Spirit, he lives in you. You are healed in the name of Jesus!'
Tom looked at him thoughtfully, then dipped in his pocket and brought out a container of pills.

'So I won't need these?'

'You must keep them until you have seen a doctor, and he stops their prescription.'

Almost regretfully, Tom returned them to his pocket and said, 'I know the unit brought me to terms with my life, but I agree, God's healed me. I can remember periods of real anger in my life, and I know I hurt Clare, but it doesn't matter anymore. Was it some sort of final fit I had last night?'
Helen glanced at Frank, but Tom intercepted the look.

'Oh, I understand. You cast him out.'
Everyone was stunned, he wasn't supposed to know yet.

'It's not always best to know. We wanted to be sure you were ready.'

'It's no problem. In a way, it's made it easier knowing I was under an evil influence. It's gone, and I suppose you've just been checking, but I know every cell in my body is clean. I've never been free of fear. I've spent all my life running. Now I'm going to stop and let Jesus take over!'

'Really?' exclaimed Helen, still shocked.

Tom had said nothing about his experience to her, beyond how happy he felt. The sense of unreality and shock remained with Helen for the next few days. It was all her dreams realised yet it seemed like a film being shown to he; her part was on the periphery.

Tom was so excited that he wanted to rush about and tell everyone. Frank counselled him to wait. If he turned up at the unit in his present condition, he'd be put back in again for religious delusions. He just suggested Tom have a check-up with a local Doctor who was also a friend which he did. Blood tests and regular check-ups over the next couple of weeks confirmed the symptoms were gone. Everyone saw he was a completely different person. The hotel staff remarked on his cheerfulness, he walked with a bounce in his stride, ate like a horse and no longer needed hours of sleep. Tom began to grow a beard which made his face seem genial, no longer secretive and inward-looking. Gone were the nervous gestures with his hands, and when Helen saw inadvertently into his room one day, it was in complete disorder.

Frank spent a lot of time with Tom, counselling him and answering all his questions. When he wasn't at Frank's, he was in his room reading the Bible and all the books Frank lent him, in a growing desperation to keep pace with the questions.

Helen found her own faith being tested. She'd thought it was a tried and honed thing, but in the light of Tom's zeal, it seemed frail and ill-considered. Why hadn't she been like this? Their original plans for the holiday remained. Each morning Tom would be bouncing around with excitement at his arrangements for the day, and somehow Helen was never included. She began to feel irrelevant and lonely.

One evening found Helen sat in the rose garden, watching the stars come out with fairy light intensity. Why were they so blurred she wondered? Then realised she was weeping - weeping with self-pity, and she felt cross with herself.

Tom seemed to have no need for her, he was so full of joy. What if he was set on a solitary course? Then she'd just have to continue on her own. She managed before and she could now. The Lord would find her a new task; her faith would manage that. So why did the tears keep on flooding down? It wasn't as if she sought his eternal gratefulness, to bind him to her, but the love she felt for him was undiminished. She didn't know what he felt for her.

By sheer force of will, Helen stopped the tears, blew vehemently into her hanky and went inside. On her way in, she booked the rooms for another fortnight. It was postponing the inevitable, but she wouldn't let go yet. Helen nearly bumped into Tom as she left her room the next morning. He had a strange look on his face.

'How do I pay for this?' He handed her a Hotel bill. Helen snatched it away. The manager must have sent them up before she re-booked.

'Don't worry about it, leave it with me.' She turned to put it back in her room.

'You've paid for everything haven't you, and I've never given it a single thought.'

'You weren't expected to.' He followed her in and sank onto the bed.

'I'll make this up to you.'

'There's no need. It's a gift.'

'That's not the point. I've just taken you for granted. You stuck by me throughout everything, never complained, fought for me, never let me down despite all the things I've done. I've used you.'

'I never expected payment,' Helen repeated. 'Ever since you picked me up out of the dirt, I've wanted to return the care you gave me. Now we're quits. Don't say any more. You still need to sort yourself out, don't feel beholden to me.'

'So where do I go now?' The bleakness in his voice made Helen look him in the eye. The joy was extinguished. She came and sat beside him.

'I never looked beyond this holiday. I was so thrilled to have you all to myself that I never thought it through. I suppose I had a vague idea of us living in my house in Birmingham. I can see now that I was wrong to think of trading on our past relationship, too much has changed.'

'I never realised it either. The unit mentioned a hostel. I suppose I'd better go there. Helen, did you want to repay me only in money?'

'No!' Helen forced the next words out. This was make or break for them. 'I love you and now you're healed, you're twice the person you ever were before and that scares me. I don't see any space for me in your life.'

'Helen, I can't have any future without you.'

Helen was in his arms, engulfed in that sweetness she'd been wanting for so long. The strength in his arms was enough to love her all her life. Tom's face was buried in her hair.

'I've been so wound up in myself, I forgot how I needed you. It's not gratefulness, it's not a tie. It's the feeling I had for you when I came back from work and saw you curled up in that armchair. It hasn't changed, it's been there all along, submerged in all the dross. Together we have so much to do. I want to meet the world I've run from for so much of my life. I can't do that alone. Can I come to Birmingham?'

Helen stood up and felt overwhelmed with shyness. Tom was beaming.

'I've just booked for two more weeks, but I don't want to stay here anymore. I want to go home too,' said Helen.

She looked up into his mesmerising blue eyes and couldn't wait to show the world the Tom she'd found.

CLARE
1993

Clare woke early on the day of her wedding when the birds had scarcely begun to wake up. She saw the elegant dress hanging from the wardrobe door, and could barely believe it was real. Somehow her fantasies had never got as far as marrying, and now she saw only the day itself, nothing beyond. Clare knew the main joy would be in sharing the night with Chris, no longer having to wave goodbye on the doorstep. The preparations had gone ahead with such a speed, that Clare had spent the past couple of months in a whirl. Chris had taken charge, and she had been swept along in the tide. He'd refused to let her pay a penny out of her own small savings. At first, Clare had resented that, until she had seen the size of the bills and realised her own contribution would have been but a drop in the ocean.

The emerald ring she wore caught the first ray of sun. Clare felt a plunge of pure happiness. She'd spent a lot of time admiring her left hand in the past months, it was a confirmation of something nebulous. Being in love had changed Clare, the ache inside her was filled at last; she felt her personality expand in that new freedom. She no longer worried what people thought of her and she had the strength to stand up to people like the Harrisons. Having her own man stopped Clare looking at men with that speculative gleam. She relaxed in their company and found they reacted differently, treated her as a person, no longer with the uneasiness she'd generated before. Life was good, and Clare found happiness in all she did; down to the most tedious of tasks.

Every day she learnt more about Chris. He was basically gentle, with that strong sense of humour, but on rare occasions, his temper did flare up. Every time Clare entered the garage, she saw the dent he'd made in the wall by throwing a spanner in frustration. Clare learnt patience too. Whatever time he estimated it would take to finish a job on the Land Rover, she had to double it and add extra cups of tea. Chris at last found his appetite and was visibly plumper, although he would never be fat on his wiry frame. Dreamily content, Clare had even bought a cookbook, and found concocting new dishes a way to pass the time while he played with the Land Rover.

Aggie had been hauled home and repaired enough to be roadworthy; a rebuild for her was on the list for after the honeymoon. The Club had held two more rallies which Chris and Clare had attended as spectators. Again, competing was shelved until later. Clare enjoyed the easy camaraderie of Chris's friends and had even told Jane about her misjudgement, which had caused a certain amount of hilarity.

Chris had fallen in love with Peacehaven. He went round with a more objective view than Clare and had seen its faults, such as the dry rot and collapsing window frames. When Clare heard the owners price for it, she realised it would have been way beyond her reach. To her surprise, Chris had haggled, his accent growing broader along with his obvious enjoyment of the deal. He came up with every argument under the sun. By the end, Clare was convinced the place was a slum. The men shook hands on a price nearly half the original demand and all went home pleased. Clare hadn't known the villa was sold and the profits from that covered the repairs and acquisition of Peacehaven. In her mind's eye, she saw scaffolding encasing Peacehaven, and couldn't believe that one day it would be ready for them to move in.

Helen and Clare had lived in the cottage in an uneasy truce, Sylvie was in London. When the news about Tom being sent to the unit was announced, Clare tried not to show her relief as Helen packed her bags. Having Chris eased her hate and anger at Tom; all she felt was sorry that Helen had to waste her time on someone who would be in a mental hospital for the rest of his life.

The plans for Clare's Agency were shelved. It seemed everything was on hold until after the wedding. Everyone Clare worked for was full of good advice about it too. Even Mrs Lock in a moment of rare intimacy told her 'it wouldn't be too bad' on the wedding night. Clare no longer cared about the mundane nature of her work. All her misgivings about its lack of a future seemed to have evaporated.

One weekend Chris's parents arrived on a flying visit. They were en route for a Caribbean Cruise. Tactfully they never mentioned Pam, and Clare had the conviction that they'd lost interest in Chris a long time ago. They were far too busy enjoying their retirement. Chris said that his father had worked long hours, to put away savings and his childhood had been dogged by demands for thriftiness. At times he remembered this and was careful with money, yet he was quite likely to blow a ridiculous amount on a Land Rover spare the very next day.

The visit unsettled Clare. She wanted her parents at the wedding, her father to give her away, it was the correct thing to do. She wanted everything perfect at the start of her new life. Chris' daughter Tamsin was at college near Clare's old home. They wanted her to be a Maid of Honour and Clare felt they should ask her in person. It was difficult enough to think of herself as a wife, let alone in the role of stepmother. A trip north was necessary.

Chris suggested they write to Clare's parents first and warn them they should expect a visit. Clare took a long time in writing a conciliatory letter and with it, she enclosed a cheque for £100; the amount she had stolen all those years ago. They allowed a week between posting and the visit, during which there was no reply. Clare remembered her parents would only go to the bank once a month and wasn't surprised when the cheque not cashed.

Early one Saturday morning they set out on the long drive. Clare felt a deep sense of foreboding. She tried to imagine how her parents would look, but she was unable. All she hoped for was that the years had mellowed them, and they would forgive. The motorway ran past the village of Boarwiden, and so they had to backtrack from the next exit. In the country, little seemed to have changed, it had simply shrunk. Boarwiden itself still boasted only one shop, and the only concession to new times was a newly painted school. They turned past the Chapel which caused Clare to shudder and then they were by the farm.

Time had stood still. Cows, although they bore different markings were just as thin and the muck heap steamed with a familiar reek. The house looked worn out, greats cracks in its brickwork by the eaves looked like the creases of old age on a face. The windows appeared black and threatening. Clare gripped Chris's hand as they walked up the uneven path and round the side to the kitchen.

'Hello?' Clare called cautiously. If the latest dog was as vicious as old Sam, they may have to make a quick retreat. There was no answering growl. They had just reached the door when it was snatched open, and a pitchfork was pointed in their direction. Clare's parents came out. They seemed to have shrunk. Along with their surroundings, they looked old and beaten by the elements and somehow even looked alike. Clare instantly recognised the look in their eyes. She had seen it so many times when a beating was in the offing.

'Jezebel!'

'Wicked harlot!'

'You've broken the commandments. Thou shalt not steal! Honour thy Father and Mother. How dare you come back here, with all your vile sin? You're no child of ours, you're a devil!'

'You're no kin. Evil one. You were bad right from the start.'

'Begone Satan!'

Chris and Clare backed rapidly away from the two-man act. If it hadn't been so evil, it could have been funny. Finally, Clare found her voice.

'Mum, Dad. I'm sorry. Can't you forgive me? I've repaid the money. I've said I'm sorry, what more do you want?'

'Nothing. Go back to your nest of vipers,' they hissed in unison.

Clare's father fished in a dirty pocket, took out Clare's letter and threw it. Clare let it lay where it fell, she wasn't going to give in.

'Can't you even meet me half way and come to the wedding?' Clare pleaded again.

'Never will we mix with the devil in disguise. We know you're a thief and a slut.' Clare's Dad lunged violently with the pitchfork. Fortunately, the gate was open, so Clare and Chris ran to the car jumped in and drove off with a flurry of mud. Clare caught a glimpse of her parents, still brandishing their weapon; a triumphant look on their faces.

'I should never have tried. 'My suspicions were right on how they would behave. I wanted everything perfect.' Clare tried not to cry.

'You've tried. All the responsibility lies with them now. They're obviously off their rockers and you're better off without them. Forget it, you've managed for years without them. Besides, you've got me now!'

Clare saw his lopsided grin and realised he was right. All she could do was wash her hands of them.

'Who will give me away then?' Clare wailed, the practicality of the situation coming home.

'I've been thinking about that. Promise not to laugh. Bill or Mr Harrison!' Clare exploded into laughter born of tension. Somehow Bill seemed too young for that role. Mr Harrison did seem a more likely candidate. He had been sympathetic in his own way when she had returned to work, even patting her on the shoulder like a pet dog. He would do. Clare wanted everything perfect, but she was coming to see there would have to be compromises. They pulled into a lay-by, and Chris pulled out a roadmap.

'We're only an hour from Loughborough. How about going on to Tamsin now?'

'Shouldn't we call first, she may be in lectures or something?' Clare didn't want another disastrous meeting.

'I've breezed in before and it's been fine.'

Chris pulled out of the lay-by and accelerated away. The hall of residence was distinguishable from the others only by the name emblazoned over the door. They were hit by the throb of a heavy bass beat from one end of the corridor and the smell of burning food from the other. They strode down the corridor, a few students eyeing them in mild distaste. Clare felt old for the first time in her life. Hammering on the door, they heard a muffled, 'come in.'

The door pushed open, and they saw Tamsin on the bed, book in hand. The small room was in a state of total disorder; books and clothes lying in equal abandon everywhere. Tamsin leapt up, a furious glow of embarrassment on her face as she tried to pick up the carnage.

'I didn't expect you until tomorrow. I was going to tidy up.'

Clare leant down to help, scared that this was going to end in another argument. Unfortunately, the first thing she picked up was a pair of men's boxer shorts. Clare caught Tamsin's eye, and they froze. A conspiratorial grin appeared on Clare's face as she hastily pushed them out of sight under a box. Chris was looking out of the window, the angle of his shoulders belied the beginnings of anger. At last things were in some sort of order. Clare plumped down on the chair.

'You can stop the angry father business now Chris, it's tidy.'

He turned, and she saw him check what he'd been planning to say.

'I suppose this is an attempt to blackmail me into a frock to be a bridesmaid,' stated Tamsin.

'Wouldn't dare. We were thinking of Maid of Honour, but I can't think of any colour that would go with those boots!'

Tamsin roared with laughter and at last the ice was broken. Chris held his peace while his women made friends.

The smile caused by that reconciliation stayed on Clare's face as the alarm clock began its furore. She groped around, hammered it off and looked at the time. From now on there wouldn't be a moment for grief or anger; this was her day. It was going to be perfect after all…

Sylvie's job wasn't quite what she'd expected. The interviews with the magazines had come to an end when she began to recognise the interviewers as teams who'd already interrogated her. Numb with disappointment, Sylvie had gone home and examined her motives by putting them in writing, and found them dominated by salary. It was while she was recovering from the shock that she saw the advertisement for a Night Assistant at a Christian women's hostel. With nothing to lose, she went for it and got it.

Now she sat in the wine bar, bleary-eyed from her day's sleep; clock-watching so she wouldn't keep Brenda waiting. Why was Duncan always late? Some nights the job was boring, the women either sleeping or non-communicative. On others, there would be the excitement when the Police brought someone in, and Sylvie felt she was being of some use. There had been some talk of swapping shifts to give her more experience, but Sylvie was very much having to prove her worth first. She had never thought to find satisfaction in anything except journalism and so was now rejoicing at the unexpected path that God was leading her on.

Sylvie was sharing a bed-sit with two nurses and their paths rarely crossed to their mutual satisfaction. She was even toying with selling the cottage once Clare and Helen had vacated it, now that she seemed to be heading for a long stay in the smoke. Sylvie's elbow slipped, along with her head and she nearly knocked over her drink. Why on earth had she agreed to meet Duncan? Before all the excitement had died down, he'd reverted to his usual brittle self; even flirting with the policewomen. There seemed to be no hope for him.

Duncan was thinking along very much the same lines as he swung through the double doors into the smoky atmosphere. He could have been with Veronique or Sally, who would smile and pretend to be surprised at his well-rehearsed raised eyebrow and nod towards the bedroom. However, it was urgent to meet this celibate, cross-patch who would probably doze off at the end of a sentence, if the plans were to succeed. He had arrived, so he shrugged and ploughed in.

The peck he gave Sylvie on the cheek was just about permissible, and he was careful not to let his arm linger too long on hers. He'd been right, she was heavy-lidded with sleep.

'Can't understand the attraction in your job. You'll be nocturnal before long and start growing fur,' he drawled. She didn't see the joke.

'Duncan, you invited me here. Why wouldn't a phone-call do?'

'Well, I need your help!' He did his best smile.

'Wonders will never cease,' Sylvie yawned.

'Helen's dumped the big reconciliation scene on me. She's over bothering the lunatic asylum, visiting Tom, and just hasn't got the time. I've had to arrange three sets of social engagements to meet at the same time, the same place, without telling them what it's all about.'

'But you've done it, so where do I fit in?' Duncan winced, he'd hoped to build up to the next question gently.

'Well, I need you to come and act as mediator!'

'What!' exploded Sylvie, fully awake.

'If there's someone there from outside the family they won't dare misbehave, and it might make things just a little calmer.'

'Might they just not look pained and ask if I'd like to use the loo, then lock me in while they beat you and Helen senseless?' This was the Sylvie Duncan identified with.

'You'll do it then?' He grinned, switching the Duncan charm on full blast. Sylvie found herself powerless.

'Oh, alright. Do I get a chance to look at my social engagements?'

'Sunday evening. I've booked a suite at the Savoy. We're all having dinner, then once they're mellowed, we'll go upstairs and Helen will float in.'

'Good grief Duncan, I haven't got a pair of jeans without a hole in them, let alone a posh frock! My salary barely covers food and electricity, let alone a Selfridge's account.'

'Go to Harrod's and charge it to me.'

'You're kidding.'

'It'll go some way to pay the debt of gratitude I owe my referee.'

For a moment they met eye to eye, then both ducked away.

'I'm going to be late.' Sylvie swigged the last of her mineral water.

'Does that rust bucket of yours still go? You can give me a lift to work, and to the wedding as a payment.' She marched out before he could reply.

On Sunday evening Sylvie felt a total fraud as she stepped out of the taxi and marched into the Savoy. She carried 32p of change in her purse, her perfume was borrowed along with the shoes she teetered on. Duncan was waiting, debonair in his dinner suit, hair slicked back. There was no sign of the family. Momentarily she wondered if this was another of his amorous traps, then felt swamped with guilt when she saw Peter leaning against the bar behind him. Duncan took her arm and with a conspiratorial grin, swept her in.

'Peter, old chap - remember Sylvie?'

He swung around and Sylvie was horrified to see from the distant look in his eyes he'd already been drinking.

'Sure - remember the old sheep-dip we all used to swim in?' He was able to turn on the charm as well as his brother. Sylvie found herself handed a gin and tonic, which she sipped gingerly, she was out of the habit.

'Well, here's Ma and Pa, right on time for a change.'

Sylvie turned around and saw the Harrisons peering around the end of the bar until they spotted Duncan. They glided over with relieved 'ahs' and 'how lovely to see yous'. Sylvie was swept into a maelstrom of chat and gentle questioning as they were led into the dining room. By the end, she was out of depth and finding cold feet.

Her reporter's instinct knew the game. She was being gently, tactfully cross-questioned and examined, to see if she met the mark. Her anger started to rise because Duncan made no attempt to dissuade them from their conclusions and to some extent encouraged them. By the time they walked to the lift, she was simmering enough to give Duncan a swift kick on the ankle when they weren't looking and subject him to her fiercest glare. He replied with a blank look as if totally innocent. Sylvie wanted to murder him.

In the lush sitting-room, they all sank to seats while Duncan served them with liqueurs. At last, he cleared his throat and all the eyes swivelled expectantly to him.

'Well, I imagine you've all been wondering why you were called here tonight. You've been guessing too, but I say now you're all totally wrong.' Sylvie tried not to glare at him again.

'There's a lot of talk about sheep returning to the fold in the Bible - you remember Rev Anstay used it a lot in his sermons.' They now looked bewildered, a bit lost, a little like sheep themselves.

'There is someone here who wants to return to the fold.' Duncan swept over to a large pair of doors and with the air of a conjurer, flung them open. In walked Helen, made up, dressed to kill, a small diamond crucifix shining in the black bodice of her dress.

There was a long stunned silence. The first one to move was Mr Harrison. He leapt up from the sofa, and ran to Helen crying, 'my girl' repeatedly as he hugged her, kissed her, then stood back to look her up and down.

'You look magnificent!'
He grabbed her arm and pulled her back to the sofa. Mrs Harrison sat, her face ashen.

'I thought I told you to never, ever come back again,' she said in a steely voice.

'That was a long time ago. I'm still your daughter. I'm not on drugs, drink, and I'll never ever embarrass you like that again,' Helen stated firmly, hanging onto her father's hand.

'Mother, can't you forgive and forget, so we can be together again?'

'But you've wrecked Peter's life.'

'Oh no I didn't. I set him free, didn't I, Pete?'

In the electric light, Peter looked very like his mother, his face of a similar line. They all waited for him to speak. He cleared his throat and looked around the room.

'Yes, you did. I never had the courage to tell you, Mother, because you were so involved in being angry at losing face. The marriage would never have worked. We got engaged at a very drunken party and neither of us had the courage to back out until Helen barged in. Yes, you saved me Helen, and I've never stopped thanking you for it.' Peter grinned at Helen.

'Then why did you let me go on, all these years, feeling bitter about my lost grandchildren? Feeding my hatred at Helen?' Mrs Harrison demanded.

'Because you never gave me the chance. You were so involved with anger, you never listened to anyone's opinion except your own. Mother; you must listen now. I'm sorry if you've had these years of anger, and I'm sorry for my cowardice. Now we've got a chance to make amends. I forgave Helen a long time ago, so can you forgive her too?' He stood up and walked over to his mother. He and Helen took her hands. For a moment there was a look of utter fury on Mrs Harrison's face, then the veneer cracked and she burst into tears, and hugged her twins.

It was too much for Sylvie, she really was a spare part. She rose and made for the exit. She nearly escaped before Duncan caught up with her. He swung the door shut behind them.

'You bastard,' hissed Sylvie forgetting she didn't swear. 'You let them think we were getting engaged just to distract them. I've never been so embarrassed in my life.'

'Would that be such a bad thing?'
Sylvie resisted the Duncan gaze.

'Oh no, you don't. Haven't you learnt by now? I'm not small game.'

'I know it. I'm sorry. I handled the whole thing badly. Come and have a drink with me?' By a touch, Sylvie saw his hands were shaking. The great and marvellous Duncan was upset. He did have some honest emotion in him. Sylvie forgave him.

'Alright. At least they're all catching up, and are reconciled, no harm came of it. Did it have to be so theatrical?'

'I think they appreciated the neutral ground. Especially when she tells them about her faith and then Tom.'

Sylvie guffawed.

'Haven't they had enough shocks for one night?'

'You never know with Helen.'

Duncan seated Sylvie at a corner table. To her surprise, he came back with her usual mineral water.

'Sylvie, I'm sorry,' Two apologies in one evening were astounding. All her conceptions about Duncan were in a whirl.

'Is there ever a chance you'd re-consider me?'

Duncan had known as he sat watching Sylvie adroitly field his family's questions, that here was someone who was more than his match. She was different and had that something which he'd been subconsciously searching for in his manic promiscuity all his life. He understood the regret he'd felt and now wanted to try to grab his chance of redemption. The past few weeks had found his cocaine flushed down the loo because it sickened him, and the endless succession of identikit girls a yawning bore. He'd only had the courage to admit it to himself that night.

Sylvie was feeling echoes of the thrall he'd held her in as a young girl and was enjoying the newness of the old sensation. Yes, she did want him; the inner Duncan, but not the cynical, worldly wise outer. There was only one way.

'Alright Duncan, but on my terms. I know it'll take you a long time to change your spots. Any two-timing or double-crossing, that's it. No drugs.'

Duncan jumped, he'd forgotten she knew.

'No showing off cash, or frittering it on me. I'll just put it in a charity box.' He tried to assume a face that looked humble.

'And now and then you'll come with me to Church or a meeting, but there will be no pressure.'

'Do I get any say in it?'

Duncan suddenly longed for a blank-faced blonde who wouldn't lay down the law.

'Of course, go on.' She waited, hoping she hadn't gone too far.

'Right. I reserve the right to wine and dine you occasionally, without any remarks about third world countries. The right to buy gifts on suitable occasions. You will have to understand I cannot change all of my spots, but I'll try to remove some,' he stated.

They grinned at each other and it seemed they were back at the village disco.

'Thought there was more to it than that!' A heavy hand thumped down on Duncan's shoulder. It was Peter.

'Come on, we're opening some champagne and celebrate, and you're going to tell us your part in all this young lady!'…

The longest Indian summer on record was in its dying throes on the morning that the church at Bathurst was looking its most glorious. A generous hand had swamped every windowsill and clear surface with displays of late summer flowers. The scent wasn't cloying because a steady breeze trickled its way through the door and out an open window. Outside was hot parched heat. Robins were fighting over territory in their strange autumn clicking song.

The Vicar was the first to arrive, humming under his breath as he changed in the vestry. The glorious weather and the whole feeling of the ceremony had something special about it. Yet the couple he was going to marry wasn't anything unusual. No, there he was wrong, their love was purer than that of the majority of couples he wed because they'd told him with candid honesty they were waiting until after the ceremony. The age difference sat well on them too. She'd never let go of his hand and had waited on his every word... Some would say they were plain soppy. The Vicar was jerked out of his ponderings by the sound of a large vehicle stopping outside the Church. He left the vestry to find two men in morning suits carrying pipes up the path.

'Exhaust pipes for the archway of honour!' explained the bald-headed one.'I hope they don't fall to bits!'

From then on it was a rush. People arrived in silly brimmed hats and out-of-date suits. The church filled with rustle and chat. The groom arrived, pale-faced in his morning suit. The Vicar realised he'd have looked far better in the jeans and grease that usually covered him. The clock ticked on, and excitement rose. Finally, an expectant hush settled.

The bride arrived and the organ burst into acclaim. She wore a full-length dress dotted with pearls and exquisite embroidery. Even though the veil hung low, it couldn't hide the luxuriant red curls beneath. Clare walked sedately down the aisle, hoping no-one saw the terrible shaking in her body. She clung to Mr Harrison's arm like a drowning man. At the altar, she lifted the veil, and all at the front were thrilled at her beauty. The joy of the day had added that special allure to an already attractive face. The colour began to return to Chris' cheeks.

It seemed but a matter of moments before the pair were gliding back down the aisle, with silly, radiant grins stretched across their faces, which broke into laughter when they saw the exhaust pipes. After the photographs, they were showered liberally in confetti and rose petals, and driven away in the back of an open Land Rover which was festooned with ribbons and balloons.

'Oh Chris, I want this to go on forever!' Clare hung onto her veil in the breeze.'It's everything and more than I expected.'

His response was to kiss her again. They both felt the new freedom in the embrace, the wait had been worth it. They swung into a courtyard, and Bill jumped out to open the door for them. A second vehicle drove up behind. In it sat Sylvie and Tamsin clad in pale blue dresses, looking like one of the fragile flowers from their bouquets. They shrieked with laughter because Henry had been regaling them with his best wedding jokes and tumbled into the Hotel foyer to greet the guests.

The Harrisons were the first to arrive, still glowing in their excitement from the reunion. Mr Harrison went as far as to give Clare a smacking kiss on the cheek; only Helen seemed a little sad. No doubt thinking of Tom thought Chris. Their gift was a state-of-the-art Teasmaid Clare had giggling when she saw it but looked forward to the luxury of early morning tea. The Crofts and Mrs Lock arrived together, with smiles and tears. They were followed by innumerable Aunts and Uncles of Chris's; some of their accents were so broad that Clare ended up just nodding and smiling. She found it didn't matter that she had no family, she had more than enough friends. The reception passed in a happy daze, and all too soon Clare was bundled upstairs to get changed. It was with genuine regret she took off the dress and put it back in its wraps. Tamsin and Sylvie pulled her into a two-piece suit and hustled her down the stairs. There was some joke afoot which they wouldn't explain.

In the courtyard stood Aggie, recognisable at first only by her registration number. She had been re-sprayed, repaired and made like new. Her bonnet stood open. Clare rushed over to look inside. A new engine, still unsmeared by oil sat waiting to be turned over.

'My gift to you,' said Chris appearing from nowhere. He was elegant and strange in a dark suit. Clare's insides turned like on the day she'd first seen Duncan in a dinner suit, but this time it was love, not lust.

'You can drive her to the station. Bill will collect her later.' Clare's response was to throw her arms around Chris in a mammoth embrace. A loud cheer rose from the waiting crowd. Red in the face Clare released him.

'Throw the bouquet,' hissed Chris.

To Clare's surprise, Tamsin and Sylvie fought for it, then she saw Duncan behind Sylvie watching her with an almost loving look in his eye and she understood. Tamsin won and brandished it aloft to further cheers.

'Mrs Rowan, it's time to catch the train.' Clare didn't realise Chris was speaking to her until he repeated himself.

Clare jumped up into the cab and kicked off her shoes to drive. Aggie began with a new roar and leapt away with an incredible eagerness. Clare finally understood Chris' mania for speed as they belted down to the station. It wasn't until they stopped that she saw the cans tied to the back. They only just made the train and sank into the seats out of breath.

'Well, Mr Rowan, would you please tell me where we're going?'

'Three weeks in Blackpool!'
Clare's face fell and Chris burst into laughter.
'Oh, I couldn't resist it. I meant the Bahamas!'
The train lurched out of the station and Chris kissed Clare with the new assurance of man to wife.

EPILOGUE
1994

Clare hauled herself out of the bed, automatic responses leading her to the cot at the end of the dark room. Ian's cries quietened in response to her touch. Enveloped in the night Clare slumped down on the bed and let the child feed. Her eyes began to close in response to the hypnotic sucking. Perhaps if she lay down, he would still feed and she would doze. Shifting her body made him lose his grip. He sent up an impoverished wail, so she had to sit back up again. After an eternity the sucking slowed then stopped. Terrified to move in case he woke, but wanting to sleep, Clare gingerly rose and laid him back down. He gave a brief half-hearted wail which sent Clare's fists clenching then he settled. Clare crawled back into bed; her comforting womb of warmth and sleep. Two hours later she was driven out of it again by the baby's incessant demand. Once more she went through the routine until he settled and she could sleep.

Morning light came too soon, along with the shrilling of the alarm clock. Chris stretched and yawned.

'He was quiet last night, wasn't he?' Clare wanted to hit Chris.

'No, he had me up every two hours, thank you. I feel like death warmed up, and he'll be at me again before long.' They were speaking in frantic whispers.

'Why don't you come here until he does?' Chris stretched out his arms and Clare shrank away.

'Can't you see it's like torture? My body is crying out for sleep, so shutting my eyes for five minutes knowing it can't last is a vicious punishment.'

On cue, the baby began to sniffle and cry. Chris leapt out of bed and picked him up.

'Good grief, he's soaking.'

Clare was up and taking the baby away.

'I was going to offer to change him while you lay in,' Chris said indignantly.

'You still don't understand, do you? It's too late now, I'm out.'

Holding the wriggling person away from herself, Clare put him on the changing mat and stripped his clothes. That didn't pacify him and Clare found herself trying to satisfy his voracious appetite. Her back ached, and she wished for a pillow. None was nearby and Chris was shaving with the radio blaring. Clare had to fight to keep her eyes open. Finally, he finished; she tucked him back into the cot and made her way downstairs.

Clyde, the cat meowed an affectionate greeting, stretched his claws and led the way to the kitchen. His ecstatic purr was pure cupboard love because he was expecting food. Did no-one ever want her except for what she gave them?

Clare slammed the cat food onto a dish, while Clyde contorted through her legs trying to trip her. Outside, the frost on the grass was gleaming silver, echoing the grey of the sea. A dull mist was occluding the skyline. Clare shivered despite the warmth of the kitchen. The grey weather matched her mood. Dreamily she laid the table and prepared breakfast. The toast burnt again, but they were used to that. Chris came thundering down the stairs and she winced.

'Be quiet,' she hissed as he came in. Chris was swamped with guilt because he'd clean forgotten about Ian. Pouring a coffee, Chris watched Clare inexpertly spooning cereal into her mouth. The dark shadows under her eyes and her pale skin made her look haggard, even her red hair had lost its lustre; it looked a dull brown.

He couldn't understand why Clare found it all such hard work. Pam had positively bloomed when Tamsin had been born. She had sung and carried the baby around all the time. It was so difficult not to make comparisons. Admittedly, Tamsin had been planned whereas Ian resulted from a faulty contraceptive on honeymoon. It had all happened too fast. Clare barely had time to adjust to being married before Ian was born. She hadn't wanted to rush into babies but had seemed as equally thrilled as Chris when their suspicions were confirmed. Where was the sweet girl he had married? Who was this weary, non-communicative woman?

The crunch of tyres on gravel sent their eyes towards the bedroom and Chris leapt up to retrieve the letters before they crashed through the metal letterbox. For him, there were the usual plethora of brown envelopes, but for Clare, there was a hand-written white one. She took it and read without comment.

It was an invitation from Tom and Helen to their baptism at their church in Birmingham in a week's time. Clare and Chris were invited for the whole weekend.

'It's impossible,' Clare stated and handed him the paper.

'I don't see why. After all, we did miss the wedding because of Ian. Is it because of what happened?'

'No, I don't think so. I haven't thought about it for months. I feel absolutely nothing towards Alex, I mean Tom,' replied Clare, with a lurch of her former asperity. 'Helen says he's a different person, so there would be nothing to remind me. It's not even the Church business. I can handle all the Christian stuff because I can use Ian as an excuse to walk out. No, it's the hassle. Lugging all the gear up there; then he'd probably keep the house awake all night and yell through the service. I don't have the energy or wit to organise a clean shirt, let alone enjoy the trip. I'd rather stay here.'

'You can't stay in all the time, you're becoming a hermit!'

'It's just this phase. I'm only tired. He may grow out of it soon.'

'But he's five months old and shows no signs of it.'

'When he improves, I'll go out more.' From the tone in Clare's voice, Chris knew not to push the subject any further.

'I must go now. I'll be back at about six. Anything you want in town?' Clare shook her head.

'Think about it. The change may do us all some good.'

He left before she replied, remembering not to slam the door. Clare's routine clicked into operation. She cleared the breakfast things, loaded the washing machine, then switched the television on. Clare sat for the thirty minutes she knew she had before Ian woke, struggling with her weariness, hardly hearing the voices.

Clare had thought the body-numbing fatigue was something that would pass but it hadn't. How she longed for those few carefree, idyllic weeks when it was just the two of them, enjoying their own company and lovemaking. When the sickness had begun everything had gone to pieces. Her hormones had gone on the rampage, moods swinging from deep anger to overwhelming joy within the course of a day. The time alone with Chris had been too short. She still knew so little about him. There should have been at least a couple of years while they adjusted. It had been with genuine regret she'd turned in her jobs when her growing stomach made it all too tiring. She missed the challenges, like the figurines she'd helped Mrs Lock repair and the refurbishing of the Harrisons' study where her opinion had been valued. From being just the cleaner, Clare's status had risen to domestic oracle, and she had on several occasions needed to resort to checking textbooks. Yes, it was the company too; she had also sometimes become a confidante, perhaps as a spin-off from being a domestic encyclopaedia. Clare had been valued, not drained dry like now.

The birth had been textbook, so the Midwives said, yet Clare still remembered the pain. Afterwards, she had been wound up in the excitement of the fact that it was a boy and all the presents, cards and congratulations. Chris had been more tender and loving than she'd ever expected. He'd talked of when Ian would have his own Land Rover and they'd laughed. It had been downhill ever since. Ian had such a voracious appetite which showed no signs of being satisfied. Far from going longer between feeds at night, he seemed to need more. Clare hadn't had one full night's sleep in five months. During the day he was laughter and sweetness. Despite her weariness, she forgave him. Chris couldn't help with the feeding because Ian was breastfed, which he preferred above all the other foods she frantically offered him. He would take a mouthful, spit it out, then scream for her. It was easier to give in than to go on fighting.

Clare took Ian to the clinic to be weighed on the days she shopped. The room always seemed full of happy bouncing babies with well-rested mothers, so she put a brave face on it and said everything was fine, avoiding the Health Visitor's eye. At Chris' encouragement, Clare had gone to a mother and toddler group in a nearby village. It had taken all her courage to walk in through the door only to find it filled with a well-formed clique from a nearby Council Estate. Apart from a few hellos, what's his name, and isn't he lovely, they turned their backs on Clare and continued their conversation. Clare refused to go again.

The result was Clare spent most of her time alone at Peacehaven. It hadn't been so bad in the warmer weather, she'd been able to take the pram along the beach, but the Autumn mists meant she didn't dare venture out.

Aggie was parked in the newly built garage. Chris had even fitted a baby seat. But there seemed to be nowhere for Clare to go. After doing the proud mother rounds to all her ex-employers, she didn't feel she wanted to return. The few acquaintances she made at the Club, were either older or working. Then to crown it all, the Crofts had moved to London when Mick had changed his job. Clare's day was timed by Ian's feeds and television programmes. Sometimes he would sleep for a couple of hours in the afternoon, and Clare would doze off. She'd emerge even grumpier than usual, so she would struggle to stay awake instead.

Chris' company had promoted him, so the trips abroad had finished. He was planning on competing again in the spring and for the first time, Clare began to resent the hours he spent tinkering on the vehicles. She had so little company, that she wanted his undivided attention when he was in; even if she was barely speaking to him.

The nights were bad too because when Chris turned to take her in his arms, she was usually so anaesthetised with tiredness that he would turn his back on her, muttering under his breath. Sometimes Clare pretended she was asleep. There hadn't been an open row, but the lack of physical contact was taking its toll. Clare admitted to herself that some of the problems were that she was terrified of falling for another baby, despite her mathematical taking of the pill. There seemed no solution to the problem, only time seemed the answer. Ian couldn't go on like this forever. Every night Clare put him to bed and prayed that this would be the first time he slept right through. When he woke, she wanted to weep. She was trapped; but there was security in the confines. The demand to leave it, even for a weekend scared her.

Chris arrived home that night, laden with parcels. Begrudgingly, Clare went to see. He pulled out a steriliser, bottles and tins of powdered milk, an electronic baby alarm and to her surprise, a pot plant.

'Len said their lad played up on the breast but was fine on the bottle, so I bought this. Next feed, give him a couple of ounces then gradually change him over. I've got all the instructions. I'll be able to feed him while you sleep. We can't go on like this. His cot is going in the next room; so we won't disturb each other. That's why I got the alarm.'

Clare wanted to deny him, say everything was alright really, she was managing.

Was Chris just using this to get back into her favours? Her tired mind read different reasons into his motives. Begrudgingly she agreed.

'And, we're going to the Baptism!' Chris stated.

'Don't I get any say in it?' Clare's back went up.

'I rang Helen. She's going to borrow a cot, and all the gear you'll need. There are loads of babies in their Church, so he won't disturb anything. She will even organise a babysitter if we need one.'

'I can't,' stated Clare with all the conviction she could muster.

'Oh yes you can,' replied Chris with the steel in his voice which betokened anger.

Clare backed down, knowing she was beaten.

That night Ian greedily took the bottle, only to vomit it up two hours later. Clare had to change him, the cot and wash it from his hair. She fed him, walked the miles between the two rooms and slammed herself back into bed, pulling the covers from Chris' sleeping shoulders.

It seemed the Motorway Service Station would never be reached. Ian's wails grew louder and Chris' expression grimmer as he accelerated and dodged through the lanes. Clare sat in silence, there was nothing she could do, except to hold the baby's flailing as he struggled to escape the baby seat.

At last, they drew into a parking bay. Clare leapt out of the car and ran round to the boot. Frantically she dragged at the catch until Chris appeared and unlocked it. Clare threw several bags to the ground before the truth dawned.

'Where is the blue plastic box with his bottles and feed in? I asked you to get it off the table,' she demanded.

'No you didn't.'

'I did, just as you were fetching your coat.'

'I didn't hear you.'

'Well isn't that just bloody typical!' Clare yelled. 'All you think about is yourself.'

'Hush Clare, there's no need to shout. I'm sorry.'

'That's not going to do any good. How am I supposed to feed him?'

'Can you do it yourself?'

'As you so happily encouraged me to put him on the bottle,' said Clare acidly. 'I've nearly dried up.'

She wasn't going to give him the satisfaction of knowing she'd been leaking for the past half hour.

'I'll see if there's anything in the shop.'

Clare watched him walk away. Why did he always have to give the orders, be the one who was right? Ian's cries were reaching fever pitch. Clare wrenched him out of the seat. True to his usual form, he was soaking. Hungrily he latched on and while he fed. Clare felt the damp soaking onto her lap. She felt such a strong revulsion, it was all she could do not to yank his mouth away and throw him so that she was left in peace. Clare knew she would never do that, but it didn't stop her wanting to. Under the pale neon light, she tried to think of succinct things to say to Chris. Why did he have to force her to come when she would rather be comatose in front of the television, instead of in the middle of nowhere, cold and wet? Chris climbed into the car.

'I found two bottles of this pre-mixed stuff.'

He handed them over and saw.

'He throws that up and anyway I've fed him.'

'So I went all that way for nothing.' He reloaded the boot, then sat, drumming on the steering wheel.

'Why did you have to drag me out?' Clare exploded.

'Because you're becoming an agoraphobic. You need something to drag you out of the hole you've crawled into.'

'I haven't. You're just looking for a reason to pick on me.'

'No, I'm worried about you.'

'Just because you're scared about coming home to find your meals uncooked and me not available for bed. Hasn't it occurred to you, that this might be your fault!'

'That's not fair. Don't misread the situation. I can't see why you find it so hard, Pam...'

'I knew you'd bring her in some time. Saint bloody Pam. If she'd had her sleep ruined, she wouldn't be such a heroine now.'

'It's not just the sleep and you know it. Get in the back with him.'

The cold fury in his voice silenced Clare. She got into the back and sat for the rest of the journey in smelly wetness.

The heavens had opened when they found the small street where Tom and Helen lived. Clare stayed in the car while Chris knocked. The door opened sending a yellow glow spilling onto the street. They were swept into the warmth of the house. Clare avoided making eye contact and shrank away from

Helen's embrace. She was too angry and sad inside.

Clare and Ian were ushered to a bedroom where to her dismay a cot lay at the foot of the bed. Any hope that the trip might improve things, vanished. Clare changed Ian and put him to bed, for once he didn't demand a feed, but lay cooing. The strong smell of nappies pervaded all of Clare's clothes so she stripped and unpacked some dry clothes. Everything that came out was creased despite the care she thought she'd taken earlier. She caught a glimpse of herself in the mirror. The haunted look was back, a reminder of the night she'd fled London. Chris walked in, and Clare hushed him before he spoke. The baby slept.

'Clare, whatever our differences, put a brave face on it. Don't spoil their weekend,' he whispered.

Miserably Clare agreed and went down to the kitchen. Helen was stirring something savoury in a large saucepan.

'That smells good,' Clare ventured.

'It's only a mild curry - that won't affect you feeding the baby, will it? Tom's gone down to the all-night Chemist to get you some formula and bottles.'

Clare sank onto a chair.

'Hear it was a bad trip.'

'What's he been saying,' snapped Clare before she could help it, then remembered her promise. 'Oh, I suppose it was rather fraught. His nibs shrieked practically the whole way.' Clare's eyes began to droop in the warmth. The back door swung open and Tom burst in out of the rain.

'Think I've been baptised already, it's so wet out there!'

While he shook off his parker, Clare covertly watched him. There was an energy and a deftness in his movements that Alex never had, and he was thinner.

The beard added a new dimension to his face, softening his hawkish nose and bringing out the peaceful expression in his eyes. He turned to Clare and grinned.

'Long time no see!'

He pulled up a chair to sit opposite her.

'We must start as we mean to go. I know I dealt you a lot of pain in the past. Some of which I can remember, some of which I can't. I have to apologise, say I'm sorry and ask if in any way you can forgive me!'

Clare had shrunk from his physical presence but the longer he spoke, she felt only the best that was in Alex and nothing of the maniac. His eyes were as mesmerising as ever. The small knot of anger she'd been holding inside dissolved. This was a new man, a new creation. Might it all be laid at God's door as Helen said?

'It's forgiven Alex-er-Tom. Everything worked out for the best and it all seems irrelevant to us now.'

Tom subjected her to one of his deep looks which seemed to see into her soul, then he smiled and planted a rubbery kiss on her forehead.

'Thank you... Any food going?'

'I can't keep up with this man's appetite,' grumbled Helen.'We're just waiting for Chris.'

During the meal, Clare was given a glass of wine, which to her surprise acted like a stimulant. She joined in the conversation, which was based around the work Helen and Tom were doing with the homeless. Tom announced that

Duncan and Sylvie were arriving in the morning and if the weather cleared, a picnic was planned. The baptism on Sunday would be followed by a meal in the Church hall. Then Alex pronounced triumphantly, they could all collapse in a heap. Clare was unable to see how she was going to cope with all the chat and new faces under her burden of weariness. She ducked out of the talk and began to toy with her food. The wine was sending her to sleep and Clare hadn't realised she'd dozed off until her head slipped forward, but no-one seemed to have noticed. A wail came from upstairs. Clare blundered out of her chair and made her way across the room.

'Hey, wait,' shouted Helen. 'You sit down. I'll fetch him.'

Clare sat on the settee and all too soon a squirming body was placed in her arms. This was as bad as being woken in the night. Feeling drugged Clare fed him herself, the new bottles weren't yet sterilised.

'I'm going to bed,' Clare stated when he'd finished and lurched up. The conversation paused.

'You've hardly eaten a thing,' said Helen.

'I'm not hungry,' Clare lied, 'I'll see you in the morning.'

She ignored the God bless yous and got ready for bed. While she dozed off, Clare heard them talking and hated it. Why should they have all the energy and happiness, be able to sleep all night?

The hatred was still with her when she was woken in the early hours of the morning. Chris tried to put his arms around her, but she snarled and leapt out of bed. In the empty kitchen, she found the bottles and prepared a feed. The squeaks upstairs became roars. Why didn't Chris pick him up, everyone would be awake soon. In her haste, Clare didn't screw the bottle up tight enough. It was still wet, so of course, it fell to the floor and its contents cascaded over the pale blue tiles. Out came all the most horrible words Clare knew as she inexpertly mopped up the flood. She cleaned most of it and made another bottle. This she hung onto like grim death. Chris was pacing around the room with Ian in his arms.

'What took you so long?' he asked mildly.

'I dropped the bottle, satisfied?'

'I hope you cleared up the mess?'

'That's typical of you. All you can think of is the spill, so everything looks alright on the outside. Never mind the muck inside.' Clare was close to tears.

'I only asked.'

'I know exactly what you meant. Leave me alone!'

That set the tone for when they awoke later on and during the rest of the day. Chris and Clare barely spoke to each other. Duncan rang to say they were delayed, so the five of them went on the picnic. Clare felt excluded from the beautiful day. Ian switched on the charm, convincing everyone he was a nice little boy. The talk was general, yet Clare couldn't keep up; she had nothing to say. A diet of daytime television effectively cut her off from day-to-day events. She replied to everything in monosyllables and in the end they stopped trying to get her to join in. When they arrived back at the house, Clare saw Ian bracing himself for another yell and she felt the tension rising.

'Right Clare, hand him here,' Helen demanded. 'You go and sleep. I'll deal with this little brute. I'll give you a call in time for dinner. Don't argue.' She gave Clare a shove in the direction of the stairs. Obediently, Clare went up.

Helen wasn't used to babies, but eventually got the bottle in his mouth. To her surprise, instead of guzzling, Ian fixed her with a beady stare and a broad grin. He didn't want any milk. Helen lay him on the rug with some toys.

'You're a fraud,' she pronounced, and he gave her a conspiratorial smile.

Tom and Chris came in, they'd been inspecting the engine of Helen's ancient Fiesta to see if it was time to pension her off.

'How could you let Clare get in such a state!' Helen demanded. 'Don't you ever do the feeds and let her sleep?'

'She's been feeding him herself until recently. There was trouble with getting the right formula, and anyway I have to work. She can catch up on her sleep during the day if she wanted,' Chris replied defensively.

'You know that's ridiculous.'

Chris was startled.

'You can at least do the weekends.'

'I did offer. I never had to with Pam, she seemed to cope, not go to pieces like this. Clare's turning into a hermit.'

'Well, what have you done to help - have you taken her out once in the past five months?'

'She's always been too tired. I encouraged her to go to a toddler group, but she said they were unfriendly.'

'Chris, you're as ill-suited for parenthood as Clare is!'

Helen didn't get the chance to continue due to Duncan and Sylvie arriving, closely followed by Henry, the Pastor of Helen and

Tom's church. Once the introductions were over, Duncan and Chris escaped.

Clare was woken by a burst of laughter, but the short deep nap had done some work on her. Perhaps it was being woken by joy rather than a baby's cry that made the difference. After a shower, Clare began to feel vaguely human. Downstairs, she found Ian being played with by Sylvie, all she had to do was sit and drink coffee. Chris returned later on. Shamefaced, he kissed her, and she responded by giving him a steely glare.

There was a conspiracy against Clare for the rest of the day. Ian was fed, washed and played with by the others, and when she went upstairs, she found the cot moved out of her room and into Helen and Tom's. Part of her wanted to lug it back, the rest realised she may get a whole night's sleep. The meal was another surprise. Clare had always imagined Christians to have no sense of humour and was astounded to hear Tom tell some appalling jokes at their expense. Clare hadn't laughed so much for years. There seemed no difference between them and anyone else, except for saying grace. Duncan and Sylvie seemed to have slipped into a habit of convivial banter between them, but Clare saw they were thoroughly enjoying each other's company. Gone was all of Duncan's old arrogance. However, by 9.30, the wine had its usual effect, and Clare was stifling her yawns.

'Go on up,' suggested Helen. 'We've got an early start in the morning.'

Clare didn't resent leaving this time, her desire for sleep was so strong. If they had wanted to kidnap Ian, she wouldn't have minded. She rushed through washing then lay in bed, luxuriating in the security. A couple of times in the night she was partially roused by a distant cry, but blissfully drifted back to sleep. Chris had to spoil everything by waking her with an amorous caress.

'Can't you leave it alone. I get one decent night's sleep and you expect me to be all over you because of it. Give me some peace.' She turned her back on him.

Despite feeling refreshed, Clare and Chris entered the Church with matters pretty much as usual. The building was modern, a small dais at the front with a few chairs on it. It surprised Clare that there was no altar. Directly below the dais was a deep blue pool, its colour reminded her of the pool in the Hotel on their honeymoon. She wished she was back there.

The people inside the church were a revelation. They ranged from a couple of punks to well-dressed matrons in hats. There was a great sense of friendliness, people were kissing and hugging. Clare shrunk back from any contact. They were ushered to the seats of honour at the front.

'Hello!' a young girl stood by Clare. 'I'm Shirley and I'm going to look after Ian for you during the service. Do you have a bag with his things in?' Once again the baby was whisked away and Clare felt a little redundant. Then she realised she was trapped - she no longer had an excuse to walk out. The clang of an electric guitar began the service. The congregation sprang into song and Clare looked for the hymn book. Chris prodded her and pointed to an overhead projection on the wall. The songs were simple and catchy, yet Clare kept her mouth shut. Instead, she watched the surrounding people - were they working themselves up into a fervour? The singing stopped before they had the chance.

Henry stood up and welcomed everyone. Clare sensed he meant it to each and every one of them. He prayed for the service and the concerns of the Church. Respectfully, Clare bowed her head. Her mind wandered back to the Chapel. If someone had clapped to a hymn there, they would have been thrown out. Now it seemed the congregation were making up prayers and not reading them. Clare was astonished. From the back came something unintelligible. Clare craned her ears to hear, but it was another language. Someone else said they had an interpretation of the words. It had been praise to God and His great power in changing people's lives from dark to light. Clare was impressed, they certainly put on a good show. This must be the sort of thing Sylvie had talked about. Clare realised she hadn't wanted to bolt or felt bored, all she was aware of was a slight uneasiness, and she could cope with that.

'Now friends, I'd like to invite Helen and Tom to tell us about why they're going through the waters of Baptism today.'

Clad in identical white T-shirts and trousers they stepped to the front.

'Many of you already know my story,' said Tom. 'But I will tell you again anyway! I came from a squalid home; my mother kicked my father out when I was two and had instead a succession of men who paid her and beat me when I wouldn't keep quiet. One of these men I christened the Bull because he looked like one. He hated children, so when he came I either had to hide in my room or keep away until he left. One day I could stand it no longer and went into their room, hoping to stop the relationship. He laughed. It seemed he'd known about me all along and didn't care. I had endured it all for nothing. I had one friend, a lad called Douggie, and we were very close. I had no idea that he was not of this world. Over the years we planned revenge by telling the Bull's family about my mother and murdering her.'

There were gasps of horror.

'This we duly did. Afterwards, Douggie left me high and dry, with blood on my hands. I ran away, found a new identity, became Tom, living in constant fear of being found because I still didn't understand who'd done the murder. I was in total mental shock. Eventually, I did make a friend, but as soon as that happened Douggie appeared and I ran away again. I found myself in a park with a starving woman.' He grinned at Helen. 'Who's sat by me now.'

There was a commotion at the back. Clare peered around and saw the Harrisons come in and take a seat. The joy on Helen's face was all too apparent.

'I think I fell in love with her then,' Tom continued. 'Despite my fear of Douggie, I fed her, helped her, and we shared a small flat. I thought I'd escaped Douggie, but I hadn't. He met me one lunch-time, and I tried my hardest to convince him Helen was okay, but he wouldn't listen. He also told me the Bull was in prison, so I knew I was safe. I had to prove Helen wasn't like the others so dragged him back to the flat. Douggie disappeared as soon as I went in.'

'Helen saw I'd flipped, and she wisely fled. I broke down in confusion. I no longer understood what was real and what was imagined. I drank a lot of whiskey and tried to take an overdose. Fortunately, I was so drunk, I swallowed a bottle of vitamin pills. In a daze, I

ran back to the park where I fell, causing a blow
to my head. When I came to in Hospital, I'd lost
my memory. All I could fix on was a sense of
danger from my past and refused their
treatments. I discharged myself and headed
south, took another a job and another identity. I
was asked to house-sit an empty cottage while
the owner was abroad. All was fine until another
waif turned up on my doorstep.'
Clare cringed.

 'She had nowhere to stay and decided to
move into the cottage. Sylvie the owner had left
me strict instructions to let her friends in, so I had
no choice. I felt alternatively furious and
protective because she reminded me so much of
someone I couldn't remember. I even tried to
warn her away from other men who were using
her.'
At the back, Duncan blushed.

 'After some idiotic behaviour on my part,
to my great surprise, the girl agreed to go out
with me. I'd been told to seize every opportunity
with both hands, so I did. Everything was fine for
several months. But of course, Douggie turned
up, although I was at first unaware of his actions.
He assaulted her in the house, sent hate mail,
broke the brake pipes on her vehicle and ended
by nearly killing her in one of her employers'
gardens. By that stage, I was aware of Douggie
as a separate person, and I had to protect this
woman. It culminated with me trying to get her to
run away to a place of safety with me.
Unfortunately, she went elsewhere, and Douggie
caught her. He held her hostage until the Police
resolved the situation. It was only when I they
arrested me that I heard people were calling me
Douggie. I cannot describe the confusion and
utter blackness which engulfed me then. In the

end, I was certified insane, put under the protection of a Court Order and admitted to a Secure Unit. I followed all of their treatments and they seemed to help. I came to accept that all Douggie's actions had been mine, and he was gone for good. I knew I had murdered my mother and was happy to stay put because I was a danger to everyone.'

'The terrific weight of guilt paralysed me. I began reading the Bible during that time, but it seemed nonsense. Then came the startling news that I hadn't murdered my mother. That should have helped, but it didn't. The guilt was overwhelming for my wasted life, and for what I'd done to people because of my delusions. Gradually, I got used to the shifted load. So well, in fact, they released me and entrusted me to Helen's care; solely because there was nobody else to pick up the tab. She took me to a Hotel in Cornwall, and eventually to a Church Service. During the sermon, I knew Douggie was back, but the rest is a merciful blank. Suffice it to say, I came around on the floor, with all my pain gone.'

'I tell you, Sisters and Brothers, I know what a newborn baby feels like, what the released prisoner feels, and there's only one person who can do that! No doctor. No Hospital. It was Jesus. The power of his name set me free from that demonic bondage. I am free. I am His and will spend the rest of my life glorifying his name!'

There was a round of Hallelujahs and Amens. Clare was stunned. She'd never heard the whole story before, and whether she believed it was Jesus or not, there was no doubt Tom was healed. It was too much to absorb at once.

'I can't top that,' Helen was saying. 'Except to add my own part. I come from a wealthy background and took one of the options open to that class and instead of working, I got into parties, drugs and drink. I humiliated and shamed my family until they kicked me out. I deserved it. I ran away and ended up beaten and starving when Tom found me. He was a bright knight in shining armour. He found me, fed me and in his strange way, loved me. On the day he came in with the invisible Douggie, I ran again. Later I returned to a deserted flat, wanting to help. He was gone. All I found was some money. I spent the next few years searching for Tom, but the Lord found me instead. One day, my brother Duncan found me and wanted to take me back to the family fold. Inadvertently, he took me to Tom.'

'When I saw him again, he was sat in a police cell; dead in the eyes. I knew in my spirit he was possessed, but no-one would believe me. So I prayed and waited. You know the rest. We're now married, and in return we work with the Homeless in Birmingham, to try to bring the hope we found, to them.'

There was another cheer. Henry took the microphone and asked them if they repented of their sins, turned to Jesus as their Lord and Master, and gave their lives to him. This they affirmed. Tom was first into the water. Henry baptised him in the Name of the Father, the Son and the Holy Spirit, then he was tipped backwards until he was completely immersed in the water, then he was pulled up. The whole congregation burst into song while Henry prayed and laid hands on him. Tom climbed out and stood dripping while he watched Helen, a huge grin on his face. They left the church singing fit to burst while they got changed.

Clare sat down and found her knees were shaking. She was relieved that Tom had spared her any embarrassment by not naming her; but it was more than that. The transformation in his life was amazing. How nice it would be to have her life so easily sorted, no baby, no husband. Clare pulled herself up on that, she didn't mean it at all, she wanted them, but she needed to be able to cope. There was no more time for reflection because Henry was speaking again. He was calling people forward to make a declaration of faith. A couple went up and Clare found herself almost envying them and was horrified at her reaction. The service came to a close and Clare followed the throng to a room at the back. Helen and Tom were being inundated with gifts, cards and hugs. Ian was suddenly back in her arms, clean, dry and gurgling. To her surprise ,she was glad to see him.

Chris and Clare found themselves cherished and fed; as fast as they began to chat to one person, another would introduce themselves and appear to be deeply interested in who they were and why they were here. Admittedly, there was a lot of talk about the Lord's greatness and weren't Helen and Tom a witness. To her surprise, Clare found she was able to reply to such a comment without cringing. These people meant it.

Mr Harrison waved to Clare from across the room, and she saw they were being feted too, although with worried expressions. This was no cosy chat with the Vicar. Mrs Harrison was talking to another woman wearing a silly hat; she would be alright. Peter was chatting to a tall coloured girl. Clare smirked and wondered if the Harrisons had changed their views on race yet.

Chris had disappeared, then she saw him with Henry. They appeared to be deep in an earnest conversation. The word crankshaft was uttered and Clare relaxed. Gradually people began to slip away. She hadn't realised it was getting on for 5 pm. It was a relief to return to the quietness of the house. Tom and Helen were already there, admiring their cards. Ian slept on in the buggy.

'He's drugged,' said Helen. 'He stuffed his face with bits from my plate. He needs a diet of vol-au-vents, sausage rolls and sandwiches.'

'But he's too young, he's still on the first stage food,' Clare exclaimed.

'I talked to Rosie, the girl with six kids. She said Sam, her eldest was just like Ian until she caught him wolfing the cat food and realised he needed a more solid diet. She says it's all bad habits and he can be cured.'

Clare stared in disbelief.

'Did you hear all this, Chris!'

He nodded.

'We've got something to say to you two,' said Tom. 'Come and sit down.' Obediently they did.

'After you'd gone to bed last night, we had a talk about your situation. What we've decided is you need a holiday. Together. Alone. No baby.'

Clare's heart fell, she'd been looking forward to returning to her haven.

'You two can't have had much of a chance to get to know each other, with Ian on the way so quickly. We can see the effect it's had on you, even if you can't. The first thing in the morning, you two are off to Wales. We've booked you into a small holiday village in the middle of nowhere, and you'll have to sort yourselves out because there's precious little else to do there.

Ian will stay here. Rosie's going to help sort him out. No arguing. You can afford it, Chris, just don't buy another bit for that Land Rover.'

Chris and Clare sat open-mouthed, and the state of surprise continued all evening! Several people from the Church arrived, and another party took place. Halfway through Clare realised that despite the intense noise, and the freely flowing wine, no one was drunk or behaving like a fool. Another nail in her preconceptions about Christians. Clare found herself in the kitchen with Sylvie, washing the glasses.

'What are you up to at the moment? I haven't had a chance to reply to your last letter,' asked Clare before Sylvie could give one of her famous ticking offs.

'The Hostel has finally put me on days, and that's twice as rewarding as nights. There are noises about a new one in Tottenham Court Road, and they may put me in charge of that!'

'Oh, that's brilliant. What about you and Duncan then?'

'It's swings and roundabouts. He's quite a reformed character in some ways, but he still goes off with the old crowd, shooting, Ascot and all that. We'll get there one day. Did you enjoy the service?'

'It was OK.'

'You still think we're a bunch of cranks?'

'Is that Ian crying?'

Clare backed out of the kitchen, not wanting to admit her changing views. A second full night's sleep continued its healing upon Clare, but she still shot out of bed before Chris was properly awake. They'd both accepted their orders without question and packed in silence. The other four came to see them off. Clare had some qualms about leaving Ian, but it was only a few hours away on the motorway. He'd been passed around like a parcel for the past few days and not turned a hair. It was more of a problem to think about what she had to say to Chris. A lot of her antagonism towards him had gone, now she was refreshed, and she saw more clearly he had been concerned rather than angry with her.

The village was set on the lower slopes of a mountain and the chalet nestled in a grove of firs. It contained a bed, settees, and a small fridge. They needed nothing more. Once they had dumped their bags, Chris and Clare felt awkward. Chris came close.

'May I put my arms around you?'

'Don't be so silly, you know you can.'

'No I don't. You haven't wanted me near you since Ian was born. Don't blame me entirely for him, it was both of our faults.'

Clare blushed remembering the passion. Could they ever recapture it?

'Yes, I do want you to. I want that feeling back. I didn't like beginning to hate you,' Clare admitted with all her old honesty.

His response was to take her in his arms. Clare felt once again his kiss that was so right and knew it wasn't too late.

'Chris we can't go back to things as we left them.'

'I know. Come and sit down. We've both made mistakes. We have to talk every day about what we've done, what we've felt, however angry that may be because we know what happens if we don't. We must go back to where we were on the day we married.'

He took her hand and looked at the double rings.

'You're right,' Clare agreed.

'And, I think we should sell Peacehaven,' said Chris in his deadliest voice. Clare snatched her hand away.

'Oh no. I love that house!'

'Can't you see, it's part of our problem? In the middle of an estate, there'll always be a neighbour to talk to, someone to help with the kids, you can do the Playschool run together. Ian will have plenty of friends - there's no-one within two miles of the cottage,' Chris reasoned.

'Oh, please don't sell Peacehaven. I know, why don't we let it, for fabulous amounts to holiday-makers, then we can use it for our own holidays?'

Chris mused. 'We would have to charge a lot to cover two mortgages.'

'Chris, listen to me,' the eagerness was back in Clare's voice. 'We're being completely honest. I'm not cut out to be solely a housewife. I've been trapped by the boredom as much as the tiredness. I'm not saying I want to go back to cleaning. That's a contradiction, but I still want to run my Agency. That could be operated from a spare room at home, at first anyway. The income from that would help our costs.'

'Oh alright, alright. It might just work,' Chris admitted.'There's one more thing and this you're not going to like. When we do find our estate with loads of kids and friendly people, I want it to be near a church like Helen and Tom's.'

Clare remained silent, so he ploughed on.

'I don't know if you felt the love that was there. They all seriously cared for each other. They got something out of the service, they hardly wanted it to stop. Even that woman in the big hat kissed the punk. I want some of that in my life. I had a chat with Henry...'

'So it wasn't all carburettors?'

'No,' he grinned roguishly. 'I want to know more about why they're different. I want a piece of that cake. There must be other Churches like that if this is what Christianity is all about.'

Clare was silent for a long time.

'You know what I feel about religion,' she said at last. 'The transformation in Tom was quite a shock to me. It rocked a lot of my convictions. Remember how he used to dislike you, and yesterday he hugged you like a bear. He sneered at Christianity far more than I ever did. The change must have come from something spiritual. No Hospital could fill a man with such joy. I can't help but think that somewhere my parents have gone terribly, terribly wrong. They missed something vital out. So I have to agree, I felt there was something different. I've got a lot of reservations but I'll follow you as long as I'm not forced into anything.'

'Do you think they would?'

'No, perhaps you're right,' Clare had to admit.'I think they'd accept you for whatever you are.'

'Are you hungry?' Chris demanded.

'Starving.'

He leapt up to raid the fridge. Clare watched the angular lines of his body and was overwhelmed with a surge of her old love. Things had been put right. She knew some would say the Lord's hand was in it. Now they had a fresh start. For a moment she longed for Ian, but realised this time alone with Chris was more important.

'Chris, I'm sorry for being so horrible,' she began to apologise.

'And so am I. I'll never compare you to Pam again. Clare, we've got so much, and to think we might have blown it if we hadn't gone to Helen and Tom's. I'll never cease to be thankful to them.'

Chris placed some fruit and cheese on the table, but suddenly the food didn't seem important when he saw the light was back in Clare's eyes which he'd thought was gone forever.

Here are the tasters for my other books!

COMPROMISE
Sometimes, things just can't get any worse, but
for hardworking Mollie, they do!
Not only does she have to leave her job at the
stables, but she also has to find a new home for
herself and the dogs. Then a chance encounter
with old friend Chris at the Hazeley show brings
a solution; compromise living. Mollie gets a new
start on his farm and Chris gets freedom from
being harassed by the riding club ladies.
But will this just make things worse? As tangled
emotions and hurt begin to surface, Mollie has to
make sense of her past and Chris has to come to
terms with his deeply hidden sexuality and faith.
None of this is helped by the cows and Keith, a
slightly dippy stallion, whose combined antics
and dramas cause confusion and heartbreak.

CHAOS

Chris and Mollie thought it was time to move on;
change is good, isn't it?

But in going their separate ways, they just hit
more problems and complications. Chris leaves
the farm to meet his mentor Alan. But his dream
of a happy time sorting himself out in the
Christian community on the Dorset coast is
ruined by a terrible accident. Chris must return to
work with horses to make amends. Returning
home brings more shocking revelations throw
new light on his troubled gender identity. More
trapped than ever before, can he find a way out?

Mollie starts her dream of boarding girls from her old school but finds herself out of depth and struggling with the teenagers' demands and moods. It seems the idea is a disaster for all. But maybe, Ann from the stables has a solution.

Galloping through all these misadventures is the equestrian sport of Vaulting and the struggles of Keith, the stallion who has caused the two so many problems. Strange arrivals, a new horse, a Nun and Mollie's mother all combine to bring even more chaos to the struggling pair. The journey for all ends in a shattering conclusion but will Mollie and Chris finally get their happy ending? Does it need God to step in and change things?
A standalone follow on to Compromise.

CHALLENGER

Would you ride your precious horse too hard, just so you can beat your best friend?

Joanna did, driven by the ghost of her highly competitive mother. Remorse and fear engulf Joanna when she finds her best friend, Diane had disappeared on that same day. Joanna walks away from everything to do with horses to run the county show with her Dad.

Years later, Challenger returns, bringing to a head the series of events that has burst Joanna's little bubble. He seems determined to savage her, every time she goes near him. Diane also returns, but Joanna cannot quite trust her. Does she really want to re-kindle the friendship or does she have an ulterior motive?

Joanna's worst fears are realised on Christmas day when Dianne makes the ultimate betrayal. Her life must be rebuilt once again. Is all as bad as it seems? Will the horses and dogs she meets on her journey help her to heal and finally find love? Can Challenger forgive her?

Also available: Collection: Animla short stories
Christmas: A holiday novella that follows on from Chaos
Ponies: A shaggy short story

Printed in Great Britain
by Amazon